TRESPASSING ON HIS HEART

MARY J HICKS

Trespassing on his
Heart
Mary J Hicks

Publisher's Note: This is a work of fiction. Names, characters,
places, and incidents are a product of the author's imagination.
Locales and public names are sometimes used for atmospheric
purposes. Any resemblance to actual people, living or dead, or to
businesses, companies, events, institutions, or locales is
completely coincidental.

marehicks4@gmail.com
www.maryjhicks.com
Trespassing on his Heart/Mary J Hicks. -- 1st ed.
ISBN 978-0-9963488-0-5

To Myron L. Hicks, whose unconditional love and support gave me courage and the freedom to be me. Though no longer at my side, he is ever on my mind and alive in my heart.

To our son Greg, and his family—the wonderful people he's brought into my life.

And to our daughter Gayle, who keeps me smiling.

I love you, and I'm thankful for all of you.

Let the words of my mouth and the meditation of my heart be acceptable in Your sight, O Lord, my strength and my Redeemer.

~PSALM 19: 14~

CHAPTER 1

respassing

LAUREN HELD her speed steady as the scenic winding road threaded through the countryside. Basking in the glorious morning, she paid little attention when a flame-red Mazda appeared in the rearview mirror. The sports car was quickly closing the distance between the two vehicles. The driver wouldn't be able to pass her in the stretch of no passing zone they'd entered, yet the car continued to move closer—too close.

The driver appeared to be a young woman.

Lauren neared her turnoff, and with a quick glance in the mirror she put on the turn signal. The orange-red light flashed a warning—Mazda girl ignored it.

"Come on lady, back off. Can't you see my signal?"

The moment she tapped the brake and began slowing, the sleek Mazda nosed from behind. Lauren's breath caught. "Oh, you're not ... !"

The driver stomped the accelerator and the red car roared

into the forbidden zone. As it blasted past Lauren, a pair of wide dark eyes peered out the rear side window from under the brim of a pink softball cap.

The Mazda disappeared safely around the next curve. Only then did Lauren breathe again with an explosive, "Crazy, irresponsible person!"

Irresponsible.

She'd learned the word early in childhood and it invariably prompted a reminder at unexpected times.

Lauren had come to a stop on the side of the road. She gripped the wheel and sat for a moment. A glance through the passenger window drew her back to the cool April morning and the stillness of the countryside. No sound stirred but that of her own breath and a distant songbird celebrating spring.

Gathering her collar closer to her neck, she forced her attention to the woods that lay beyond the rugged field next to where she'd parked.

Winslow, the small black and white terrier on the seat beside her brought a smile to her mouth and restored her spirits. Opening the door to the brisk air, she slid from the warm leather seat to wade the dew-wet grass to the passenger side of the Range Rover and opened the door for Winslow. Excited to be included in the outing, he leaped to the ground and buried up to his belly in the damp grass. She smiled down at him and reached for the bottle of water on the seat and dropped it into the holder at her waist.

Winslow's excitement ignited her own as she turned toward the scrubby field. Rusted barbed fence wires sagged and clung to rotting posts that barely stayed upright. Lauren carefully grasped the wires, stretched an opening between them and slipped into the field. She gauged the distance to the stand of trees to be twenty-minutes, maybe? Rubbing a finger over the snag her shirt had just suffered, she soothed the sting where the barb nipped her shoulder. Studying the dense woods at the far side of the field, thoughts of grabbing Winslow and getting out of there flashed briefly. Instead she snapped her fingers and moved forward.

"Winslow, let's go!"

Years of neglected overgrowth slowed her progress across the wide patch of earth. But half an hour later she stood gazing up at the tall trees cumbered with briars. She breathed deep, pulling the fresh air into appreciative city lungs.

Her first glimpse of the steep roofline that she now searched for, happened one morning. As she'd made the last curve in the road that straightened into the long stretch toward Valley Ridge, she saw it. The roof-peak had shimmered through the distant treetops as the pale early sun caught it just right. She'd never noticed it before.

Obsessed with the hidden house from that moment on, that last curve became an automatic signal to slow the Range Rover and search for an entrance or private drive to the property. Not even a cow trail had surfaced to indicate a way to the house. Crossing the field on foot seemed her only option.

"Winslow! Here boy, come!" When he ran out of the woods she knelt and filled her hand with water. "You could wait for me, you know." He lapped the water and darted back into the underbrush. She wiped her hand down the side of her jeans and raised the bottle to her lips.

Turning back to the formidable barrier of undergrowth, she gave her ponytail clip a securing tug and plunged in. Deep into the woods, briars as big around as her thumb trailed high into the ancient trees.

"Wicked things!" Lauren cringed and dodged, but knife-sharp thorns pulled strands of dark hair from the silver clip. She pushed at a limb, causing a mass of tangled briars to graze her hand. Instinctively she jerked, digging the thorns deeper into her flesh.

Chills shivered along her spine as she stared at the thin line of blood that curled across her knuckles. Lauren pressed the back of her hand to her faded jeans and bit her lip at the stinging pain.

Sobered by the briar attack, she cautiously forged ahead. As she attempted to hold a sapling out of the trail with her foot, it slithered from under her boot like a snake and sliced through the air, striking her in the face—tears gushed instantly from both eyes, blurring her vision to zero. She crumpled to the ground and jerked her arm up to use the soft shirtsleeve to stop the flood of tears.

Sitting on the cool bed of leaves and moss, bleary eyed, she gazed about checking her vision for damage. Suddenly, blinking rapidly, she stared. Not sure she wasn't imagining it—a hundred feet ahead the warm color of brick flickered and beckoned through the tangle of foliage.

Lauren scrambled to her feet and charged forward, too excited to care that the briars tore at her hands. She emerged from the woods onto what had once been a great lawn. Pushing tangled hair back from her face, she stood mesmerized by the stately mansion standing in the large opening. Winslow startled her when he streaked after a squirrel. "Silly boy, you can't catch it!"

The scene before her resembled an English countryside estate. The house was the one of her dreams. The great lawn had given way to aggressive weeds and thistles, but nearer the house a tenacious patch of yellow flowers thrived.

"How beautiful!" she murmured.

"Excuse me ... ?"

She whirled at the voice, stumbled, caught her balance and stared into the puzzled eyes of a tall man standing several yards away, hands in his pockets, frowning.

"Oh—you scared me!" She laughed, a nervous hollow sound. "I didn't hear you walking up."

"How did you get here?"

"I hiked across that field." Lauren waved in the general direction of the main road and smiled. "I probably shouldn't have come without permission, but I felt ... I just *knew* the house was vacant, and I didn't know how else to get here. I'm intrigued with this place."

He glared without comment until his eyes moved beyond her to the house. He stared, as if forgetting she was there.

Lauren observed the man quietly for a moment then she raised her voice slightly. "It's been abandoned."

His gaze never wavered as he replied in a low voice, "Yes ... it appears that way."

At least he'd heard her.

"Do you know who owns this house? I'd like to get permission to come back and do landscape studies." Lauren pursed her lips. "I'm an artist, and I'm always looking for new locations to paint."

The man ignored her question. What was wrong with him? At least he didn't look threatening. She firmed her voice. "I may be interested in buying this property." She reached up and tightened her hair clasp and scratched an insect bite on her arm. She immediately regretted mentioning an interest in the house—what if he was there for the same reason?

He rubbed a hand over his face and lowered his head, shutting his eyes. He stood for a moment before looking up to once more allow his gaze to sweep the house and grounds.

Lauren shielded her eyes for a closer look. He was above average height with distinct features that bordered on being perfect, yet masculine. Not pretty as some handsome men tend to be. His eyes expressed an emotion other than anger, as she'd first thought. An outdoorsman, in spite of the khakis, chambray shirt, and loafers he wore.

She guessed him to be middle to late thirties. He pushed one hand deep into his pocket, while the other hand raked through longish, sun-streaked, dark blonde hair. His shoulders slumped as his gaze continued roaming the neglected yard. He turned gray-green eyes back to her and for the breath of a second they registered surprise.

With a muffled groan, he squared his shoulders and said, "You need to leave—this is private property!"

He spoke in a low voice, making her strain to catch his words. He averted his eyes, but not before Lauren saw misery in their depths.

She softened her tone. "Sir, I only wanted to—"

"Please, just ... just leave!" He pushed his hand through his hair again and shook his head as if confused. He wheeled abruptly, and long strides carried him along a stone footpath that led beyond the house.

Lauren stared after the tall figure hurrying away. After he disappeared from sight she exhaled, her body sagged with relief. "How rude!" She steadied her hands and once more brushed at the straggling hair around her face. Twisting around, she scanned the yard for Winslow. "Winslow, come!" Why hadn't he barked a warning? She threw her hands in the air and focused once more on the house.

Leave without looking inside? She couldn't do that. Spreading her fingers, she winced at the deep red scratches and figured she'd earned a peek inside. Her gaze traveled down her worn white flannel shirt to faded jeans now stained with dried blood and on down to her scruffy boots. She rolled her eyes, no wonder he'd hurried away.

Picking her way through the overgrowth to one of the large windows, Lauren cupped her hands to the dusty glass and peered inside. Surprisingly the room wasn't empty as she'd expected. Indiscernible shapes of draped furniture set scattered about a spacious room. A beautiful Aubusson rug covered most of the fine hardwood floor. The rug was celadon green with pale-peach cabbage roses woven throughout. Trailing along the rug's wide borders were leaves and vines of dark green.

The owners appeared to have just walked away. Lauren

moved to another window, stopping short at her reflection in the glass. Her ponytail hung half in and half out of the clip, framing her tear-streaked face. A fiery red welt marked where the limb had decked her. For all that poor guy knew she could be an escaped lunatic.

With the side of her fist she rubbed a clean circle on the window—just one more peek before starting the walk back. After a long wistful look at the lovely interior she brushed her hands on her jeans and tore herself away.

"Winslow! Hey boy, come!" He darted from the brush and loped along in front as she trudged back across the used-to-be lawn. Reaching the shade of the trees, she sat on the ground and patted her leg for Winslow to come. "Hey, bud, why didn't you warn me somebody else was here too? You thought you came along just to chase squirrels?"

Winslow searched her face, his tail in action.

"Come on, let's have a drink before we tackle those briars again." Lauren twisted the top off the water bottle and filled her hand. Winslow lapped two hands full of the cool water before Lauren raised the bottle to her lips for a long drink.

Dreading the hike back, she rose, replaced the water bottle in its holder and entered the woods. A muffled sound halted her step. A whisper of unease prickled along her back and up her neck, sending chills to her scalp.

Holding her breath, she listened. He was still there.

Stepping back into the open, she stared at a large mound of foliage a good distance from the house, the direction the sound had came from. The mound appeared to be an explosion of climbing roses. They'd completely enclosed a large arbor or some other structure. She stared at the mound for several moments before turning toward the house and blowing a kiss, then darting into the woods.

Her heart pounded as she hurried to the Range Rover. The thrill of discovery sent her nimbly dodging the briars and limbs this time. "We've found it, Winslow. Our new home." Her voice carried in the quiet of the woods.

Barely slowing down at the fence, she made a running attempt to straddle the wires this time. A barb snagged the seat of her jeans causing an abrupt stop. She pitched headlong into the ditch, leaving blue threads dangling on the wire. Winslow had reached the Range Rover where he sat by the passenger door, watching.

Lauren pointed a finger. "Don't say a word!" She scrambled to her feet and helped him into the seat where he plopped exhausted. "City boy." She scoffed.

Heading toward Valley Ridge and her realtor, the speedometer quickly hit the far side of the speed limit. Adrenaline pumped the foot pedal.

From the very first glimpse she'd known—this was the one. The home she'd been searching for ... dreaming of. Ever since the age of four when her father had died.

CHAPTER 2

auren

A BLACK LINCOLN sedan sat next to Thelma's Cadillac. The Lincoln clinched a bet that Thelma, Lauren's realtor, had a client in her office. Lauren stepped onto the stone pathway and slowed her step. Colorful blooms set off the rustic beauty of the stone cottage. A dark green sign read WADE REALTY. Up the two wide steps to the polished oak door, she paused a second before entering.

Voices mingled with laughter drifted from Thelma's office. Cindy, Thelma's secretary, spoke into a phone hooked on her shoulder as she riffled through a stack of papers. Lauren raised an eyebrow and tilted her head toward the office. Cindy gave her a quick nod confirming that Thelma was with a client.

She flashed Lauren a smile and mouthed, "Sorry."

Lauren gave a thumbs-up and stage whispered, "Thanks." Outside in the SUV, she touched the silver watch on her wrist, eleven forty-five, perfect time to run by and collect her mail.

Minutes later, parked in front of the post office, she pulled the visor down and glanced in the mirror. The red welt where the sapling had smacked her appeared to be growing. Lauren flipped the mirror back up, planted a kiss on Winslow's head and tugged the sunroof partially open. "I'll be back in a few minutes."

She pushed against the thick glass door of the post office and entered the cool interior, braced for the talkative postman, Jonas Bond.

He flashed large white teeth. "Good morning." And after a brief glance discreetly looked away.

Lauren hid a smile at his swift inventory of her disheveled appearance. "My dog and I took a walk in the country." She pointed to her face. "I tangled with a tree."

"Oh mercy," he sympathized.

As she thumbed through the stack of mail, her spirits lifted at the sight of a pale yellow envelope. *Clair! You always know when I need you.* She stuffed the mail into her leather tote. She'd have Clair's card to look forward to later. Lauren turned to confront the postman's expectant expression. He leaned on the counter poised for conversation. Lauren returned his smile. What did a few minutes matter? He meant well.

"Mr. Bond, I have an hour to kill. Any suggestions?"

The postman brightened. "Have you seen much of our town yet?"

"No, I really haven't seen anything, I'm sorry to say. The move to the cottage has taken all my time."

"Well then, you might consider the Opera House or the little historic church building first."

"Oh, great idea! I've heard of the primitive church building."

"Yes, it's one of the oldest buildings in three counties. It's over on The Avenue. If you like primitive, you'll love it. As a matter of fact there's several neat church buildings. We have new walking trails in the city park located right in the center of town. There's the art gallery, Montgomery Fine Art, on The Avenue. You can't miss it. Main Street is mostly shops and tea rooms."

He appeared to search his mind for a second. She jumped when he snapped his fingers.

"Ah, yes, the old theater is worth a visit too."

After all that, he reached across the counter to a crowded rack and pulled out a limp brochure.

"It's all in here, Miss Ashby."

"Oh, thanks a lot. This will be a great help." She smoothed the slip of paper and headed for the door.

Lauren tossed her bag onto the back seat and climbed in up front with Winslow. He roused briefly from his nap. She absent-mindedly stroked his head and scanned the brochure. Church buildings first, she might even find the congregation where she'd choose to worship.

The brochure located the oldest church building on the same street as the art gallery, and since the gallery came first, she might as well check it out. Most small town galleries consist mainly of a place for local artists to display their work so family and friends could gather to admire the local talent and socialize a bit.

Just minutes from the Post Office Lauren guided the Range Rover into the paved, tree-shaded parking area of the gallery. Stunned, she sat motionless, both hands wrapped on the wheel until Winslow rested his paws on her arm. She stroked his head without taking her eyes off the modern building. It certainly didn't resemble anything she'd expected.

Her good friend, Charlie Weston, had told her about this small community, that it boasted a lot of old wealth. It looked as if Charlie, as usual, knew what he spoke of. The owner of the gallery not only exhibited excellent taste, *but* it seemed, also enjoyed their share of the old wealth.

Lauren shifted her gaze and poured her hand full of water for Winslow. He lapped gratefully, drying her hand with his tongue before he settled back to his nap. With the sunroof open and the tall shade trees surrounding the parking area, the interior would stay cool. Strolling toward the gallery entrance, her step lingered. She admired the landscaped beds and life-size bronze works displayed along the wide brick pathway. The choice of shrubbery and trees set off the building beautifully.

A sign of burnished brass read MONTGOMERY FINE ART. The front entrance spoke of unpretentious elegance. The door opened soundlessly as bells chimed softly deep within the interior, alerting the proprietor.

Whoever the gallery's designer and decorator had been, the airy, spacious showroom testified to their excellent taste and knowledge of presentation.

A tall, slim man dressed in dark slacks and a crisp blue pin-stripe shirt, strolled casually toward Lauren. He gazed from the bluest eyes she had ever seen, and he had a gorgeous smile. He pulled his hand from his pocket as he strolled toward her. Lauren quickly hid the hand she'd just watered Winslow with, attempting to give it an extra swipe on the backside of her leg.

"Hello, I'm Matt. Welcome to the gallery. Looking for anything in particular?"

She placed her hand in the one he held out and willed herself not to fidget. An urge to pat her hair, tuck in her shirt, and hitch up her jeans all at the same time was overwhelming.

She regretted stopping here today of all days.

This neat, handsome guy zoomed in sharp focus on her deplorable, woodsy state. She longed to jerk back the offensive just-licked-hand and apologize for even being there. But Matt kept his eyes on hers, much to her amazement, and like a gentleman he refrained from a curious once over.

"Hello," she said. "Don't let me keep you, I'm just killing time." The instant the words passed her lips, a hot flush rose to her face, she darted a look at Matt. Had she actually said she'd just dropped in to kill time? She'd been as rude as that man at the abandoned house.

Matt smiled graciously. "Great—we like for people to drop in and kill time with us. Don't rush, and I'm happy to answer any questions."

She glanced about. Good sense said she should thank him and leave, but curiosity about this wonderful gallery wouldn't allow that. And since she'd already blown the chance for a good first impression, she might as well stay.

Matt commented on several of the artists' work and tried for small talk, but when Lauren remained non-communicative, he pointed to the door he'd come out of earlier saying, "I'll be in there, but if I can be of any help." His eyes lingered on her face for a brief moment before he returned to his office.

Of course she would meet someone like this Matt person on a day she resembled the tail-end-of-summer. It credited his trust in humanity that he'd even leave her alone with the art.

Surprised at some of the names represented in the gallery, Lauren recognized many of them, some of whom she moved in the same social circles.

She strolled toward the office door, Matt walked out as if summoned. Lauren smiled. "I'd like to get a couple of business cards if I may. I didn't see any out here."

"Of course. Did you enjoy the paintings?" Matt reached for a small silver cardholder on the nearby table and held it toward her. "Take as many as you like."

Lauren looked at the cardholder, then back to him. His mouth didn't smile, but those blue eyes danced. He'd not make a poker player. At exactly the same moment they burst into laughter.

"You'd have to know the morning I've had to even begin to understand." She laughed and reached for a card.

Matt chuckled. "And I could have been kinder and gotten cards from the office, but this was more fun." He continued to smile, but his eyes held a question as he studied her battered face.

"A tree limb got me earlier as my dog and I hiked through some woods. He's in the car, probably wondering if I've deserted him." Lauren took a second card and started to leave, but hesitated. "Are you the owner?"

"I'm part owner, along with Jackson Montgomery"

"Montgomery. So the gallery is named after him?"

"Yes ... it's named after him."

"My compliments to the designer and the decorator. You have a wonderful gallery." Lauren glanced around the spacious showroom. "I confess I almost didn't stop. I never expected a gallery like this in a town this size."

"Thank you. I'm glad you did stop, and I'm glad you like the gallery. We ... we did have a wonderful designer and decorator." Matt's voice grew quiet. He glanced around the showroom with the look of someone grown used to his environment, but suddenly awakened to see it again through fresh eyes.

Lauren studied his face.

When he spoke again, his tone had returned to his normal, pleasant voice. "I'm Matthew Williams. Just call me Matt. And I didn't get your name?"

"Lauren Ashby, from New York City."

He looked doubtful as to whether she told the truth. No doubt he'd never encountered another New Yorker in the gallery who looked as ragtag as she did.

"Welcome to our town, Lauren."

Matt Williams had mastered the art of graciousness. He made her feel comfortable in spite of everything as he smiled and toyed with the ring on his little finger.

"Thank you, Matt. I've got to run, but I'll be back when I have more time." And with as much grace as she could muster, Lauren patted her hair and pointed her scruffy boots and torn jeans toward the door. She hoped the missing plug of denim wasn't too revealing.

No sound of movement came from behind as she neared the front entry. She glanced back. Matt remained in the same spot. With a quizzical smile he watched her. Lauren half turned toward him. "There's a small painting in the back, in the far left corner that I think I must have."

"I believe we have several small paintings in the back." He teased. "Which one do you refer to?"

"Oh, yes, of course." Lauren laughed. "It's the exquisite little still life of the daffodils. Could you hold it for a day or two?"

Matt raised his chin, his blue eyes darkened.

She met his gaze and smiled. Matt dipped a slight nod, but didn't return her smile as she turned to leave.

ld Church

LAUREN FROWNED as the heavy door closed behind her. Matt's expression had changed when she mentioned the painting. She was sure of it. Climbing into the Range Rover, she sat for a moment, puzzled. Automatically her hand reached to caress Winslow. Could the painting be sold and he'd forgotten to remove it? Maybe it waited for delivery?

Matthew Williams didn't strike her as a businessman to fall short when it came to details.

She hoped not. The small still life would fit beautifully in her new home. Thoughts of her new home sent a shiver of excitement that trembled her body. Lauren calculated the short distance and turned to swing by Wade Realty once more on the chance that Thelma might now be free. The white Cadillac was gone. Better call Thelma for a meeting first thing in the morning.

That man in the woods had given the impression of being interested in the house, informing her that it was private property. Of course it would be private property; she knew that. Had that been to put her off? She had foolishly let him know that she was interested in it. She hoped he hadn't already spoken for the house. Surely he'd have said something if he had?

With a glance at her watch she pointed the Range Rover once more toward The Avenue to continue a search for the oldest church building in Valley Ridge. She smoothed the crumpled brochure that looked as if Winslow had decided to have a go at it too. The primitive church should only be one or two blocks past the art gallery.

Lauren drove slowly along the wide, tree-lined street. Up ahead a gleaming white steeple rose above a grove of trees. That would be it. Minutes later, parked in front of the small structure, Lauren's breath faltered for the second time that day over a building. She stepped out of her vehicle, gazing at the scene.

"Good morning. May I help you—needing directions?" An older man walked toward her across a patch of thick, lush lawn.

"Oh, hello." She pursed her lips and shook her head. "No, this is what I was looking for. I love this building! It's so quaint and charming."

"Yes, it is, isn't it?" The man tossed a hand trowel on the ground and walked closer, pulling off his yard gloves.

"I'm Ed Blackwell. Preacher and sometimes gardener for this congregation." He smiled, holding out his hand.

She returned his firm handshake. "Lauren Ashby. I'm new in Valley Ridge."

"Then let me be the first to welcome you and invite you to worship with us."

She liked Ed Blackwell. "Thank you. I probably will."

"Good. You'll find the people here are very friendly."

Lauren turned again to study the scene before her. "I'm an artist, and I'd like to do some sketches. Do you think it would be okay?"

"Of course, any time and as often as you like." He glanced as if trying to see the building through her eyes. Lauren could almost hear him wondering why she'd want to do a painting of this plain little structure. Non-artists often expressed that thought aloud.

"Thank you, Mr. Blackwell. I'll let you get back to your work." She turned to leave and the preacher stooped to retrieve his garden tool.

"I hope to see you on Sunday," he called after her.

"Yes, I'm looking forward to it." She waved good-bye and Ed Blackwell nodded and raised his trowel in affirmation as she climbed into the Range Rover. "Let's head for home Winslow. I'm starved, and you've got to be hungry too."

Since she'd decided on getting with Thelma later on the phone, she headed the Range Rover toward the country road. Her mind switched onto autopilot as events of the morning crowded her anxious thoughts. That guy in the woods must know something about that property. Could he be considering a purchase also? Why else would he be there? Panic threatened.

She *must* talk to Thelma first. In no time she wheeled into her own driveway. Not bothering to pull into the garage, Lauren jumped out and grabbed her tote. Suddenly remembering Clair's card, anticipation quickened her step. But first things first—call Thelma.

Fumbling the front door open, she swung it wide for Winslow. He lagged behind, sniffing each flowerpot on the wide porch. "Oh, you rascal." Impatiently she scooped him up. He'd learned that dawdling got him a ride every time.

Inside, Lauren set him on the floor and headed to her bedroom. She plopped the tote on the foot of her bed and rummaged its depths for Clair's card—while also trying to scan for Thelma's name in her phone list. She touched the number— Cindy took her call and scheduled a meeting with Thelma for early the next day.

Winslow streaked off to the sunroom where he thumped his

stainless food bowl and ran back to the bedroom door and tilted his head.

"Sorry sweetie. Give me just a few minutes." Winslow knew what "Sorry sweetie" meant. He scrabbled at the side of her bed until she pulled him up next to where she'd settled for a relaxed, comfy read.

Lauren tore into the yellow envelope. Clair had jotted a short note asking a favor. Would Lauren please check out a gallery in Valley Ridge? The owners of *Montgomery Fine Art* wanted to represent Clair's work—she was only considering it because her dearest friend now lived there. Lauren grinned at the three smiley faces following the last sentence. She clutched the note and fell back on the bed. Wonderful! The idea of Clair showing in a gallery right here in Valley Ridge erased her anxious thoughts about the house for a time as she recalled the warm spring day when she first met Clair Weston. The memory flashed across her vision as clear as if it were yesterday.

The day she broke the rules.

When Lauren turned eight, she had begged her mother into letting her stay in their townhouse without a sitter for the last three hours before her mother got home from work. The house-keeper came at eight in the morning and stayed until two in the afternoon—then the sitter came and stayed until her mother got home at five-thirty. She would only be alone a little over three hours. Her mother finally gave in and rules were set. Lauren was never to leave the townhouse and never talk to strangers or open the door to strangers.

That particular day, when she met Clair, happened to be a beautiful spring afternoon. What possible harm could come from sitting outside in the warm sun for a few short minutes? Lauren brushed away guilty thoughts of the promises she'd made, something she'd never done before.

Perched at the top of the townhouse steps, Lauren watched a young woman park a bright yellow Volkswagen convertible across the street. From the back seat of the Volkswagen, the young woman gathered an armload of canvases, a tote with brushes poking out the top, and a large black folder. An artist! With her arms loaded, she bumped the car door shut with her skinny hip and turned to cross the street, straight toward Lauren.

Long, thick, curly hair the color of new pennies sparkled in the sun and floated about her shoulders. Her skin looked like Lauren's Barbie doll, smooth and perfect. She paused at the lower step and smiled up at Lauren. She had happy green eyes. Lauren thought her the most beautiful creature she had ever seen, outside of television.

"Hi, I'm Clair. You must be my new neighbor."

"I am?" Lauren dared not believe this fairy-tale creature could be her neighbor.

"Yes. I'm moving into 125. How about you?"

"129." Lauren could hardly breathe as she whispered the numbers.

"Why, you're almost right next door. Want to come have a Coke with me?"

Lauren nodded, stricken dumb with sheer happiness. She dismissed her mother's second rule without thought, or hesitation. No punishment she could have imagined would have kept her from having a Coke with the beautiful artist, that warm spring day—because Lauren secretly dreamed of being an artist too, someday.

Lying on her bed with her eyes closed, she felt the sun on her face and smelled Clair's perfume—all that she chose to remember of that fateful day.

Stuffing the card back in the envelope, she jumped up and tickled Winslow awake. "Hey, pal, did you give up on din-din?" She snuggled him up and buried her face against his wiry little body and meandered to the kitchen. Thoughts of Clair lingered. She hadn't realized until years later that Clair, so worldly wise to her eight-year-old mind, had been little more than a child herself that day. Having just celebrated her eighteenth birthday only four days earlier, she'd begged and twisted her father around her little finger until he relented, and she got her own place.

Lauren set Winslow on the floor while she prepared his food. She often wondered how different her life might have been had she not broken the rules ... if she'd been as responsible as her mother trusted her to be, as she'd always been before. What if she had not sat outside on the steps? A melancholy sigh slipped past her lips. If not for Clair, where would she be? Probably not in Valley Ridge in a panic about the house of her dreams.

Lauren set Winslow's food on his mat and breathed a second sigh. With her whole being, she believed that fate had placed her on the steps that day ... in the direct path of Clair Weston.

CHAPTER 4

 ackson

JACKSON'S BRAIN operated from a jumbled mire of emotions as he headed back to Valley Ridge. For the first time in a long time he'd been shaken to his core. Why had he gone to the house today?

He gripped the steering wheel. Why today? He knew why. The last five years he'd lived behind a facade of pretense. Neither Matt nor Ally, the two people closest to him, suspected a thing. Today marked six years ago that his world had changed. The day Jenna died. The first year after her death he'd lived in denial.

He'd not planned on going to the lake today. He often tramped in the woods and around the lake. Walking along the shores of the lake where his dad had taught him to fish never failed to restore his shaky balance, but he never went farther than that, never to the house. But today someone had been prowling around the house.

If only he had left sooner he'd have missed the trespasser, and not have had to deal with her. If only he hadn't taken his rubber boots out of the truck for a cleaning and left them in the garage. If only ...

His walks usually ended at his mother's old rose arbor for a rest and water break. But without his boots, he'd gone straight to the rose arbor to think and meditate, to be alone.

As he'd sat in the rose shrouded arbor, his mind buried in the past, a soft murmur gradually penetrated his consciousness. He poked a small hole through the tangled rose vines. A young woman of twenty-three or twenty-four stood staring at the house. She talked to a small black-and-white dog that sat at her side until a squirrel taunted him and he took the bait, streaking after it.

The old home place had never before been bothered with trespassers—he didn't like the idea of it starting now.

Jackson braced himself to approach the girl. She stood at the south side where Jenna's daffodils grew. As he approached the house a rush of memories unexpectedly flooded his vision. They slammed the breath from his chest and left no time to think. He'd reacted as if it were someone else, not him.

Jackson shook his head and gripped the steering wheel as he tested the Dodge around the curves. His knuckles bunched into white knobs. He drew a ragged breath and glanced at the speedometer, seventy-eight in a sixty—

Easing off the accelerator, he glanced at his watch. "Getting stopped is all I need now," he muttered.

Of all days for Ally to plan lunch at the club, why had he agreed? He groaned and thumped the steering wheel. He'd stayed too long at the house, making him late getting back to town.

Jackson's thoughts kept returning to the incident. He'd never seen the girl before. She must be new. What makes a person pick up and move to a new town? He could never leave Valley Ridge. His memories, his roots were here. *Jenna was here.*

He wheeled into the employee parking and hurried into the office.

Matt glanced up from his desk. "Whoa! What's the rush? I thought you and Ally were having lunch?"

"We are, and I'm late. But I wanted to check first to see if I'd heard from that artist. I'd expected to hear back today. I hope to get her signed on before summer." He quickly scanned his emails.

"Jackson. We need to talk. I didn't realize you had this on display." Matt swiveled his chair toward Jackson.

"What's on display—?" Jackson turned. His jaw hardened when he saw the painting in Matt's hand. "I want it displayed. Does that bother you?" Jackson winced. He never spoke sharply to Matt. In all the years they'd never had a harsh word between them.

Thankfully, Matt didn't rattle easily.

"You know it doesn't bother me. But it does present a problem when someone wants to buy it."

"It's not for sale. You know that." Jackson reached for the painting, his voice testy. "Did one of your clients inquire again? They should know by now, I won't sell it."

"No, not one of my clients. A lady who's new to the gallery expressed an interest in it. She just brought it to my attention."

Jackson's face tightened.

Matt sighed. "If you want it here in the gallery just mark it sold or not for sale. It's no problem either way."

"It's not for sale, and I don't want it marked anyway at all." Jackson turned away. His actions were childish and unreasonable. But he couldn't seem to stop. He liked having the small painting in the gallery; it kept Jenna close. But Matt didn't understand. How could he?

"I don't have time for this, Matt. Ally will think I've stood her up." The rough edge to his voice wasn't lost on Matt who simply nodded and turned to his computer.

Jackson made a quick exit from the office, taking the painting with him. He sat in the truck holding it. He wanted to hug it to his body and mourn. He gazed at the small canvas. The last one Jenna had completed. Placing it face down on the seat beside him, he pulled his old jacket over it. He slumped back for a moment, weary. He'd lingered at the rose arbor as long as he dared, to gain control of his emotions.

It hadn't been long enough.

Now he was late and Ally would sense something had happened if he didn't cheer up.

Jackson turned into the country club parking lot and pulled up next to Ally's white BMW. Her disdain for his pickup made him smile. He brushed at his clothes for any debris he might have picked up from the woods. Once in the club he zigzagged between tables, making his way to where Ally sat at their usual place.

She glanced up with a fake-smile—he was late.

"You're late, Jackson."

"Twenty minutes is not late, Ally. Thirty minutes is late." He grinned at her.

"Anytime I get here before you, makes you late."

He reached across the table and patted her hand. Jackson knew she hated it when he was even a minute late. "It's good to see you too."

"Oh, I'm sorry. And I'm impatient. But knowing that, why do you test me?" She switched on a real smile.

Glad to end the exchange, he tackled the dilemma of ordering lunch. Food ranked at the bottom of the list of things he wanted right now. The morning still gripped his stomach with an iron fist. The scene at the house had been bad enough, but snapping at Matt ... he sighed. Closing the menu, he hoped Ally would follow his lead. He glanced up at the waiter. "I'll have the Caesar Steak salad and tea."

Ally continued to peruse a menu she had memorized.

Finally she glanced up. "Jackson, you're getting awfully thin."

Concern darkened her hazel eyes. "Are you sure that's all you'll have, just a salad?"

Not up to this, he lightened his tone before speaking.

"I had a large, late breakfast." As soon as the words were out, he knew it wouldn't fly.

Her eyes widened. "Since when did you start eating breakfast? Much less a large one."

"Ally, choose something. We're holding this young man up." He glanced at the waiter and forced a chuckle. Jackson had eaten breakfast—dry cereal in a mug with a splash of half-and-half to float it. They were out of milk. Brooke refused to drop an empty container in the trash. His irritation spiked, remembering the talk with her.

Ally smiled and placed her order. Gazing across the table she spoke softly. "Never mind me, Jackson. I had a bad time at the Art Council meeting this morning. Marla Turner will be the death of me yet. You'll never guess what she brought up ..."

Jackson concentrated on Ally's voice, hoping he contributed appropriately to the conversation.

But his thoughts roamed to the country house, remembering a pair of violet-blue eyes with the longest black lashes.

CHAPTER 5

n Guard

LUNCH FINALLY ENDED, and they strolled across the parking lot to Ally's car. Jackson hugged her lightly. "I'll call you later."

"Are you terribly busy today?" She lingered with her hand on his arm.

His guard rose. "Not so much, why?"

"Oh, you just seemed preoccupied all through lunch." She spoke softly and opened her bag to search for her car keys.

"I'm sorry. I guess I am a little distracted. I've been working on a deal. A new artist for the gallery." He ran his fingers through his hair. "I can't seem to get it tied up. I'll call you later this evening. We could see a movie if you'd like?" He raised his brows.

Ally nodded.

Jackson held the door while she gracefully slid into the seat. He closed her door, waved and walked to his truck and climbed in. Mean and unfair, that's how he felt as he watched her sports car pull out of the parking lot.

Ally deserved better.

For the life of him he didn't know why she continued to bother. Ally Parker could be described as beautiful. She was tall, slim, with hazel eyes and soft chestnut-colored hair that swung just below her ears. They'd been friends since grade school.

Ally put up with a lot from him and Brooke. Lately Brooke whined and acted resentful when Ally spent time with them. He didn't know why she behaved that way or what to do about it. Ally hinted that he spoiled Brooke, and maybe he did.

After Jenna died, Brooke had been his reason for living, his reason to get up mornings. All he'd wanted was to hide from the world and grieve. If not for Brooke and her needs, he'd have done just that.

After he'd floundered for a year, Matt sat him down one day and talked straight. Reminding him that he didn't have options. Brooke was three years old, a baby, and she needed him. That's when he started pretending. Pretending that he was fine, back on track.

He kept his grief private, hidden.

The people who loved him just wanted him to be okay again. How could he ever be okay again? Jenna was gone.

Pretending had made it easier. His friends and family breathed a collective sigh of relief. And they left him alone. At times he even fooled himself. He stayed busy allowing very little time to reflect on the past.

And he'd allowed Ally to gently press her way into his life. This morning at the house his reaction surprised him. Strangely enough it wasn't so much the trespasser as seeing the deplorable state of the house and grounds. That shook him to his core. Jackson had looked past the girl, appalled. What had he been thinking, neglecting it that way? What would his mother and father think if they could see it now? The incident forced him to take a hard look at the cowardly sham of a thing he called a life.

Could he find the courage to live life for real?

The short distance from the club to the gallery seemed farther than normal. Suddenly the need to smooth things over with Matt urged Jackson's speed. He parked beside Matt's silver Lexus and made his way to the employee entry.

Matt looked up from his desk. "Hmm, quick lunch."

"Yeah, the club wasn't busy and we had good service." Jackson ran his fingers through his hair. "Matt, I'm sorry about earlier. This hasn't been a good day." Jackson gazed at Matt then glanced away and swallowed the lump in his throat.

Matt nodded. "I know. Hey, my timing wasn't good either. I should have waited about the painting. This day is always a hard one."

They were quiet for a moment. Jackson stuck his hand out to Matt. "Is everything okay then?"

Matt reached and gripped Jackson's hand. "No problem, all's well, friend."

Jackson cleared his throat, relieved. "So tell me about the new client you had this morning." He settled on the corner of the large oak desk that had been his father's.

Matt swiveled his chair and faced Jackson.

"Oh, just a pretty girl browsing, said she had some time to kill." Matt grinned.

"That's a good sign."

"What's a good sign?" Matt frowned.

"You smiled when you mentioned her. She must have made an impression." Jackson grinned back at Matt.

"Yeah, she made an impression all right. She looked like she'd been cutting brush on the back forty or something." Matt laughed.

"I thought you said she was pretty?"

"Yeah, she was pretty, in spite of everything."

Jackson shot a puzzled look at Matt before turning on his

computer. "And the only thing that caught this pretty girl's attention happened to be the daffodils?" He could have bitten his tongue.

"Come on, Jackson, be fair—everyone that sees it, wants it."

"Hey, sorry again. Don't mind me. I'm taking the painting home." He glanced at Matt over his shoulder. "So then, this girl, she was pretty like how?"

"I don't know, just pretty." Matt shrugged.

"Have any luck getting a phone number?" Jackson grinned.

"Nope, I didn't even try. She's too young for me."

At forty-one Matt was three years older than Jackson.

"But now that I think of it, you might have liked her. She had that outdoorsy, windblown look. Your type." Matt laughed.

"What do you mean, *my* outdoorsy type? Ally considers the sidewalk to the department store a hiking trail." They laughed when Matt agreed with him.

"And when they're too young for you, pal, they're too young for me too. Besides, I'm not looking." He raised his eyes expecting to see Matt's easy-going smile, but instead, a strange expression lingered on Matt's face, one Jackson had never seen before.

Matt quickly looked away.

The outer bell chimed in the gallery showroom. Maggie hadn't gotten back from the bank so Matt hurried out, looking relieved for the excuse.

What was all that about? Jackson tapped a rhythm on the desk with the side of his thumb. He recognized deep-down unhappiness. He'd seen it often enough in his own mirror. The thought that Matt could have problems was troubling. He'd never thought of Matt as unhappy in any way. What did Matt have to be unhappy about?

"Want to take in a movie with Ally and me?" Jackson offered when Matt returned to the office.

"No, thanks. I have big plans with my TV and an exciting documentary on whales." Matt spoke in his normal, easy manner.

"You sure?" Jackson probed. Had he been mistaken? No, Matt's expression had been real.

"Yeah, I'm sure, besides Karen's coming over to watch on the big screen."

"She's the one who's just a friend?"

"Yes, just a friend. Same as she was the last time you asked." Matt gave Jackson a let-it-go look.

"You've been seeing her for some time, haven't you?" Jackson trod on shaky ground.

"No, I don't *see* her. She lives in the condo next to mine. We're friends. We knock around some, that's all." Matt turned to his computer, ending the conversation.

Matt never lacked for female company, so why hadn't he married? He possessed all the trappings that women tend to go for—good manners, a sense of humor and financial security. Jackson sneaked a sidelong glance at Matt. And yeah, he looked as good as the next guy.

Ally might have more insight into Matt's affairs of the heart. He'd ask her. Maybe one of her friends would like to meet a nice guy and settle down.

They worked the rest of the afternoon with the office in relative quiet until the back entry bell jangled off the wall.

Jackson checked his watch, hurricane Brooke, eight, going on eighteen. She hit the back door full throttle.

"Hey Pumpkin, what's up?" He closed the file he'd been working on.

"My bike needs air in the front tire. It nearly killed my legs peddling uphill."

Her tone accused. Somehow it was his fault that the private school she attended four blocks away, was downhill to the gallery. Jackson ignored the whiny undertone and attempted to head her off. "We'll pump those tires up first thing in the morning, okay?" He rushed on before she could whine that he would probably forget. "Want to go to the early movies this evening?"

"Can I pick?" Chin squared, Brooke had the same determined, dark amber gaze of her mother.

"*May*, you pick. Maybe we should check the listings and all decide together." He didn't breathe.

"Who's all?" Her chin inched higher. A challenge gleamed in her eyes.

"Brooke, you know perfectly well who's all."

"Never mind. It doesn't matter." She deflated like a pricked balloon and dragged the words to emphasize the unfairness of her life.

Matt saved the day when he returned to the office.

"Hello, Sunny Girl. Want to watch the whales on TV tonight with Karen and me?" Matt sat in his chair.

Brooke loped to his side, slid an arm across his shoulders and latched it around his neck. Her eyes brightened. "And eat pizza?" Brooke loved Uncle Matt, and he returned the feeling a hundredfold.

"Sure, why not," he said.

Matt had given her the nickname Sunny when she was just a toddler. Everyone else had naturally picked up on it. Even her mother had called her Sunny when the two of them were being playful. Jackson always used her given name except for the occasional, Pumpkin.

"Dad, is it okay if I watch TV with Uncle Matt and Karen? It's the whales program. You can pick me up later." Brooke asked permission and gave instruction, all in one breath.

"Sure. I'll get you on the way home from the movie. And don't eat too much pizza."

He caught the smirk that passed between Brooke and Matt. Brooke would eat pizza until she popped. Jackson ran his fingers through his hair. At least Ally would enjoy the evening with just the two of them. Brooke could get on anyone's nerves at times.

Jackson stood. "If it's okay with you, Matt, I think I'll cut out a little early."

Matt nodded. "Sure thing. Sure you're okay? Today's been—" He stopped at Jackson's look, and patted Brooke's arm and started chatting with her about school.

Jackson had one more thing to do before the day ended.

CHAPTER 6

ome

THE DAY GOT off to a strange start and it had continued in that mode so far. He swung the truck door shut and slumped over the steering wheel, his forehead pressed onto the back of his hands. Time to deal with the past; he had already put it off far too long. Today had marked a turning point.

Had it been instinct or fate that guided him to the house this particular morning?

Jackson exhaled wearily and straightened his shoulders. He cranked the engine and backed out of the gallery parking. Taking a right turn he headed toward Old Elm Road.

Late afternoon sun streamed through the windows. The sun's warmth and the hum of the engine gradually relaxed his tense body for the first time since morning. His thoughts drifted back to the house, as they'd been doing off and on all day. He remembered he'd left his stainless water bottle in the arbor. After he'd asked the girl to leave he practically ran from the house and circled through the trees, slipping back into the arbor on the side concealed from the house.

He hadn't been able to think, much less talk, on seeing the condition of the grounds. The girl must have thought him an idiot.

He'd sat on the bench giving her time to leave. Several moments later he stood and peeked through the hole he'd made earlier. What ... ! She stood with her face pressed against a window and as he'd watched, she turned and made her way toward the woods, calling for the dog.

Ready to leave himself, Jackson watched the girl for a moment before reaching for the water bottle. The bottle had slipped from his hand, he grabbed, but the steel thing clanged against the stone floor like a fire alarm. He jumped to the vines and peered out, hoping the mass of greenery had muffled the noise.

The girl stepped out of the trees and gazed in his direction. Jackson quickly drew back.

She *had* heard.

She couldn't possibly have seen him, but he'd felt exposed under her stare. He peeped out again in time to see her blow a kiss in the direction of the house. How strange.

So, for the second time that day, he was headed for the house that had once been his home. The steady throb of the engine lulled his tired body, pulling him down. Violet-blue eyes drifted across his vision . . . long lashes and a very pleasant voice . . . *'I came across the field. I wanted to see the house.'* Jackson startled, jerking the wheel dangerously. He shook his head. Her voice had sounded as clear as if she sat next to him in the cab.

He straightened and gripped the wheel. His heart pounded, he'd dozed off. He quickly put the window down and thrust his face into the rushing wind. Soon the turn off to the private drive come into view.

Jackson turned onto the driveway and dread squeezed his heart. The truck slowed to a crawl up the long drive and stopped at the heavy iron gate. The keypad had been disengaged years ago. He reached into the glove box for the key to open the gate manually. His fingers groped several familiar objects: his dad's old pocketknife, a small flashlight, a handful of pecans, and then the key ring with three brass keys.

His and Jenna's keys.

Old memories tightened and squeezed his breath. He fingered the keys. No more pretending, no hiding from the past. His unsteady hand inserted the key into the lock.

Frozen from long days of silence, the heavy gate creaked and shuddered under the strain of movement. He'd not been back to the house since that day. Six years ago.

Almost a year after Jenna's death, his mother, knowing he wasn't coming back any time soon, had closed the house. She'd handled all the details for him. They'd kept the gardener on the first few years. Until his arthritis forced him to retire.

Since then nothing had been done about the yard.

Jackson coaxed each side of the gate back against the unkempt hedge. Behind the wheel again, he touched the accelerator lightly, and the truck crawled up the wide familiar drive to the front of the house.

Warm afternoon sunlight filtered through the trees, casting long shadows that played across the big house like restless fingers. He parked and sat in the truck while memories rushed over him like a great flood. This house had been his birthplace, his home. He touched the third key on the ring, feeling the smooth worn brass. He caressed it with his thumb. His key for after school, just in case he needed it, which seldom happened. He'd felt grown-up when his parents presented him with his own key. They'd *trusted* him.

His eyes swept the neglected grounds and for the second time that day, his heart ached. He'd broken their trust. But it wasn't too late to make things right.

Jackson stepped out of the truck, hesitated then quickened his steps. A walk through the house would satisfy the vow he'd made to himself. One small step at a time he'd promised.

Jenna would want him to move on.

The key slid smoothly into the lock on the carved front door. The bolt hammered solid as it released. Furtively he stepped into the wide entry. The musty smell of rooms long closed up enveloped his senses. Gone were the wonderful smells from the days when this house had been home. Moving slowly as an intruder might have, he found his way to the great room. He looked past the random shapes of draped furniture to scenes from the past. In this room he and Jenna had sat on the floor playing with Brooke, their bare feet together, their legs spread to form a safety barrier as she'd played back and forth between them. They'd laughed and delighted in the miracle of their baby daughter.

In the silent, darkening room Jackson whispered.

"Jenna, she's independent just as you were. She's you all over." He slipped off his shoes and sat on the rug Indian-style. His arms folded across his chest, his head hung. Deep sobs racked his body, and the tears came. The pain gripped fresh and raw as it had that night when Jenna slipped away.

Time stood still until his emotions drained, and his heart found peace.

He raised an arm and wiped his sleeve across his eyes. A final, deep sigh shuddered his spent body. He breathed deeply. This strange day had brought him home.

Home. The years melted away.

He felt Jenna's presence. Jackson embraced the peace that settled over his tired body, and he gave thanks.

God had heard his prayers.

Dusk approached, but he didn't want to leave. He leaned back and stretched out on the rug. He'd dreaded the day when he would have to come here again. But he'd found his way back. And knowing in his heart that he still belonged here, filled his senses with a deep peace.

Jackson took a deep cleansing breath and sat up. He slipped his loafers back on and rose from the floor. After moving to the large windows, he stood gazing out. Long shadows streaked across the shaggy lawn. His gaze wandered to the edge of the woods where he'd found the girl.

The deep shadows on the grass blurred. Giving way to violet-blue eyes with thick black lashes. She had touched her fingertips to her lips and blew a kiss toward the house. He'd not seen that gesture since his mother used to do it when he was a kid and he and his dad would be leaving on a fishing trip.

A blue jay suddenly flew toward the window and veered from the glass just in time. Startled by the bird's close call, Jackson glanced at his watch and groaned. *Ally*. He'd only suggested a movie because he felt guilty. Now he had to go sit through it. And he couldn't be late again. Not twice in one day.

He wanted to linger here now that he'd found his way back. Change stirred deep in his heart. Healing had begun.

* * *

Bell-chimes echoed softly in the distance. While waiting for Ally to answer the door, the truth hit him like a punch to the stomach. Jackson loved Ally, but he was not in love with her. Clarity of conviction jolted his body. He took a deep breath.

Ally opened the door with a smile. "Hi, Jackson, come in while I grab a jacket. Sometimes the theater gets a little cool."

Ally never kept anyone waiting. She'd been punctual since first grade when his mother carpooled them to school. His lateness was a real contention with her.

"I had the same thought." He lifted his elbow indicating the sweater he'd hastily pulled on at the last minute. His voice sounded hollow as he swayed under the finality of his feelings. Ally didn't seem to notice anything.

"Did Brooke not come?" she asked.

"No. The whales won out."

She raised a questioning brow.

"Uncle Matt invited her to watch TV with him and Karen—and pig-out on pizza. We didn't stand a chance." Jackson reached to open the door.

Ally laughed as they stepped outside and closed the door. "You know how she loves her Uncle Matt."

She patted his arm to comfort him for losing out.

"About Matt, remind me to tell you something later."

"Can't you tell me as we drive?" she asked.

"I'd rather talk later, over coffee. Okay?"

"Sure. But we can't linger over dinner if we plan to catch the first show."

Bone-numbing tiredness settled over his weary body. He glanced at her mother's big Lincoln sitting in the drive. "Are we taking your mother's car, I hope?"

"Yes." Ally smiled. "She won't be needing it."

Jackson stretched his long legs and welcomed the comfort of the luxurious leather seats. His mind was still in turmoil. He had never mentioned marriage to Ally. But she let it be known in small, subtle ways that she expected they would eventually marry. He cared deeply for her. He had even tried to be in love. Ally had just always been there. He didn't expect to ever have the same feelings for anyone else that he'd shared with Jenna.

"Jackson, did you hear me?" Ally touched his arm. "We could cancel the movie if you're too tired. Really, I wouldn't mind."

"No, Ally, I'm fine. It's been a long day, that's all."

"I have a suggestion."

"Okay. What's your suggestion?" He leaned his shoulder closer to hers.

"How about a leisurely dinner and coffee afterwards. We'll skip the movie and you can tell me about Matt."

"I confess that does sound great to this selfish person. The best suggestion I've heard all day. But are you sure?"

"Absolutely. I'm tired too."

He took Ally's free hand and held it in both of his. "And by the way, have I ever told you what a thoughtful person you are?"

Her soft laughter told him she was happy that he appreciated her thoughtfulness.

Later that evening Jackson stirred half-and-half into the strong coffee and brought up the subject of Matt.

"Ally, have you ever thought that Matt may not be happy? That he might wish his life was different? I don't know, maybe a wife and kids?"

"Jackson, most people do want a home and family."

Ally gave him the look she reserved for when he really pushed the late thing, and said, "Why would Matt be any different?"

"Then why hasn't he married Karen? They spend lots of time together."

Ally drew back slightly and gave him a pointed look.

"What? What did I say?" Then the look she gave him answered his question.

"Oh, Jackson, nothing. And I don't know why he hasn't married Karen." She added another sugar to her coffee.

Jackson ducked his head and gulped the hot coffee. Ouch! He deserved a scorched tongue. She had every right to wonder the same about their relationship.

"How do you think we could find out if he is unhappy or lonely?" Ally asked, her eyes full of genuine concern for their mutual friend.

"I don't know, fix him up with one of your friends?"

"Matt knows most of my friends, and he's never paid any particular attention to any of them. It would thrill Carol Beckett to death if he showed some interest."

"Why, what's wrong with her?" Jackson frowned.

"What do you mean, wrong with her?" Ally drew back. "It's Matt. He's not interested." She held her cup.

Jackson sneaked a look. She looked tired and she'd lost her enthusiasm for the evening.

After a while he said, "It's getting late, and maybe I'm wrong."

"If you think it would help, I'll come up with a project and ask Matt to help me with it, that way I could spend time with him and take the opportunity to snoop." Her face brightened. "Actually, Gram does need help cataloguing her art collection."

Jackson's brows went up. "Ally, that's a clever idea."

They rode in silence on the drive back. A heavy silence, the kind that makes you nervous, like maybe the other person knows what's on your mind. He gave her a sidelong glance. She seemed deep in thought. He searched his memory over the last two years. Ally had been persistent in a soft, determined way. She'd made herself a comfortable part of his life. And he'd allowed it. Ashamed to admit that he'd taken the easy way out.

Ally parked in her parent's driveway. "Coming in?"

"Thanks, Al, but I'd better go collect Brooke."

Walking around to her side of the car, Jackson gathered her in his arms and held her tight. He did love Ally. He couldn't imagine the pain and loneliness if she hadn't been there after Jenna died.

Ally pulled away from his embrace and searched his face. "Good night, Jackson," she said and reached up to kiss his mouth softly. "I'll come by tomorrow and get with Matt about Gram's collection."

"Good deal. You can find out what's going on with the big lug if anybody can—with your powers of womanly persuasion." He spoke with tenderness.

"Oh, really? I don't see that my womanly powers have such a great track record."

Jackson had no comeback. He sneaked a guilty glance as they walked to her door.

"I'll call to make sure Matt's free and to give him a rundown about the collection." She gave Jackson a quiet look, said good night and went inside.

He jammed his hands into his pockets and walked to his truck. He glanced at Ally's closed door and then looked up into the night sky. To the list of guilty and selfish, he added old and sad. Yet another emotion stirred deep in his soul. Relief. Somehow, his load had lightened.

Tomorrow he'd call Thelma Wade about finding him a groundskeeper. He would need one.

It was time to put his life back in order.

CHAPTER 7

 auren

LAUREN PACED, arms tightly folded, aware that Thelma waited patiently. "If the elderly gentleman who owns the house died, why isn't the house for sale?"

"It's just not that simple, Lauren." Thelma studied the pen in her hand for a moment before she looked up.

"It belongs to his heir."

"Have you seen the place lately?" Lauren heard the edge in her voice and softened the tone. "It's shameful. If the heirs really cared, they'd live there and take care of that wonderful house."

"Like I've explained, there are reasons, and there's only one heir—"

"Thelma, please try once more." She sat on the edge of the chair she'd just plopped onto. "I have errands to run. But I'll be home this evening. I'll wait to hear from you." She rose and hurried from the office. Out of the corner of her eye she saw

Thelma raise her hand, palm up, and then drop it back to her desk.

Poor Thelma. That was a mean thing to do to her.

Winslow's eyes followed her as she crossed in front of the Range Rover. Lauren smiled and waved at him. Climbing into the driver's seat she leaned and kissed the top of his head.

"We'll get our house, even if I have to find the heir and badger the gentleman myself."

Lauren headed for the gallery, but a glance at her watch reminded her that Matt would probably be at lunch. Instead, she'd run by the little church and do a few quick sketches and catch Matt later.

In the shade of the SUV, a watercolor board and paper on her lap, the paint palette on the ground, Lauren sat on the grass with her ankles crossed and dipped a half-inch sable brush in the water jar. Within minutes color flowed onto the paper. Soon she breathed easier, lost in the ebb and flow of the fluid sky and the white building with mauve shadows. As always, time stood still when she had a brush in her hand.

"Wow! I wish I could do that."

She made a bobble on the cloud she'd just added. Lauren didn't mind peoples' curiosity and comments as she worked. But the child's voice startled her. She hadn't heard her approach.

"Oh, you could with enough practice." She corrected the stroke and looked up into the face of a little girl.

"Have you ever tried to watercolor?" She smiled, welcoming the interruption.

"No," the child answered shyly.

"How old are you?" Lauren had not been around many children. None, as a matter of fact and she didn't have a clue when it came to guessing ages.

"Eight. Until my birthday." The little girl's eyes brightened.

"Oh, when is that?"

"September 16."

"September sixteenth is perfect for a birthday. My name is Lauren. What's your name?"

"Brooke." She glanced over at the bike parked on the sidewalk. Lauren glanced at it too, and back to Brooke.

"Well, Brooke, at just about your age I started art lessons." Lauren watched closely to see her reaction. As she'd expected, hope, excitement, doubt, and fear all mingled in the large, amber eyes.

"I have to go. Lunch period is over." She ran to the bike and then turned back to Lauren. "Will you be here tomorrow?" She twisted the fringe that dangled from the handlebars.

"Um, yes, I will. Same time." Lauren decided in a heartbeat, whatever came up, it wouldn't keep her away tomorrow. This child intrigued her. With her huge amber eyes and long blonde hair, she would make a wonderful little model.

"Bye, Lauren. See you tomorrow."

Lauren waved and watched her peddle down the street at record speed. The short interruption had been enjoyable. She noted the time—a little after twelve-thirty. She must remember, same time tomorrow. Lauren's desire to create images had never gone away or dimmed with time. The child brought it all back fresh and new.

Brooke reminded her of herself at that age. It might be fun giving the child art lessons.

Winslow woke and barked from the window above, he'd had his nap and wanted to join her on the grass.

"Hey, boy, did you have a good nap? Winslow, wait, and I'll help you out." She laughed as he all but threw himself out the door. With his leash clipped to his collar she tossed the end next to her paints. He meandered about for several minutes sniffing the grass before he plopped at her feet.

A new sheet of paper inspired her to paint for the rest of the afternoon. It kept her mind off the house. Why hadn't she thought to get the owner's address? Thelma probably wouldn't give it to her. She chuckled and Winslow's ears perked up. He watched her face.

"Oh, Winslow, it's just me being silly," she reassured him and dragged a brush loaded with color onto the pristine paper.

* * *

HOURS LATER, long shadows crept across the church lawn.

"Good grief, Winslow!" Lauren scratched his head. "Why didn't you remind me of the time?"

Was there time to do another study? Or should she try to catch Matt at the gallery? It would be rude to run into the gallery right at closing time. Besides, violet shadows on white buildings looked the most beautiful in late afternoon light.

Lauren glanced at her hands. The scratches would be almost healed by tomorrow. Recalling the first time she'd met Matt, Lauren hoped to be more presentable the next time she saw him.

Doing another study won out.

* * *

LAUREN PULLED into the same spot she'd parked in the last time, flipped the mirror down and applied a light touch of warm-rose lipstick. The welt near her eye had healed. She looked normal again. She'd dressed casually, but with care, in wheat colored linen slacks and a silk sweater of periwinkle blue. Clair had remarked once that the sweater matched her eyes. She wore her long hair loose, casually back from her face.

"You get to go too, Winslow."

She gathered him into her arms and crossed the parking lot. Inside the gallery she sat Winslow on the marble floor. Across the room Matt conversed with a young woman over some papers the girl held in her hands.

"Come Winslow, let's browse until Matt's free." She reminded herself to stop talking to Winslow in public.

Before long Matt walked toward her. Recognition lit his eyes. He smiled, held his hand out, obviously glad to see her again.

"Hello, Lauren. I almost didn't recognize you at first." He flushed, as he must have realized how that could be taken. He released her hand and quickly knelt to speak to Winslow. "Hey guy, are you an art lover too?"

Matt looked up at Lauren. "Does he ever disagree with your taste in art?"

"I don't think Winslow cares much about style and genre."

They laughed and Matt stood. "You do look different today." He smiled. "And may I add you look great, as a matter of fact." His eyes were direct and appreciative.

"Thank you. I'm glad you didn't recognize me. I looked a mess the other day. I'm not fully recovered from that adventure." Lauren smiled down at the little terrier. "Winslow and I are both adjusting to country life."

Matt pushed his hands into his pockets and tilted his head to one side. "Do you hike often? Isn't that what you said you were doing the other day?" He looked puzzled.

"Yes, we were, but I'm not into hiking for fun, I just like trees." She vowed not to mention the house again until after she had it bought.

"You were looking at trees in the woods?" He grinned. "Um, logical."

Lauren laughed. "I like to study trees—certain trees." That should be enough information to satisfy his curiosity. "I came back to get the small painting that's in the back. Did you find information about the artist for me?"

"Uh, Lauren, about that particular painting, it wasn't supposed to be here. It belongs to someone who doesn't want to sell it."

"Oh, really?" She allowed herself a pout. That little still life had been intended as a reward for herself, the first purchase for her new home. "Oh, well … are there any other pieces by that artist that I could see? I loved the style and the brushwork."

"I'm sorry, Lauren. Really, I … we don't have anything else."

Matt looked so uncomfortable and regretful about the painting that she swallowed the lump of disappointment.

"It's okay, I just fell in love with the brushwork and colors. But I'll find another one." She smiled to prove she meant it.

"I'm really sorry. I hadn't noticed that it was back there." Matt pressed his fingertips together and shifted from one foot to the other. "If I can do anything else, I'd like to make it up to you."

"Please, don't worry about it. But you should definitely carry that artist's work. I have a friend who I hope will be in town soon, I'd have loved for her to see it. I'll bring her in to meet you. Lauren looked at her watch. "Oh! I've got to run." She scooped Winslow up.

"Great, I'll look forward to meeting your friend. But before you go, let me get you our brochure of events. It covers every-thing for the next month. Maybe there's one you'll be interested in." Matt hurried to grab the printed material. He returned, handing her an elegant booklet. She practically snatched it from his hand.

"Thanks, I'll have a look." It was almost time for her to be at the church. She didn't want to miss her little biker friend after promising she'd be there.

Sliding to the curb in front of the church, Lauren parked and bailed out. She rummaged for the old paint apron she kept in the back, not wanting to ruin her sweater and slacks. While search-ing, she chatted to Winslow. "You get to meet a nice little girl today and she's going to love you." Finding the paint-spattered apron, she whipped it on. Settled on the grass, she applied bold strokes of color to her paper. Lauren practiced a warm up before starting a painting. In minutes Brooke's bike whispered to a stop on the sidewalk. Lauren glanced at Winslow. He tensed, his ears perked and his eyes bore into hers as he listened.

"Hello, Brooke. You made it." Lauren smiled.

Brooke's eyes immediately fastened on Winslow.

"Is this your dog?" she whispered and fell to her knees next to Winslow.

Winslow's tail thumped the grass, but he didn't move a hair. Lauren set her drawing board aside and moved closer to Winslow. "Yes. And I think you two should be introduced. Winslow can hardly wait to meet you." Lauren watched a big smile spread across the child's face.

"Really? He wants to meet me? How do you know?"

Lauren smiled and lifted her brows. "I just know."

Brooke clasped her hands close to her chest almost under her chin. Her eyes sparkled as her gaze locked on Winslow. Lauren couldn't tell which of the two was most excited, the child or Winslow.

"Winslow, I'd like you to meet Brooke, my new friend. Brooke, this is Winslow."

"Can I pet Winslow?" Brooke twisted her fingers.

"Yes. You *may* pet Winslow. I think he's waiting for you to make the first move."

Brooke gently petted Winslow's head. In a flash he found her lap. She giggled and hugged him close.

Ten minutes into the visit, Lauren glanced at her watch. She mustn't cause Brooke to be late getting back to school. Obviously this child didn't have a pet of her own. Lauren recognized the hunger in her eyes. Growing up in the city, it wasn't practical to have a dog. Her mother had reminded her of that every time the subject came up. She never got a dog. But this child didn't live in a big city.

"What time do you need to be back at school, Brooke?" Lauren observed how gently she stroked Winslow's body. He had managed to wiggle completely onto the little girl's lap and reveled in the attention.

Brooke's eyes grew large. "Last bell is at twelve forty-five."

"You just have time to make it. Winslow wouldn't want you to get in trouble at school." Lauren smiled and lifted him off Brooke's lap. "You better run."

Brooke quickly kissed the top of Winslow's head and ran to her bike.

"Bye, Winslow." She grabbed the handlebars and as she got on the bike she looked back. "Will you be here tomorrow, Lauren?"

"I can't make it tomorrow, things to do. Maybe the next day?"

She needed to meet Brooke's mother. A child shouldn't have friends their parents weren't aware of.

"Okay. I'll watch for you." She flew down the street, her legs a blur of motion.

Hours later, as Lauren loaded her painting gear the cell phone rang. She'd forgotten it for an entire afternoon. A glance at the screen and her stomach tightened. She uttered a prayer and held her breath. "Hi, Thelma. Any news?"

"Lauren, can you come by tomorrow afternoon, around three?"

"Sure, of course. Can you tell me if it's good news? Or ... bad ... it's bad, isn't it?" Her heart sank.

"I'd rather not go into it now. I have a client due any minute. I may have another property you'd like, and I'd rather not go into it on the phone. I'll see you tomorrow."

Thelma said goodbye before Lauren could protest. Jerking the phone away from her ear, she glared at it.

"That hateful man *is* after my house." By the time she had her gear loaded and Winslow settled in his seat, she'd worked herself into a state. "Okay, Winslow, let's have some water and calm down."

Winslow, as cool as a cucumber, tilted his head. She smiled and lightly scratched the top of his head. "Okay, lets have some water and *I'll* calm down."

The sun lingered on the horizon as she drove past the gallery. Several cars sat in the employee parking. Lauren's foot hit the brake—there sat the red Mazda that had almost run her off the road.

Lauren wracked her brain to recall some detail of the driver. It had been a girl, she remembered. Why hadn't she paid more attention? She guessed she'd been more concerned about how close their bumpers were, than the color of the driver's hair. The gallery just got bumped to the top of tomorrows to-do-list.

CHAPTER 8

he Guest

IT HAD BEEN A LONG DAY, but one that ended well when Lauren convinced Clair to hop a plane and come see Montgomery Fine Art gallery for herself. Clair promised to call back once she'd booked her flight. But even the excitement over Clair's visit couldn't dismiss Lauren's worry about the house in the woods. She would absolutely refuse to look at any other properties. Tomorrow she'd make that clear to Thelma.

After a hot shower and a solitary supper, an early evening beckoned. Turning the covers back, she climbed into bed, weary and anxious.

The soft music alarm sounded early the next morning, easing Lauren awake. The good night's sleep had done wonders for her outlook and her damaged hands. She hummed as she brushed her dark hair until the warm highlights gleamed. Gathering her hair into a smooth, low ponytail, she fastened it into place with a round silver clip. She'd taken extra care with her appearance, more than she'd taken in a long time, since before the move to Valley Ridge.

A quick turn in the mirror proved the results. The pink fitted linen dress she'd picked up two years ago in Italy still looked great. The soft color set off her dark hair.

She gave one last glance in the mirror just as the front bell chimed. Grabbing her earrings Lauren hurried to the door.

"Good morning Mrs. Wilkes." She smiled at the housekeeper. "If you're sure you don't mind, I'll leave Winslow with you while I'm out." Lauren worked the backs onto her diamond studs.

"Oh, sure. Mr. Winslow will be fine." Mrs. Wilkes had taken a fancy to Winslow.

A brisk coolness lingered in the April air. The pale sun was welcome on her bare arms as she drove into Valley Ridge. First stop, the gallery.

Lauren eased off the accelerator and turned onto The Avenue and cruised past the gallery's employee parking. The red Mazda was parked in the same place it had been the day before. Now what? Did she storm the gallery, point a finger at one of Matt's employees and accuse them of being a reckless driver? Lauren laughed. Put in that light, it was funny. Still, her curiosity needed to be satisfied. She had to know who drove the red sports car, and in such a way as to endanger a child's life.

Speeding up she continued down The Avenue searching for a turn around.

Lauren claimed the familiar spot where she'd parked before. She sat for a moment and imagined the view through Clair's eyes. The landscaping and stone walk leading to the entry was a work of art in itself.

The outside of the gallery reflected the elegant taste that followed inside. And Clair, who had traveled the world and seen the best, would love it.

For the third time in a week Lauren grasped the heavy polished brass fixture and stepped into the cool wide entry of

Montgomery Art Gallery. A large arrangement of fresh flowers graced an ornate table that stood in front of a wide mirror set in a heavy gold frame. The table and flowers filled the space on the right side of the spacious entry. On the left wall, a large beach scene flooded the foyer with sparkling light. Lauren stepped closer to the flowers enjoying their fragrance. Fresh flowers in a gallery on Friday meant an event over the weekend.

She'd forgotten to look at the program Matt had given her.

"Lauren! I almost didn't recognize you again." Matt chuckled. "You look different every time I see you." He moved to her side.

Lauren laughed softly and relaxed. Today she had no need to hurry. "Well, I haven't been hiking lately." For some reason she felt shy with Matt. "The flowers are beautiful. Is there an event?"

"Yes, a reception for one of our artists on Saturday evening. Did I not give you a program? I'll grab you a bio of his work." Matt strolled across to a table and gathered up several pieces of literature. Lauren frowned when another man stepped out of the same office Matt used. He stopped to speak with Matt. He looked familiar ... the way he pushed his hand through his hair—

Lauren gasped and whirled her back the two men. He was the man from the house! She glanced toward the entry. Could she reach the door without Matt's notice? Don't be foolish, breathe deep and calm down. *He* had been the rude one, not her. Maybe he would leave without noticing her. She took a step closer to a canvas and pretended interest.

Matt touched her lightly on the shoulder. "Lauren, I'd like to introduce you to the other half of the gallery."

Dread slowed her actions. Lauren pasted a smile on her mouth and turned.

"Lauren, this is Jackson Montgomery. Jackson, Lauren Ashby. She's just moved to Valley Ridge."

Shock registered in his eyes the instant he recognized her. Jackson stiffened. He looked as frozen as she felt.

Matt looked from one to the other.

She recovered first and offered her hand, "Hello, Jackson, It's ... it's nice to meet you."

Jackson clasped her hand. "Yes. It's nice to meet you too, Lauren. I didn't recognize you. You look *different*. I mean ... I'm sorry about the other day."

"Hey, don't tell me you two know each other!" Matt's blue eyes danced as he waited to be clued in.

Lauren gave Jackson time to speak, but he gave no indication of doing so. Her face felt warm, flushed, she stammered, "I ... uh, we met at that big house outside—"

Jackson came to life and jumped in, "Yes, Matt, we met in town this past week. I was in a hurry as usual, I'm afraid I behaved rudely—for which I'm very sorry." The stunned expression hadn't left his face. He slid both hands into his pockets.

Lauren's gaze went from Jackson to Matt. Matt frowned, clearly puzzled, as his gaze shifted from Lauren to Jackson.

"At a house?"

Matt's frown deepened as he glanced back to Lauren and they both looked at Jackson.

"Oh, really, Matthew, does it matter where—"

"Jackson, may I speak with you?" A young woman tapped his shoulder, rescuing him. Their conversation didn't last long, and as the girl turned to leave, Matt motioned to her.

"Maggie, come meet Lauren Ashby. She's a newcomer to Valley Ridge. Lauren, Maggie Sands, our best salesperson and Jackson's right hand man ... uh girl."

Maggie favored Matt with a dazzling smile before turning cool green eyes on Lauren. Tall, slim and very pretty in a smart, blonde-girl sort of way, Maggie gave the illusion of looking down from her four-inch heels, on Lauren. Attitude oozed from her cool stare.

"Hello." Clearly she didn't give a fig whether Lauren returned the greeting or not.

"Hello, Maggie. Do you drive the red sports car parked

outside?" Lauren startled herself when the question popped out unexpectedly.

"Yes." Maggie's chin inched higher. A trace of curiosity or more likely annoyance flickered in the green eyes. "Why?"

"Just curious. Those cars are fast, aren't they?" Lauren smiled and held her gaze steady. Maggie returned a cool smile and sauntered away without comment.

"A pretty girl." Lauren glanced after Maggie

"She's spoiled rotten, but good in sales," Matt said. "Her parents are friends of mine. We're just lucky she is good in sales." Matt laughed and rested his hand on Jackson's shoulder. "Jackson also pays her extra to run errands and things like that for him. She leaves for college in the fall."

Jackson smiled at Matt's remark and glanced at Lauren. "Good to see you again." He nodded and turned to leave, but hesitated and ask, "Did Matt tell you about the reception Saturday evening?"

"Yes, he did." She indicated the literature Matt had handed her.

"We'd like for you to come, so please feel welcome." He touched Matt lightly on the shoulder before he headed back to the office.

Jackson seemed anxious to get away. Guilty conscience? Why had he been evasive about the house and where they'd first met?

"I'm intrigued that you two had met earlier," Matt commented as they moved along the display wall. "Jackson never mentioned it. He said something about being rude? I find that hard to believe. He's not a rude person." Matt's puzzled expression returned.

"He really wasn't rude. Like he said, just in a hurry." Jackson Montgomery had certainly put her on the spot. Why had he not wanted Matt to know they'd met at that house? He *must* be trying to buy it. But why would he not want his partner to know?

She remembered her appointment with Thelma at three. "Um, Matt, do you know Thelma Wade?"

"You don't live in Valley Ridge and not know Thelma. Why do you ask?" He slowed to a stop.

"Just wondering. I've enlisted her help in finding a house. I guess she's very ethical?" A sidelong peek at Matt told her people didn't question Thelma's integrity.

"Thelma? Ethical? That's almost laughable. Matt crossed his arms and one hand came up to stroke his chin as he smiled. "Yes, you can trust Thelma with your life."

Lauren figured as much but it made her feel better for someone to vouch for Thelma's integrity. If she got a bid on the house first, she wouldn't have to worry about it.

"Lauren, there's a great salad bar and coffee shop over on Main Street. May I buy your lunch?"

"Oh, I'd like that. What time?" They both turned their wrists up. "I could go anytime," she said.

Matt studied for a moment. "It's eleven thirty-five. I prefer an early lunch, what about now?"

"Great. I'm free until three o'clock."

"Let me check with Jackson. Back in a sec." He disappeared into the office.

Lauren browsed, enjoying the art as she waited.

He returned. "I'll bring my car around to the front."

"Great! I'll wait for you." Lauren smiled. She might learn why Jackson had been in the woods and why he'd spied on her. She strolled toward the foyer to wait for Matt, her gaze wandered toward the office.

Jackson stood just inside the office doorway.

Their gaze locked for a moment before she hurried into the entryway. Something about him ... she recalled the unhappy encounter at the house and reminded herself that he was the enemy.

Hurry up Matthew. Lauren moved deeper into the foyer and farther away from Jackson Montgomery's intense gaze.

* * *

AT THE SALAD BAR they sampled most of the fresh veggies, piling bright colors onto the dark leafy greens until the generous salad bowls could hold no more. Matt chose a table and they set with their masterpieces, laughing and comparing the mountainous creations.

Lauren spread her napkin on her lap and sprinkled feta cheese on top of the large salad.

"Bet lunch tomorrow you can't eat all of it." Matt teased.

"No way I'd bet, if I won I'd be too sick to collect on it!" Lauren grinned and shook her head.

After a lot of small talk she ventured onto the subject of houses. "Where do you live, Matt? I don't mean to be nosy, I just wondered if you live in an apartment or a house in town or in the country?" She glanced at him and then kept her eyes on the salad. "I mean the country around here is so beautiful … "

"It is pretty country. But I'm a city boy. I have a townhouse. I moved to Valley Ridge in my freshman year. I like living with restaurants close by and I enjoy a movie now and then. How about yourself? Have you found a place yet?" Matt proceeded to demolish his mountain of salad.

"Not yet. I grew up in a townhouse in New York City. But all my life I've planned to get back to the country. I moved here at the first opportunity. I've leased a place for a while." She blotted her lips and dared to smile, salad greens could be tricky. "Um, where does Jackson live? Is he a town boy too?" Her question didn't sound casual even to her ears. She felt a warm flush spread up her neck and face. She hoped Matt wouldn't notice, or think her interest personal.

"Oh, he has a townhouse. Jackson is his own person. You said, 'get back' to the country, yet you grew up in New York." He paused from his salad.

"I lived in the country as a child, and I've always dreamed of moving back." Lauren didn't care to share her past with Matt, and she had eaten about all the salad she could handle. Obviously he didn't intend to talk about his business partner. Sighing, she pushed the salad away and shook her head. "No more. I can't do it."

The conversation had gone nowhere. Jackson's interest in the house remained a mystery. She'd eaten her weight in salad for nothing. Matt had said that Jackson owned a townhouse, but he didn't mention him having a wife. As a handsome, successful man, it would be highly unusual for him not to be married.

"You did better with the salad than I expected. You put a good dent in it." Matt grinned.

"Thank you. I've never eaten a better salad."

They chatted awhile longer until Matt glanced at his watch. Lauren gathered her small purse and sunshades and they made their way toward the door. Even in her three-inch heels, Matt stood a head taller than her.

Back at the gallery, she pointed out the Range Rover to Matt and he pulled up beside it.

"Thank you, Matt. I really enjoyed lunch. I'll see you Saturday at the gala if I can possibly make it."

"You're welcome, Lauren, and I enjoyed lunch too. I do hope you make it on Saturday."

She stepped out of his car and unlocked the door to her own. Matt waited until she started her engine before he drove to the other side of the gallery.

Lauren checked her phone and listened to several messages before backing from the parking spot. At the street she glanced both ways and did a double take. A small figure disappeared down the hill in the opposite direction, a familiar sight.

Lauren lifted her wrist, twelve forty. She watched the flying legs and streaming blonde hair until the bike disappeared out of sight. Brooke must live close by.

Lauren wondered again if the child's parents would allow her to take art lessons? She must remember to ask Thelma if she knew Brooke and if she had any idea where the child lived.

CHAPTER 9

 Shock

JACKSON HOPED he hadn't looked as foolish as he felt as he hurried away from Matt and Lauren Ashby. Thoughts of her had lingered on his mind ever since running into her at the house, but he never expected to see her again after that. It was all he could do not to stare. And what must she think of him? He'd told Matt a bald-faced lie about meeting her in town.

He'd seen the confusion in her eyes—but she'd kept quiet and gave nothing away.

That girl brought out the worst in him. He'd been rude in her presence and now untruthful. Matt had been right about her looks, though, the word *pretty* fell short in describing her. And beautiful didn't apply only to her appearance. Lauren Ashby projected a beauty of manner as well. All he'd remembered from the brief time at the house that day was her eyes and her voice. The violet-blue eyes fringed with long lashes made him recognize her when Matt introduced them. And when she spoke, he remembered the voice. She likes Matt, but he's too blind to see it. Maybe things were starting to look up for Matt after all.

Jackson pushed his hands through his hair and denied the twinge of envy twisting his insides.

Maggie posed in the doorway. "Jackson, where's Matt? I need him to look at my computer."

"It'll have to wait, Maggie. He went to lunch with the new girl." Jackson glanced up to see how Maggie would take that. He suspected she had a schoolgirl crush on Matt, and now her lips compressed into an unhappy pout.

"How am I supposed to work with my computer messed up?"

Maggie whined almost as well as his eight-year old daughter. "He won't be long. Want me to have a look?"

"*No*. Matt knows this program better than you do." She flounced off to her office.

Uh-oh, sounds of her flouncing back.

"Tell Matt I need him as *soon* as he gets back. Okay?"

"Yes, Ma'am, I'll tell him."

The back entry bell jangled. "Hey there, Pumpkin. Aren't you a bit early?" He looked at his watch.

"Yes. I hurried and cleaned my desk so I wasn't the last one to leave. Is lunch ready? What did you bring today?" Brooke leaned on his desk, her cheeks pink. The bike ride from school got oxygen pumping in her blood. Jackson hated that she wasn't growing up in the home where he grew up. Guilt plagued him over it. Jenna had loved the country house.

But things were about to change. He hadn't said anything to Matt about putting the house and yard back in shape. He wasn't ready to share his plans with anyone yet.

"I believe Aunt Willa made chicken salad for us. With grapes and nuts the way we like it. Yum, aren't we lucky?" Jackson shuffled his desk into a semblance of order and followed Brooke to the break room. He enjoyed lunchtime with her.

"Dad, could we get a dog?" Brooke fidgeted in the chair, swiping stray hair from her face.

"A dog? What brought that up? A dog is a big responsibility Pumpkin. We've talked about that before, haven't we?"

"Uh-huh, but can we?"

Jackson set the chicken salad and wheat crackers on the table, along with a container of chopped fruit, two plates and forks. "Tea or lemonade?" He held two glasses filled with ice.

"Lemonade, please. Can we?"

"Let's have lunch first and you can tell me all about class this morning. I'll think about the dog. Fair enough?"

"Are you sure you'll think about it and not forget?" She fidgeted anxiously.

"I promise, if you'll stop squirming." Jackson let Brooke ask the blessing on their lunch.

"Where's Uncle Matt? Is he having lunch with us?" Brooke liked it when Matt joined them in the break room.

"Uncle Matt is having lunch with a very pretty lady at The Salad Bar." Jackson tapped the edge of Brooke's plate, which meant quit dawdling and eat up.

"Is she his new girlfriend?" Brooke muffled through a mouthful of food. "I like his old girlfriend."

"No, the lady he's having lunch with is not a girlfriend. He just met her. I didn't know Matt had an old girlfriend?"

"*Karen* is his old girlfriend." Brooke rolled her eyes. "I have a new friend too. She's got a dog. And I want one just like hers. Just like Winslow." She giggled and watched to see what he thought of that news.

"Really, where did you meet this new friend?" Jackson watched his tone, careful to keep it normal and conversational. Brooke closed up like a clam when she thought he disapproved of something.

"On my way to school."

Brooke would see nothing wrong in taking up with a nice 'normal' person walking her dog. "Oh, I see. She walks her dog?"

"No, *Dad,* she's a painter. I stopped and watched and I met her dog too." Brooke giggled again and thumped her foot against the table leg.

He gave her three thumps on the table before he asked her to stop; quite often she quit on her own.

"I'd like to meet your friend and her dog. Maybe she could help us find you a dog." Jackson didn't like the idea of Brooke making friends with people along the street.

"You mean it! I can get a dog?" Brooke jumped from her chair and threw her arms around Jackson's neck. She planted a sticky kiss on his face and announced that she wanted to get back to school in time to tell her teacher about her new dog. Just as she'd washed her hands and skipped to the door, Matt walked in and the two of them did a high-five before she scooted out.

"Who lit a fire under her?" Matt helped himself to a glass of tea.

"I think I may have just promised her a dog." Jackson gave Matt a bewildered look.

"Well, it's about time she got a dog. Sunny Girl needs a dog. Where are you planning to keep it though?" Matt grinned.

"Oh, I'm not sure. Brooke says she has a new friend, some woman who paints, you know anything about it? Jackson frowned. "You don't think she's making up stories, do you?"

Matt sat at the table with his tea. "She's never made up stories before, has she?"

"Not that I know of. But she's never been eight going on nine before either. I don't know what girls that age do."

"Have you talked with Ally about this?" Matt glanced down at his glass.

"No, Brooke just now mentioned it. She said she had a new friend and this friend has a dog. She might have made up a story just to bring up the dog. We go through the dog thing ever so often." He glanced at Matt, trying to read his thoughts on it.

"Doesn't sound like Brooke to make up stories. She'd just come out and ask for a dog. Eight-year-old daughters don't seem to have many scruples about brow-beating a dad to get their way." They laughed at the truth of it.

"That's for sure. She told me the name she's already picked out for it. The same name as her new friend's dog." Jackson grew thoughtful as he cleared the table. Matt walked out shaking his head and grinning.

Later, sitting at their desks Matt swiveled around in his chair. "What's the name Brooke has picked for her soon to be dog." He raised his tea glass to his mouth.

"A cute name, actually. Winslow." Jackson turned to grin at Matt in time to see him jerk his glass, spilling tea on his shirtfront.

"Winslow!" Matt rose from his chair brushing at the tea. "Did you say *Winslow?*"

"Yeah, Brooke said her friend's dog is named Winslow. That's what she wants to call her dog. Why?"

"Jackson—Lauren Ashby has a dog named Winslow. But where would Brooke have met Lauren?" They stared at one another.

Jackson recovered first. "Brooke said the woman paints and she stopped to watch. Brooke hasn't been anywhere except to school and back." Jackson's brow pulled into a furrow. "That morning at the ... " Jackson glanced at Matt. "When I first saw Lauren I remember she said something about being an artist."

Matt shook his head, "I don't know what you're talking about, but I do know that Lauren calls her dog Winslow. What would be the odds of another dog with that name?" Matt sat back down. He glanced down at his shirt, still brushing at the tea stains. "I need to get a clean shirt. Ally's coming around about one-o'clock, she said something about her grandmother's art collection."

"Yes. She mentioned it to me, and I told her you'd probably be happy to help her with it." Jackson's thoughts lingered on the situation with Brooke.

"Look, Jackson, if you're worried about Brooke, I'll talk to Lauren and find out what's going on. She's meeting with Thelma at three." Matt glanced at his watch.

Jackson felt the stab again. "Is she? You two are getting to be fast friends rather quickly, aren't you?"

"I wouldn't say we're fast friends. She's new in town and could become a client *and* a friend. She's easy to talk to, and I like her." Matt rose and headed to the break room where he always kept a spare shirt.

Jackson's gaze followed Matt. He likes her, she likes him ... Jackson drummed on his desk, he should feel happy for Matt, but it wasn't happiness churning in his stomach. Just as Ally walked through the door, the phone rang. He waved to Ally and checked caller ID. It was Thelma returning his call.

"Hi Thelma, thanks for getting back with me. I'm awfully busy right now. Could I call you back in just a few minutes? Thanks, I'll not be long."

"Don't let me keep you from anything, Jackson." Ally made herself comfortable in the soft leather chair next to his desk. "What's Thelma up to?"

"Oh, I just needed to speak to her about some ... um, property." He lowered his voice, "Are you here to see Matt?" They shared a conspirator smile.

"Yes, I am. Is he with a client?" Ally lowered her voice as well.

"Nah, he spilled tea on his shirt and went to change." Jackson raised his voice when he heard Matt returning.

"He takes forever primping. Each button and each crease must be *just* right."

"I'm back, Jackson, you can stop making me look bad to my favorite person." Matt smiled at Ally and turned a glare on Jackson.

Laughing, Jackson reached for the phone. "I'll leave you two to get on with your business. I have a couple of calls to return."

Matt ushered Ally to the private office at the back of the showroom where they handled sales and client meetings.

"Jackson. I asked you to send Matt to my office as *soon* as he got back from lunch." Maggie deliberately interrupted him and with no polite 'excuse me, please' as she stood in the doorway with her hands on her hips.

"Oh, Maggie, I'm sorry." Jackson put his finger on the end call button before it could ring Thelma. "I had something else on my mind, and Matt and I got to talking and I forgot."

She glared at him and whirled away, her heels clicking sharply on the marble floor. Jackson shook his head and grinned. He wasn't the only one suffering pangs of jealousy. Maggie didn't like Matt with Ally. That upset her more than a messed up computer.

It would be a relief when that young lady did leave for college. He returned to his phone.

"Thelma, I'm sorry I couldn't talk when you called. I need to talk with you about … the house. I want to have the yard restored."

"Jackson, that's wonderful news. I take it you want me to find you a yardman?"

"That's exactly what I need. And I'd like to get the inside cleaned and any repairs that need to be made. I want to put everything back to the way it used to be." Jackson breathed deep, scared, but it felt good to be moving forward. He felt alive for the first time in a long time.

"Jackson, are you preparing the house to live in?"

Only Thelma Wade could ask any question she felt needed asking and not worry about it being taken the wrong way. Jackson thanked his lucky stars for Thelma's friendship. "I hope to, yes. And Thelma, I haven't told anybody else about this."

"You know as soon as work starts out there word will get around."

Silence traveled the connection.

Jackson sighed, "Yes, I know."

"Will you be needing a housekeeper too, or does Willa plan to be there with you."

"I want a housekeeping crew to make the house ready to open. Aunt Willa's home is with Brooke and me, but it wouldn't hurt to look around for someone to come in several days a week, that's too much house for Willa to keep by herself."

"I'll find you someone. But be prepared, Willa may throw a fit. You may be her favorite nephew, but she won't hesitate giving you a piece of her mind." They shared a laugh and he agreed.

"But she'll get over it."

"When do you want all this to start?"

"Yesterday?"

"Now don't act like a typical client, okay." She laughed. "I'll get right on it and let you know when things are lined up."

"Thanks a bunch, Thelma."

"Jackson, you must remember, word gets around fast."

"Yes, I'll take care of that, and thank you again, Thelma."

"You're very welcome and I'll call when—"

"Thelma, I almost forgot. Do you know someone named Lauren Ashby?

"Yes … I do know Lauren … why do you ask?"

"I believe somehow Brooke has met her. Brooke mentioned wanting a dog today at lunch. She said she has a new friend who has a dog that's named Winslow. Have you seen Brooke or talked with her lately? I need to find out what's going on." The pause on the other end of the line puzzled him.

"I don't know anything about them meeting. But I know that Lauren is a very nice person, and you'd have nothing to fear for Brooke's sake."

Jackson couldn't understand the caution he heard in Thelma's voice. Was she covering for Brooke in some way? He sighed. Did the whole town watch out for Brooke? He had abandoned his house, not his child.

"Thanks, Thelma. I have met Lauren Ashby too, but I was just wondering … well, let me know when things are lined up, okay?"

"I will. And Jackson, I'm glad about the house, I think you're doing the right thing."

"I'll take that vote of confidence, Thelma, I need it."

Just as he clicked the phone off he heard Matt and Ally approaching the office, talking and laughing. Matt opened up and allowed his fun personality to show with Ally more than any other person he knew. Jackson puzzled over that as the two entered the office.

"Well, did you get everything figured out?" He rocked back in his chair, noticing that Matt looked more animated than usual. What flea had Ally put in his ear?

"Jackson, Matt has some wonderful ideas about how to catalogue Gram's paintings. We're getting together with her to schedule work time for the project."

She turned to Matt. "I can't tell you what a headache this takes off me. Mom and Gram were expecting me to handle this. I dreaded the job so much, I kept putting them off."

"How long do you expect it to take from start to finish?" Jackson looked at Ally and she in turn lifted her brows at Matt.

Matt spread his hands. "Oh, couple of months possibly. We'll have to work around Mrs. Parker's schedule also. Being elderly hasn't slowed her down any." They laughed and agreed.

"Matt, when you come out tomorrow to have a look, we could plan lunch there at the house. It would save time, what do you think?"

"That's fine, makes sense to me. We decided to start at ten o'clock?" he asked.

Jackson couldn't resist. "Oh, and Matt, don't be late. Ally's grandmother is where Ally gets her penchant for being five minutes early, that way everyone else is always late." Jackson teased, but with a grain of truth.

"I've never known Matt to be late. That's your favorite character flaw, Jackson." Ally leaned and kissed him lightly on the forehead. "See you later, call me, okay?"

"As soon as I get home. Promise," he said.

Ally gave him a private smile and closed the door behind her.

Matt stood next to Jackson's desk. "What's wrong with Maggie? She looked fine while helping a customer, but as soon as they left, she passed Ally and me without a word. Now her door is closed. She never closes that door unless she feels wronged. Have you done something to upset our diva, again?"

Jackson lowered his voice. "I had strict orders to send you straight to her office when you returned from lunch. But we started talking about Brooke's dog, then Ally came in and I forgot all about Maggie—I've had my chewing. Your turn now."

"Uh-oh, I better go see if I can soothe troubled waters." He headed to find Maggie.

With the office quiet again, Jackson turned his thoughts to his own problems. Now that he'd set things in motion, fear and dread settled in his stomach

Matt could be counted on to be supportive of opening the house. Ally was the one he dreaded telling. She wouldn't be happy about him moving back to the country and the home he and Jenna had shared.

Opening the house might also give the impression that he expected to move on in other ways too. And make other commitments. His stomach looped and churned, he needed time. A commodity he didn't have.

He had to be honest with Ally, and soon.

CHAPTER 10

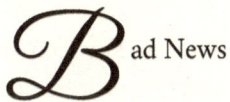 ad News

LAUREN DIDN'T NOTICE the flowers or the pretty cottage as she normally did. She hurried up the stone path, anxious to see Thelma. A whispered prayer for good news trembled on her lips. What if the news was bad, what then? That house had drawn her to it. How could she settle for anything less?

"Hi Cindy. Is Thelma ready for me?"

"She is Lauren. Go right in." Cindy always looked as fresh in the afternoon as she did first thing in the morning.

Lauren knocked lightly on the closed door before pushing it open and smiling brightly at Thelma.

"Come in. Have a seat Lauren." Thelma glanced down quickly, shuffling a stack of papers into neat form before smiling back, too brightly.

Not good.

Lauren sat in the chair across from Thelma and swallowed

against the tightening in her throat. She waited for Thelma to lead.

"I know this won't be what you had hoped to hear, Lauren—"

"Thelma, before you start, I'm not interested in looking at more property. I'm tired of house hunting. I've found the house I want. Surely you can persuade the elderly owners to sell a property they apparently have no interest in anyway." Lauren's glance fell to her hands knotted in her lap. She relaxed them and glanced up. "Why wouldn't they rather have the money the house would bring? They have even chosen not to live there."

"Lauren, there is only one heir, and he is not elderly. I have spoken with him this past week and things are changing." Thelma's eyes searched Lauren's face.

"What do you mean? Changing how?"

"I believe you have met Jackson Montgomery? The house belongs to Jackson. His father and mother moved to a retirement community shortly after Jackson married, and they gave him the big house then." Thelma sat quietly for a moment. "Jackson's mother passed away four years ago and his father just two years later."

Lauren struggled to comprehend the words coming from Thelma's mouth. "Jackson Montgomery? *He* owns that house?" *So, he is married.* It took moments for all that to sink in. "But why doesn't he live there? It's only six or seven miles from his business, yet he doesn't live in that wonderful house?"

"He's had his reasons … " Thelma groped for words.

"Could *he* not be persuaded to sell?" Defeat edged her voice.

"Jackson has just asked me to find a yardman to restore the grounds. He plans to open the house and move back. It's where he grew up," Thelma said.

"Oh, I see." Lauren's shoulders rose and fell in deep regret. She reached for her bag. "Well, I guess that's that. I'm sorry to have troubled you about it." She gave another deep sigh making no move to stand, her body numbed with disappointment. She'd stay in the lease cottage. She wanted no more house hunting.

"I don't know how you feel about the house you're in, Lauren. About buying it I mean. It's a very nice house. I've talked with the owners and they would consider selling."

Her head jerked up. "What? No, I'm not interested in buying that house." If she had wanted to buy the house she was in, she would have talked the owners into selling it long before now.

She looked away from the concern on Thelma's face. "I may close the cottage and travel in Italy with a friend. I have clients there. I may do that until I decide if I want to build or not."

Lauren felt a moment of selfish satisfaction at the fresh wave of distress on Thelma's face. The moment of satisfaction passed as quickly as it came, leaving a stab of guilt. Thelma's distress was that of a true friend.

"I'm sorry, Thelma. Thank you for trying. I'm being unfair. But I've never wanted anything more than I wanted that house." Lauren glanced out of the office window and back to Thelma. Blinking hard for a moment. "More than just the house, it's what it represented." She hooked her bag on her shoulder and stood. The excitement and fun of finding the perfect house the last week suddenly vanished. She hoped never again to see Jackson Montgomery's face.

Thelma stood also. "Lauren, I have some free time and I'd like to show you my favorite coffee shop. Could you take time for coffee and the best Black Forest cake you'll ever taste?"

"Well, that does sound wonderful. We deserve coffee and cake. And now I'm at loose ends the rest of the day." She had hoped to be touring her new home this afternoon.

"Great. We'll take my car. I have to come back by the office anyway."

* * *

"OH, THELMA, THIS IS A NEAT PLACE!" Lauren's spirits lifted as she admired the colorful tables and chairs in the outdoor sitting area. Thelma chose a table that sat tucked under a canopy of leafy green vines and tall trees. The small café, The Coffee Bean, embodied the Tuscany atmosphere. It reminded Lauren of a place in Italy, a café near Clair's villa that they went to often on late afternoons. The little café served the strong, smooth coffee that Clair loved. She reminded herself to bring Clair here when she arrived.

Thelma glanced up at the waiter and gave him their order and then touched Lauren's hand. "May I ask you a personal question?"

"Yes, I suppose so."

"Have you by any chance met a little girl named Brooke? She rides her bike everywhere." Thelma's expression softened.

Lauren puckered her brow, puzzled over the question. "Yes, I have. I planned to ask you about her. I can't remember to find out what her last name is and where she lives. But how did you know?"

"I didn't know. That's why I asked. Brooke mentioned to her father that she had a new friend who owns a dog, named Winslow. Of course it concerned him that his child had made friends with someone he didn't know. He asked me if I knew anything about it." Thelma smiled and inhaled the fragrant steam rising from the cup the waiter had placed before her.

"Oh, I fully agree. Parents should know their children's friends. I planned to say something to Brooke the next time I saw her." Lauren sipped the hot coffee. "Brooke seems interested in art. I thought I'd meet her parents and offer art lessons. But if I travel for a while ..." Already she regretted that she'd blurted out about traveling.

"Oh, Lauren, art lessons would be so good for that child, she needs a friend to encourage her in that direction. I believe Brooke is talented. But for some reason she holds back. I do hope you stay in Valley Ridge." Thelma started to speak then hesitated.

"What? Is there a problem with the parents?"

"No, it's not that. Brooke's mother passed away when Brooke was two. And her father, well her father ... he's Jackson Montgomery."

Lauren jerked her hand from her cup and sank back in the chair. "No! Brooke—Jackson's daughter? I don't believe it. Is that man connected to everything and everyone in this town?"

"Probably. Matt told him that your dog's name was Winslow." Thelma sighed. "Jackson's a great guy, active in church and the community. Give him some slack, Lauren." Thelma sipped thoughtfully. "He floundered for a long time after his wife died. And then his mother passed away. And his father died two years ago. That's why he couldn't live in the house. There was so much sadness, too many memories."

They sat quietly.

"I'm sorry to hear that. Has he remarried?"

"No. But he's restoring the house and grounds and moving back." She took a bite of the rich dessert and sipped her coffee. "Please don't repeat what I've told you about him moving back to the house. There are several people he wants to tell first, before word gets out."

"How can he keep something like that a secret? I wonder if his partner knows?" Lauren's thoughts strayed to Matt.

"You mean Matt Williams, one of my favorite people. If Jackson has told anybody, it would be Matt. They go way back, since high school I believe." Thelma looked at Lauren as if trying to decide if there might be something between she and Matt.

"Yes, I've met Matt and I like him a lot. And I like Brooke, especially now that you've told me about her mother." Lauren was thoughtful. "But giving her lessons would be unthinkable since I'd have to deal with her father. I couldn't do it."

"Before you make a decision, consider Brooke. You'd be doing her the favor, not Jackson. Brooke talks to me a little since her great aunt is one of my closest friends. Brooke needs a friend who is young enough to actually remember being eight-years old." Thelma gave a wistful smile.

Thelma couldn't know she had twisted a knife in Lauren's heart. Lauren remembered that age all too clearly. She hadn't lost her mother; it had been her father, when she was four. After he died her life changed from happy times in the country where they'd had apple trees and laughter, to the sad quiet home in New York City. Her mother worked in a law firm six days a week and never stopped grieving over the loss of her husband. In a sense Lauren *had* lost her mother too.

Yes, she remembered being eight years old and alone except for the housekeeper and babysitter.

Thelma broke the long silence. "I can't have another sweet thing for a whole week after this cake."

"Oh, me too! I just consumed my sugar quota for the whole week, and I enjoyed every bite."

They laughed and Thelma signaled their waiter for another refill. Reaching across the small table she patted Lauren's hand. "Don't be hasty in deciding what to do. And don't let disappointment rush you into making the wrong move, please?" She looked thoughtful for a moment. "There's a reason for everything. And sometimes, Lauren, when the Lord says no to one thing, it's because He's preparing something so much bigger and better than what you asked for."

"Thelma, you're a jewel. Thanks. This has been nice and you've made me feel better. I'll give serious thought before I decide anything."

* * *

Sitting on the carpet in her favorite pink sweats, Lauren gathered Winslow into her arms and buried her face in his soft fur. This day couldn't be over too soon for her. Without a few minutes of calming time with Winslow, her brain cells couldn't function another minute.

"Winslow, we have decisions to make, and you have to help me," she murmured against his face. Winslow snuggled in her arms, his eyes half closed in pure pleasure. He liked Mrs. Wilkes, but this was what he lived for.

The phone rang Clair's distinctive, 'See You in Paris' tune. Lauren hugged Winslow tight and jumped from the floor. Her brain cells suddenly charged, raring to go.

"Clair! What? Oh, that's wonderful! You'll be here in time for the gallery event Saturday evening." Lauren got comfortable on the sofa and settled in to hear the details of Clair's arrival.

Clair's flight didn't arrive until three o'clock Saturday afternoon. *Tomorrow afternoon!* It would be close, and they'd arrive a bit late, but at least Clair would see the gallery in action first hand, and meet Matt.

As soon as they ended their call, Lauren made a note to order a rental car for Clair as she'd asked her to do. Then hurrying to her tote, she searched for the business card Matt had given her. The gallery had closed an hour ago, but his business card had his personal number listed too. She'd call and find out if they needed tickets to attend the gala.

Ringing on the other end continued ... four, five ... Matt's machine picked up and she left a message. Of course, Friday evening, a charming, handsome man like Matt would have an active social life.

Sighing, she reminded herself that *most* do people have a social life.

lair Arrives

LaGuardia Airport buzzed with activity as usual. The crowds of passengers bumped and weaved along the busy terminals. Some murmured apologies while others appeared dazed, unaware of being jostled. Seated in a sandwich shop next to the walkway, Lauren people watched and waited.

She glanced at her watch. Waiting fueled her nervous excitement. In her rush to get away, had she left fresh water for Winslow? Thinking of Winslow brought a smile to her mouth. A man hurrying by misinterpreted her smile. Lauren ducked her head, pretending to search her purse, hoping not to get tickled. Who said New Yorkers were not friendly?

Another impatient glance at her watch and she jumped to her feet. Pacing burns energy, she'd go pace where Clair would exit the plane.

"Lauren!" Clair strolled toward her smiling, a book in her hand and a small bag on her arm.

"Clair! You're early! You must have been the first person off the plane. I can't believe I didn't see you." A warm embrace assured them they were really together again. They talked on the phone regularly, but it had been eight months since Lauren had vacationed with Clair in Italy for four months.

"Are you hungry? Shall we get a bite of lunch? I valet parked—"

"Lauren, slow down." Clair placed her hand on Lauren's arm. "I had lunch on the plane. Right now I'm more anxious to see your new home and meet Winslow than I am in food." Clair guided her to the luggage claim as Lauren chatted non-stop.

It took skill and nerve to maneuver through the traffic and pedestrians on the streets of New York. Lauren did both expertly. She explained the whole time about the gala and how she couldn't wait for Clair to meet Matt Williams.

"So, is there anything going on with this Matt guy?" Clair never played games. She asked what she wanted to know and offered opinions when she felt she had something that might be of help—and she did it in the most inoffensive way.

"Oh, no. You know me, Clair, no serious responsibilities tying me down. But, I expect Matt and I will become friends."

"My dear, one day you'll meet the guy who will challenge that kind of thinking. You sure you haven't met him?" Clair glanced sideways at Lauren. "You're just ten years younger than me and time *is* marching on."

"I doubt that will happen, Clair, but thank you for reminding me of how old I am." She gave Clair a rueful smile. "I'm happy with my life. I *was* at least until this past week. But I'm glad you're here. A good visit with you is just what I need to take my mind off a great disappointment."

Oh, did Mr. Right turn out to be Mr. Wrong" Clair peeked at Lauren.

"Really, Clair, what's happened to you? Do you have romance on the brain?" She glanced at Clair. "But I seem to remember that every time you fall in love you want everybody else to be in love too." Uh-oh. Lauren groaned as Clair grinned, her face glowing— love had struck.

* * *

THE RANGE ROVER came to a stop on the ocher tinted, crushed rock driveway. Clair took her time viewing the house and grounds before she turned to Lauren with a surprised expression.

"This could be anywhere in France. I love it. But I thought you had a small cottage."

"I know. I just like the idea of a cottage, humor me." They laughed happily as they'd been doing all afternoon. "In the mean- time, we have a party to get ready for."

Parking valets hustled as Lauren cruised up to wait her turn. She had never seen the gallery in this light. It looked as impres- sive in late evening as it did in bright daylight. She glanced at Clair, relaxed but alert; her critical eye missed no detail. She wasn't her father's daughter for nothing. Charlie Weston enjoyed the reputation as one of New York's sharpest attorneys, and he'd taught his daughter a thing or two.

"You were right, Lauren, I needed to see this first hand."

"I'm glad you think so. I think you'll be favorably impressed. I want you to meet Matt first thing."

"Yes, yes, I must meet this Matt, *first thing*."

Clair looked impressive in a slim white sleeveless dress. No jewelry, except large diamond stud earrings, and four inch black patent heels to complete her outfit. Her copper hair in natural loose curls reached her jaw-line, framing her face and accenting lively green eyes. Her appearance belied her thirty-six years.

The crowd of collectors, art lovers, friends, and acquaintances moved in small circles talking amid laughter and serious art discussions. Lauren searched the room for Matt with no luck.

Someone touched her on the arm, "Lauren? Is it really you?"

"Oh—Brad Scott! It's been years—Estes Park Colorado? The paint-out?"

Brad grinned and rolled his eyes. "I'd hoped you'd forgotten that disastrous outing."

Another artist they both knew joined the conversation and before long a group had gathered. Engaged in talk about galleries in Italy with another artist, Lauren suddenly remembered Clair. She excused herself and went to find her. Oblivious to anyone else when she finally spotted Clair's bright curls through the crowd, she rushed to hug her, "Clair, forgive me, but I ran into—"

"Lauren, do you know Jackson?" Clair turned, smiling to him.

"Yes, of course we've met." Lauren glanced briefly and nodded in his direction.

Jackson's expression was that of a man who'd rather be somewhere else at the moment, but he spoke politely.

"Lauren, It's good to see you again. I'm glad you could make it. I didn't know you were friends with the famous Clair Weston." His remark, intended to lighten things, fell flat. He smiled uncertainly and ran a hand through his hair, glancing from Clair to Lauren.

"There's never been any reason for me to mention my friendship with Clair." Lauren didn't hasten to ease his discomfort. Had Clair not seen Matt yet? "Clair, have you seen Matt? Did you have a chance to talk with him?" Lauren lowered her voice to exclude Jackson from the conversation.

"Yes, I did meet Matthew. And I have an appointment to visit with Jackson on Monday. We've—"

"Jackson? What about Matt?" Lauren managed to maneuver between Jackson and Clair, cutting Jackson out completely.

"Lauren, Please!" Clair hissed under her breath. "You're being rude. What *is* the matter with you?" Her green eyes flashed.

"But I thought you wanted—" Lauren turned at the familiar voice behind her as someone patted her arm.

"Lauren, it's me." Brooke beamed up at her.

Lauren stared for the breath of a second before she gasped, "Brooke."

Brooke giggled. "I'm dressed up. This is a new dress. Aunt Willa picked it!"

"Oh My goodness! Brooke, you look beautiful. I almost didn't recognize you, so grown up you are." Lauren returned her hug when Brooke shyly slipped her arms around her waist and snuggled her head against her. Lauren leaned and placed her cheek against the pale, shiny hair. Lost in the moment, she didn't give a thought to what Jackson Montgomery might think about her familiarity with his daughter.

She looked up at him when he touched Brooke's shoulder and gently pulled her away.

"Brooke, run tell Aunt Willa it's about time you should be heading home. Okay, sweet?"

"Yes, Daddy." She threw her arms around Jackson and snuggled her head against him in the same manner she'd hugged Lauren. Then she skipped from the room.

Brooke's affectionate actions ignited an electric tension between Lauren and Jackson. Everyone in the small group sensed it. Including the pretty, dark haired woman who had walked up to Jackson and slid her arm through his, as Lauren and Brooke hugged.

"Al ... Ally, this is Clair Weston. Clair's the new artist I've been trying to get in the gallery, and Lauren Ashby, her friend. Clair, Lauren, my good friend, Ally Parker."

The women exchanged greetings before Ally informed Jackson he was needed elsewhere. They excused themselves and left, leaving Lauren and Clair to eye each other warily.

"So, what just happened?" Clair struggled to hide a smile.

"What?"

"That child, Brooke, and Jackson. What was that all about?"

"Nothing. What do you mean? Oh, I'll tell you everything

tomorrow. I'm taking you to a place for coffee that you'll simply love. We'll talk then."

"I won't let you forget." Clair threatened as they moved along to view the art.

Lauren took Clair's arm. "And you can tell me what you're so happy about or should I say who you're so happy about?"

Deep into a discussion of the palette preference used by the artist whose work the show featured, they didn't see Matt until he spoke.

"Lauren, will you ever forgive me for ducking out on you? I have excuses lined up if I need them." Matt looked penitent.

"Oh, Matt, I'm the one who needs to apologize. I ran into some old friends and left poor Clair on her own. I'm glad you found her. Did you introduce her to Jackson? And why is he meeting with her on Monday?" Lauren frowned at Matt.

"Yes, of course I took her to meet Jackson as soon as I recognized her as the artist he's been after for the gallery. She's Jackson's client. They've been talking on the phone and emailing for months. Why didn't you tell me your friend is the celebrated Clair Weston?" Matt's tone bordered on a reprimand.

"I'm sorry, Matt. I didn't think about it. Clair is just my friend." She laughed at his expression. "I didn't know it was Jackson talking with her about the gallery."

Clair joined the conversation. "Matt, do you know the portrait painter, Sara Collins?"

"I know of her, but we've never met. She's in demand in Europe as well as here I'm told. Her work is beautiful. Have you met her?" Matt smiled politely at Clair.

"Yes, I know Sara Collins. I notice you don't have much portrait or figurative work." Clair turned slightly away when Lauren glared at her.

Matt looked slightly startled. "You're acquainted with Sara Collins?"

"Oh, more than acquainted. We are very dear and close friends." Clair's eyes darted briefly at Lauren.

"Wait until Jackson hears that. He admires her work tremendously." Matt scanned the crowd for Jackson.

Lauren excused herself and hurried away, afraid of what Clair might say next. Clair knew she'd said nothing to Matt about her painting. He had never asked about her work and she wanted it that way. She was careful not to give the impression that she might be looking for a gallery, because she wasn't.

Everyone who knew her knew that she painted under the name of Sara Collins. She had done so since the age of fifteen when the quality of her work prompted a gallery in New York to ask her mother about handling her. The gallery owner had suggested to her mother that Lauren sign her paintings with her mother's name, and she had. As she got older it did come in handy to have the privacy the name afforded her and the name she signed with had never mattered to her. She cared only about painting.

Matt found her and stepping to her side he leaned close, speaking quietly. "Lauren, did I say something to upset you?"

"Oh, goodness no, Matt. I'm just tired. I woke early this morning, then the quick trip to New York and back and rushing here … I think I'll find Clair." And all of a sudden she didn't know if she'd make it home without falling asleep. And for some reason, she felt like crying.

Matt put his arm around her shoulder. "Good idea." His blue eyes reflected concern.

* * *

DRIVING HOME, Lauren's thoughts chased in circles. So much had happened at the gallery. Jackson knew how she and Brooke felt about each other. He'd seen with his own eyes. Would he be angry with her? Would Jackson forbid Brooke to take art lessons, even if she did offer them? What was the relationship between Jackson and Ally Parker ... ?

Laughter from the passenger side startled her back to the present. "What?"

"Were you asleep?" Clair laughed softly. "I asked you a question."

"Sorry, I might have been. Ask the question again."

"Are you cross with me? I think you should tell Matt and Jackson that you paint as Sara Collins." Clair yawned.

"No, I'm not cross, but I wish you had warned me. I'll tell them when the time is right. You know that's never been a secret. I'm not hiding anything. They could easily find out."

"Yes, I know they could find out, but they haven't, have they? You haven't made it easy for people to know Sara Collins, being the recluse you are." Clair yawned again. "I really like Jackson. I probably will sign with the gallery. I think he likes you." Clair put her head back on the headrest. "And I do have exciting news to share. But I wanted to see the gallery first."

"Clair, you expect me to sleep tonight after telling me you think Jackson likes me and that you have exciting news?" Lauren swung the Range Rover into her driveway and reached to press the garage door opener.

"What makes you think Jackson likes me?"

"Umm, I'm not sure, I just feel it." Clair smothered another yawn.

"You just feel it? What kind of logic is that?" Lauren curbed the edge in her voice.

"Whoever said logic had anything to do with physical attraction? Is there chocolate ice cream?"

"Would I not have chocolate ice cream knowing you were coming?" They laughed at the absurdity of that.

"If you can't sleep tonight, we'll eat ice cream and talk. I can tell you one thing."

Starting to giggle, Lauren asked, "And what one thing is that?"

"Miss Ally Parker is in for a surprise." Clair giggled with Lauren; they'd both given in to the weariness of a long day.

Lauren's heart skipped a beat, now wide-awake, she asked, "What do you mean?"

"Didn't you see her possessive gesture? She thinks Jackson is hers, but he's far from it."

"Really Clair, how could you tell that?" Lauren scoffed, but her spirits revived. She opened the door of the mud-room that led into the kitchen, and they each struggled a large piece of Clair's luggage inside.

"His body language. She is to him, just as he introduced her … a good friend."

Lauren kicked off her shoes, and shaking her head she headed out of the room, calling over her shoulder, "Oh wise one, break out the chocolate ice cream while I grab Winslow."

Lauren's tiredness had vanished. Entering the sunroom she scooped Winslow up and held him close. He wiggled happily and pressed his warm body against her. "Winslow, sweetie, try to make a good impression on my friend. Okay?"

She cuddled Winslow, but she was remembering Brooke's arms around her waist, and her head pressed against her body. Tender emotions stirred in her heart.

Suddenly frightened, she squeezed Winslow closer.

CHAPTER 12

he Let Down

JACKSON PULLED into the garage and made his way to the kitchen. He felt for the wall switch and turned on the outside light over the garage door. Enough light filtered into the kitchen to dimly light the way, but not jar his aching head. He draped his jacket on the back of the bar chair and went to the fridge. He reached for the milk carton.

Empty.

Brooke! He jammed the box back in the fridge. Okay, Miss, we'll see how long it sits there. Miss Brooke would throw that empty carton in the trash or it could sit there from now on. The rule was that whoever drank the last of the milk threw the carton in the garbage and told Aunt Willa so she could add it to her grocery list.

Brooke refused to take responsibility.

Jackson glared at the tomato juice. He didn't like tomato juice. His aggravation at Brooke grew and he fueled it by recalling the incident at the gallery. What compelled that child? Hugging Lauren Ashby like that, a *stranger*. She'd never hugged Ally that way in all the time they'd spent with her. No doubt she'd hurt Ally's feelings with that display of affection. He tried to picture a scene like that with Ally and Brooke and he couldn't. Strangely enough, that made him even angrier.

Wearily he closed the fridge door.

Dragging a bar chair out from the wide island bar, he sat with his head in his hands still recovering from the shock that Clair Weston had actually been at the show. He'd been inviting her to come to the gallery for months. The fact that Lauren Ashby had brought her and that the two of them were close friends, shattered his hope of getting Clair's work in the gallery.

But in spite of everything, Clair had been friendly and receptive and they'd set an appointment for Monday. He suspected her of just being nice because of her friend.

The show turned out to be a resounding success. They sold seventy percent of the featured paintings. Jackson had plenty to celebrate, so why did he sit here alone in the dark, miserable and angry? He'd probably ruined everybody's mood. No wonder they'd all voted to celebrate later.

The overhead light flared on.

"I thought I heard you come in. Want me to make coffee?" Aunt Willa reached for the coffee canister.

"That sounds great, I'm too tired to go to bed. This was as far as I made it." He laughed. The last thing he wanted was to worry his Aunt.

"You had a good crowd tonight." Willa put the coffee on and sat on the kitchen stool she kept on the backside of the island while they waited for the brew to finish.

"Yes, we did. And Jim's sales were good. He'll have to get back to work now that we cleaned him out." They chatted until the coffee finished brewing. Jackson reached for the cup that Aunt

Willa pushed toward him. He dribbled half and half into the strong coffee and stirred.

"I like Brooke's new friend." Aunt Willa poured her own coffee. "She seemed to know a lot of the other artists. I thought she was new in town?"

"Lauren Ashby is new in town. But she comes from New York and would have had opportunity to meet many of the gallery artists."

Aware of the critical tone in his voice and his aunt's knowing eyes on him, Jackson softened his voice. "I didn't realize you visited with her anyway." His tone still bordered on accusatory.

"Unfortunately I didn't. But I've heard nice things, I keep my ears open, and Brooke seems to like her a lot." She eyed Jackson over the rim of her cup.

His anger cooled, thanks to Aunt Willa's good coffee. He rubbed his hand over his face and drained his cup. The mood for confession threatened his better judgment. He'd better go to bed before he got into trouble.

"Thanks for the coffee." He went around the island and kissed his Aunt on the forehead. "And for everything else you do for Brooke and me." He moved on to the fridge, reached in for the empty milk carton and dropped it in the trash compactor.

"We're out of milk. Good night."

"Yes dear. Good night." Willa smiled and reached for her grocery list. As his step sounded on the stair, she shook her head, murmuring, "Jackson, Jackson, something is sure eating at you."

* * *

JACKSON HELD the blue pinstripe in one hand and a crisp white shirt in the other. Running late as usual, he had no patience with clothing issues. Clair Weston had agreed to meet at nine o'clock. The crisp white shirt won. It would go with anything. Tan cords and brown loafers came out without further thought or effort.

"Brooke." Jackson called as he hurriedly shoved files into his briefcase.

"Brooke!"

"I'm here Dad." She stood at his door.

"Why didn't you answer me, Pumpkin?"

"I did."

"Well, why didn't I hear if you answered?"

"Because you were talking to yourself," she explained patiently.

"Do I talk to myself?" Jackson stopped and frowned.

"Yes, Daddy."

He headed to the door mumbling about becoming his father as Brooke trudged along behind. He knew that she and Aunt Willa rolled their eyes at each other as they trailed through the kitchen where Aunt Willa cleared the table. He pretended not to know.

When they arrived at the gallery, Jackson got Brooke's bike out of the office where they stashed it each evening. "Remember you're supposed to have lunch at school today. I have a meeting, and I may be tied up."

"Yes, Dad, I remember. What about my dog?"

"*Not now*, Brooke." Jackson took his turn at rolling his eyes. She'd pestered him all weekend about a dog, even asking her Sunday school teacher to pray about it. Mrs. Wilson had laughingly reported the prayer request to him after church.

Over the weekend Jackson tried talking with her about making friends with strangers. But each attempt turned to how much fun Winslow was, and when could they see about finding her a dog.

Matt pulled in and parked next to Jackson. "Morning, Sunny Girl, off to school?"

Brooke barely nodded, but her eyes spoke volumes as she straddled her bike.

"Bye Uncle Matt!" She wheeled off in a flash, leaving her dad an obvious snub.

"Is our girl unhappy with someone this morning?" Matt kept a straight face.

"Our girl worried me all weekend about her dog." Jackson grinned at Matt.

"Well, you did promise."

"I'll tell you the same thing I told Brooke. *Not now*."

Matt laughed and held the gallery door open, following Jackson inside. "Maybe this meeting with Clair will go the way we hope and you'll cheer up."

"Who knows, I'm amazed that I got a meeting with Clair. I don't think her friend likes me very much, she could be a negative influence on Clair's decision." Jackson cast a wary glance at Matt.

"Oh, I doubt that, give the girls more credit. What reason would Lauren have for not liking you?" Matt cast a puzzled glance. "But, speaking of her friend, I haven't had a chance to tell you. You'll never guess who else Clair is friends with."

They strolled to the break room, and Matt started the coffee. Jackson's nerves might not survive a guessing game.

"You're right Matt, I'd never guess, so just tell me." Jackson glanced at his watch when the back entry bell jingled.

Maggie—arriving early.

"Sara Collins." Matt spoke over his shoulder.

Jackson shook his head. "What about Sara Collins?"

Matt grinned. "Clair *knows* Sara Collins."

"*The* reclusive Sara Collins?" Jackson walked over and leaned next to Matt, his backside against the counter with his ankles crossed. "Are you sure? Who told you that?"

"I got it straight from the source, Clair. She and Sara are good friends." Matt looked at his watch "Time to open the front." He left Jackson still leaning against the counter with a dazed look on his face.

As Matt's news sank in, Jackson's brain started a search through vague memories from the past—one concerning something about Clair Weston and Sara Collins struggled to surface. He hurried to the office and pulled the bulging old file of Jenna's artists' images.

Jenna started the file when they first began to dream of opening a gallery in Valley Ridge, even before they had finished college. Over the years she had clipped images and articles of artists' work that they both admired.

After they opened the gallery, and Jenna died, Jackson had continued to add to the file. Jenna's old file had guided him many times in selecting artists to bring in. It made him feel that Jenna was still a part of the gallery.

Jackson hurriedly flipped through the file, as the memory grew clearer. He found it, a faded newspaper clipping of the very young Sara Collins. The young girl in the photo smiled tentatively for the photographer during a reception. She stood next to an attractive, solemn faced woman on one side who could have been an older sister, and at her other side stood a younger Clair Weston.

The caption stated that Miss Sara Collins and her mother, Mrs. Elizabeth Collins Ashby, along with Miss Collins mentor and patron, Clair Weston, well-known landscape and still life painter, posed together after an exhibit of record success for the young Miss Collins' first one-woman show.

Matt had been right; Clair did know Sara Collins.

Jackson closed the file. His insides churned. What Clair had not bothered to tell Matt was that Sara Collins and Lauren Ashby were one and the same.

Why hadn't Lauren told Matt? Whatever her reason for not confiding in Matt, it was her business and he'd not be the one to tell Matt. Of all people he understood about secrets. Sooner or later it would come out.

Unaware of how long he'd sat there chasing thoughts, Jackson hastily replaced the file as Matt approached the office in conversation with Clair.

"Jackson, Clair's here."

"Good morning, Clair. Good to see you again. Did you have a nice weekend?" Jackson had never been nervous around celebrities or famous people. His father had been a well-known surgeon and Jackson grew up with famous people in their home often. Yet this friendly, pretty woman had his nerves tied in knots.

"I had a good weekend, Jackson, what about yourself?" Clair smiled, relaxed and friendly.

"Yes, I enjoyed the weekend. But it flew by."

They laughed and Clair murmured agreement.

Jackson motioned for Clair to step into the showroom, and he guided her toward the back office. They chatted about Valley Ridge and the beautiful countryside.

Matt stepped to the office door as they walked away. "Would you two like coffee?"

Clair hesitated and half turned, "Oh, Matt, that sounds wonderful, just black for me please, and thank you." She raised her brows at Jackson.

"Umm, Oh, yes—please. Thanks, Matt."

Jackson suspected his nerves were due more to Lauren's influence on this meeting and not Clair at all.

elief

Jackson soon relaxed in Clair's warm friendly presence. They chatted comfortably and fear of Lauren's influence vanished from his thoughts. Clair's sincere appreciation for the gallery and the stable of artists' he and Matt had assembled pleased him. Unlike so many in the creative arts, exceptional in the creative end of the art world, but lacking ability in the business side of it, Clair Weston appeared to have it all.

They met for almost two hours. Jackson being careful not to bring up Lauren's name and neither did Clair, until just as the meeting drew to an end.

"Clair, may I take you to lunch? We have a nice restaurant at the country club. Service is usually pretty good, and the food is great."

"That sounds wonderful, Jackson, but may I take a rain check? I'm driving back to Lauren's place to get her. I believe she's already made lunch plans." Clair gathered her purse and keys then stood.

Jackson reached to shake Clair's hand.

"Of course. We'll do lunch another time. I'm very pleased that you're joining us in the Gallery, Clair. Your work compliments and adds to the quality and standard we maintain at Montgomery Fine Art."

"Thank you, Jackson, I look forward to working with you and Matt." She moved toward the door.

Matt stood from his desk as Jackson returned from seeing Clair to the door. "Well, how'd it go?"

"She's in. We signed a contract with only a couple of minor changes. Things I knew you would agree with." Jackson slouched in his chair and relaxed. "I really like Clair, and you will too, Matt." Thoughtful, he studied his scattered desktop.

"I have no doubt I'll like Clair, I already do. I like Lauren also."

Jackson glanced at Matt, but Matt kept his gaze on his computer screen.

"I might like Lauren, too, if circumstances had been different . . ." Uh-oh, he kept forgetting Matt didn't know the true circumstances of his first encounter with Lauren.

Matt turned, a puzzled expression furrowing his brow. "Circumstances? Two strangers meet, what circumstances could there be?"

Jackson grimaced, caught. Time to come clean. He'd been waiting for the right time to explain everything to Matt. Right time or not, he'd better start talking. "Matt, about that first meeting with Lauren." He slumped deeper into his chair and slanted an eye at Matt.

Matt grinned. "I knew something funny must have happened. You're not a rude person. So, what's the story behind you being rude to a nice girl like Lauren?"

Jackson swiveled his chair toward Matt. "We didn't meet in town like I said. I ran into her out at the house—"

"The country house? But you never go there."

"No, I don't normally go to the house, and I didn't plan to go that morning, the day just ... " Jackson glanced at Matt and saw that he understood. "I *needed* to be there. Anyway this girl just wandered out of the woods."

"Lauren was at your house? What in the world for? " Matt motioned for Jackson to continue.

"Don't ask me, I haven't a clue how she found it. She came in from the back." Jackson grinned. "She looked like somebody *dragged* her across the back pasture. Believe me, you would never have recognized her that morning." Jackson glanced to see Matt cross his arms and pinch his pursed lips to keep from smiling.

"What's amusing?" Jackson hesitated.

"You're right I wouldn't have recognized her. That's the same morning she came by here. It was the first time I met her and apparently right after she'd been at your house." Matt smiled. "Remember? I told you about a pretty girl who just wanted to browse and that she looked like she'd cleared the back forty?" Matt's gaze held Jackson's. "You just missed her being here that morning."

Jackson's voice dropped to a whisper. "Lauren? She was the new girl who asked about the daffodil painting?"

"Yes. She loved it. I was surprised when she said the brush-work reminded her of Sorolla's. That's a big compliment. Most people aren't familiar with Sorolla's work. Especially amateur painters."

Jackson turned his chair away from Matt. Of course she would know about Sorolla. Sara Collins was no amateur. She had traveled extensively in Spain with her mentor from a young age and studied in Europe. Spending summers there with the Weston's. He and Jenna had read all about it. His heart thrilled, Sara Collins —*Lauren*, had recognized the genius in Jenna's brushwork—the very thing Jenna had loved most and worked so hard to master.

Matt put his hand on Jackson's shoulder, "I'm sorry, friend. I know this is hard for you. Jenna would have loved meeting Clair and building up the gallery just as the three of us planned for so many years."

Jackson nodded and turned back to face Matt. He must get his mind off Sara Collins; he needed private time to think through that staggering piece of news.

"There's more I need to tell you." Jackson's throat tightened, he swallowed and cleared it. He'd better tell Matt about the move back to the house before he chickened out. "I want you to be the first to know, besides Thelma of course. I'm putting the house and grounds back in order. I'll be moving back. Thelma's hiring a groundskeeper for me, and I'm reopening the house." He gazed at Matt. He'd expected him of all people to be happy about his plans. But Matt looked like he'd been slammed. But seconds later his expression swiftly righted itself.

"That's great news, Jackson. Sunny Girl will love it out there. She'll have a place for her new dog." Matt reached for the coffee sitting on his desk and took a long drink.

That coffee had to be stone cold, Matt didn't seem to realize he'd even taken a drink of it. Jackson recognized that same look he'd seen on Matt's face last week, a deep down misery. He'd not had a chance to talk with Ally to see if she'd learned anything about what might be troubling him. "I have to say, Matt, I'm surprised at your response. You … you think it's not a good move?"

"No, I do think it's a good move. I just wondered about Ally. Have you told her?"

"Not yet. And I'd rather you didn't say anything until I've had a chance to talk with her."

"Sure, no problem." Matt shrugged, turning back to his computer. All of a sudden he swiveled his chair back to Jackson. "You never finished telling me about meeting Lauren at the house and how you were rude." He swung an ankle up to rest on his knee.

"Well, I caught her trespassing, and I more or less asked … well, ordered her to leave."

"You're kidding! You didn't really order her to leave, did you?" Matt laughed. "I wish I had been there. What did she do?"

"It wasn't funny. I found myself regretting that I'd gone out there before the morning ended." Jackson gave a ragged sigh. "She tried to talk, but I didn't really hear … I got sick at the awful sight of the yard, the neglect. I hadn't expected it to look that bad. And the memories of Jenna, it all knocked me for a loop. I had to get away. I ordered her to leave, and I ran." Jackson glanced at Matt and managed a grin. "I didn't scare her any, though. She didn't leave until she chose to."

Matt laughed. "Sounds like Lauren." He studied the heel of his shoe for a moment before looking at Jackson again. "Why did you say you had met her in town?"

"I didn't want you to know I'd been at the house on the anniversary of Jenna's death. Don't ask me why. I don't know why. I guess I thought you'd worry."

"I would have understood, Jackson. I thought about Jenna that day too." Matt sighed. "After all this time, I still think of her often. So if I still think of her, I know you do even more." Matt paused for a second, "Does opening the house mean you have plans to move on with your life?"

"Yes. I have to. And I'm ready."

Why wasn't Matt pleased, why should this decision about the house affect him like this? "Matt is something wrong, we can talk—"

Maggie clicked in and scooted onto the corner of Matt's desk, swinging one long leg over the other, and leaning back on her hands. She could have been posing for a pin-up cover.

"Matt, you promised you had my computer fixed, but it's still acting up. I think you should take me to lunch and have another look at it when we get back."

Matt looked at his watch. "Well, we could do that. But it's past your lunchtime. Why haven't you gone already?"

"I've been busy. I sold another painting from the show." She swung her leg and glanced smugly at Matt.

"That clinches it young lady. You deserve lunch on the house. Give me a second here and you can name your preference." He finished and stood. Then turning to Jackson he said, "There's nothing wrong, partner, stop worrying. And I'm very pleased and happy for you."

He stuck his hand out and gripped Jackson's. "Let me know when congratulations are in order." He took Maggie by the arm and headed her toward the door. Her four-inch heels clicked a staccato on the polished floor as he hurried her out.

That had felt like a conversation with a stranger, not a friend he'd known most of his life. Jackson feared he understood what Matt referred to . . .*When congratulations are in order.*

With the office quiet, his thoughts turned once more to Sara Collins. *Lauren.* He struggled to reconcile the two names. He leaned back in his chair and replayed the scene of her and Brooke the evening of the show. He'd seen, and felt the warmth of the friendship between the two. A friendship that developed so fast and deep in such a short time must be special.

A friendship meant to be?

His phone roused him from thought. Thelma's number flashed on the screen. "Hello, Thelma."

"Good afternoon, Jackson. I wanted to let you know that I've hired Claude Robson as your groundskeeper."

"Claude Robson? Surely he's too elderly now?"

"Oh, no. Claude Robson Jr., son of Claude Sr. He's highly recommended and very able."

"Aha, I see. When does he start?"

"I'm meeting him at the house this evening so he can look around. He's pleased to be working for you. He remembers going out and helping his dad when your parents lived there." Thelma hesitated then said, "I still have the key your father gave me years ago."

"Good. And I'm glad you hired Claude's son, I remember him. He's not much older than me. I'm happy he's there." Jackson steadied his voice. Memories of his parents in the house flashed across his vision, precious and painful, as were the other memories. "Claude will need a gate key."

"I'll have one made before I meet with him this afternoon and give it to him then."

"Good. What time are you meeting him?"

"We planned for around five. I'll get back with you afterwards."

"Thanks a bunch, Thelma. I appreciate it. Take care."

"I will. And I may ask a friend to ride out with me."

Jackson ended the call on a plan. He'd drive Brooke out to the house after school to get an idea of how she'd feel about living in his old home, with room for a dog.

He'd surprise Thelma and meet her at the house.

CHAPTER 14

lair's News

THEY'D BEEN ALL SET for an afternoon of shopping, but most of the time had been spent in the quaint bookstore, "BOOKS, PENS & PAPERS", the only bookstore in Valley Ridge. Clair had fallen in love with the book and stationary store and it's lively owner, Marta Dillingham. She had chosen to linger there until time for an afternoon break.

They headed for The Coffee Bean. An usher seated them under a canopy of green. The leaves stirred lazily overhead. Clair observed everything about the outdoor lounge area of the cozy coffee bar. Lauren waited patiently.

"This reminds me of that little café in Florence. The one down the street from the villa where we spent many hours enjoying that delicious coffee." Clair smiled. "And I confess, the coffee I'm addicted to."

Lauren sighed. "I thought the same thing first time I saw this place. When I'm here I forget that I'm just an hour away from New York and not back in Italy."

A waiter hurried to their table.

"Just coffee please." Lauren settled back in her chair. In just minutes their order arrived.

Clair leaned over her cup and inhaled deeply.

Lauren smiled. "I knew you'd love it." She poured half and half into her own cup, swirling the dark liquid into a rich golden brown. "Well? Haven't I waited long enough to hear your news?" Lauren giggled like the child she often reverted to when she and Clair were together.

Clair, intent on her cup, spoke without looking up. "I'm engaged." When she finally raised her face, tears brimmed her eyes.

Lauren leaned forward and in a hushed voice said, "Ohh, Clair, it's real this time, isn't it?"

Clair nodded, retrieved a Kleenex from her purse and dabbed her eyes. "It's real this time. You'll love him too, Lauren. He's wonderful. He's ... he's exquisite." Clair's eyes widened when Lauren began to laugh.

"For some reason I can't think of a man as being exquisite, wonderful, maybe—"

"That's just it though, he is exquisite." By this time Clair's smile had given way to laughter too.

They laughed until they both had tears. Lauren jumped up to hug Clair.

"My, this is a lively party. Sorry to interrupt ..."

"Oh, Thelma, you're not interrupting. I want you to meet my oldest and dearest friend, Clair Weston."

The women exchanged pleasantries.

Thelma turned to Lauren. "I'm driving out to Jackson's place and wondered if you'd like to drive out with me and see the inside of the house?" Her glance included Clair in the invitation.

"Thelma, I ... I don't know. I would love to see inside. But, will he be there?"

"Oh, no. Jackson won't be there, not that it would matter. I've hired Jackson a yardman and I'm meeting him at the house to get the work started."

Lauren glanced at Clair. "Would you like to drive out and see the house that captured my heart and soul?"

"How could I resist seeing a house with that kind of power? Jackson doesn't live in the house?" Clair looked from Lauren to Thelma.

"No, he hasn't lived in it for years." Thelma spoke to Clair as she looked at her watch. "I need to be there by five. That's about an hour and a half from now."

"Shall we meet at your office at four-thirty?" Lauren checked her watch. "We'll follow you."

"Good. I'll see you then." Thelma got a to-go coffee and waved bye.

"Did I sense a little tension between you and Thelma?" Clair lifted her brows.

"Not with Thelma, only me. I feel bad about giving her a hard time over the house. But now, back to you, when do I get to meet this exquisite man?"

Clair motioned for a refill. "In three weeks he's coming back to New York. His home." She flashed Lauren a contented smile.

"Home? He's American? I always assumed you'd marry a handsome Italian and live in Florence." It dawned on Lauren what this could mean. "You'll be living in New York again. With —hey, I don't even know this exquisite beings name." *Why hadn't Clair told her about this guy?*

"I know. But I was afraid if I talked about him it wouldn't work out or something." Clair grinned. "I'm not superstitious, just cautious, and his name is Drew Foreman. His business keeps him in Europe five to six months out of the year."

"Perfect! As much work as you do there, now you'll have

someone to travel with. And it's good for me too. I'll still have my home away from home when I'm in Italy on business." She hesitated. "You won't ever sell the villa will you, Clair?"

"Good heavens, no. Grandfather Weston gave it to my parents as a wedding gift."

"I didn't think you would, but I'm glad to hear you say so." Lauren glanced at her watch. "We should probably head for Thelma's office, as much as I hate to break up this party."

Clair sighed happily. "We have a whole summer to catch up. And you didn't get to explain about Brooke and Jackson as you promised." She stood and followed Lauren as they strolled toward the exit.

"There's really nothing to explain."

Clair prodded her shoulder. "When we get home, you explain everything. *Everything*, okay?" She made her point with a final nudge.

Lauren laughed, saying, "I will, I promise." They climbed into the Range Rover.

* * *

CURIOSITY MAY HAVE KILLED the cat, but satisfaction brought it back. Lauren's curiosity wouldn't be satisfied until she discovered the private road to the house, *Jackson's house*. Not getting it for her own proved to be a bitter pill she still struggled to swallow. Why in the world had she agreed to drive out and torment herself? What did it matter if she knew where his road turned off the main highway or what the inside looked like?

"Penny for your thoughts. Were you muttering to me or yourself?" Clair tilted her head, trying to look more fully into Lauren's face.

Lauren laughed. "I mutter to myself quite often."

"Nothing wrong with that, I do it too. It helps sort things out—"

"Where *is* she going?" Lauren gazed ahead. "The house is six or seven miles out of town. This neighborhood is in the wrong direction." She kept Thelma's white Cadillac in sight as Thelma turned down streets that Lauren had never been on before.

Clair commented on the neighborhood they were passing through. Most of the houses were situated on large spacious lawns, heavily wooded. "Maybe she's dropping something off to a client first?"

The white Cadillac never slowed or indicated a detour. "She didn't say anything about making a stop," Lauren muttered. The houses grew farther apart until suddenly they entered open country. They drove quietly for several minutes. "Look." Lauren pointed to her right.

"Um, what am I looking for?" Clair squinted ahead.

"There! Across those woods." Lauren bobbed her finger. "You can see the chimney from here."

"I see three chimneys. Is *that* where we're going?"

"Yes, that's the house. No wonder I could never find the entry. It comes straight from town, a short cut." No way she could have discovered the entry from the road she took into town—there wasn't one from that direction.

Thelma now led them deeper into the country. In a quarter of a mile she turned off onto another road.

Lauren noticed the highway they'd turned off of was Old Elm Road; the same highway that looped around and passed her house. Mystery of the hidden entry solved. Jackson's property that she saw from the highway, wound back toward town. She'd caught the back view of it from across the field. She had doubled back one day looking in the opposite direction, but hadn't gone far enough.

"Why in the world would you want a house this secluded?" Clair's face registered dismay.

"Wait until you see it up close, you'll love it. There's the private entry. And I plodded through that jungle."

Thelma pulled up to a tall iron gate and stepped out of her car.

Lauren braked, opened her door. "Wait, I'll help."

They huffed with the effort, but managed to get both sides of the gate opened back.

"I wanted to get here before the yardman did, he doesn't have a key." Thelma breathed deeply. "I thought you might find something out here you'd want to paint."

"Oh, I'm sure I will. But will he mind?"

"Why in the world would Jackson mind? Did you see the lake? That would make a beautiful painting."

Lauren agreed about the lake she'd glimpsed through the woods.

Back in their cars they drove slowly up the wide circular drive. Clair straightened in her seat, looking around, her eyes brightened.

Lauren sighed. Jackson Montgomery grew up in this wonderful house. The thought stirred Lauren's interest in a new way, and almost as much as it did when she viewed it as the vacant house she'd wanted to buy. A child could build wonderful memories here. Why wasn't Brooke growing up here? Irritation toward Jackson rose, *again.*

Thelma waited for them to park and meet her at the front before she unlocked the large carved door.

Lauren tentatively stepped inside. She swallowed the lump in her throat, feeling like she was doing something forbidden. They walked through the wide foyer into a spacious great room, each quiet in their thoughts. Thelma and Clair wandered ahead, leaving her behind.

Lauren recalled the morning she stood on the other side of those large windows. In her heart she had believed that when she stood on *this* side of them, it would be as the new owner. And she would be in her own home.

Tears welled.

Thelma called, "Lauren, I heard the yardman arrive. Tell him I'll be down in a minute if he comes inside. Clair and I are going on upstairs."

"Okay. I'll be along in a moment." The room to herself, Lauren lowered her body to the floor and gently brushed her hand over the rug. Her fingers traced the pale-peach cabbage roses. The rug was just like one her mother used to have. Hot tears fell unchecked.

"Oh—uh, excuse me ... " Jackson Montgomery stood in the wide entry to the room. A flush tinged his face, a puzzled, uneasy expression troubled his features.

"Oh, you weren't supposed to be here." Lauren scrambled to her feet, brushing at her tears. "I shouldn't have come—"

"No, please. You're fine." He ran his fingers through his hair. "It's just ... " He shrugged. "Nobody told me I wasn't supposed to be here."

He grinned, recovering from finding her in his house, on the floor, *talking to the rug*. He averted his eyes. Lauren appreciated his pretense at not seeing her tears.

"Dad! Dad!" They both shifted their gaze at the sound of Brooke's voice, glad for the diversion.

"In here," Jackson called.

"Dad, that's Lauren's car—"

Jackson stepped aside, putting Lauren in full view.

Brooke bounced across the room and slipped her arms around Lauren's waist. "Is Winslow here too?"

A quick glance at Jackson, and Lauren hesitantly returned Brooke's hug. "Winslow took the day off. Sometimes he simply refuses to hang out with me."

Brooke giggled.

"He's at home, snoozing I'm sure." She smiled at Brooke and patted her small shoulder. Glancing up, she caught Jackson studying them. Their eyes met and held until the sound of Clair and Thelma returning, sent Brooke dashing up the stairs calling out to Thelma.

"Thelma, did you know I'm getting a dog!"

Lauren laughed nervously, saying, "I didn't expect you to be here. Thelma said you weren't driving out."

"No. She didn't know. I decided at the last minute."

Lauren turned as Thelma and Clair entered the room. Brooke skipped ahead of them and sidled up to her dad. Thelma went to Jackson and gave him a hug.

"It wasn't necessary for you to drive out. I thought you were Claude Jr. arriving." Her sharp eyes hadn't missed the heightened color of Jackson's tanned face.

"I hadn't planned to drive out. It happened spur of the moment." He glanced down at Brooke "I thought it might be a fun outing for Pumpkin here." He smiled at Brooke as she danced up and down, then she pulled on his arm and whispered as he bent down to her.

Lauren heard him say, "Later, Brooke, *not now.*" Whatever it was about, his answer didn't please Brooke.

She dropped his hand and sauntered over to Lauren.

"Are you going to paint tomorrow?" She stood twisting her arms together and trying to lock her fingers while holding the contorted posture.

"Not tomorrow. You've met my friend, Clair." She and Brooke glanced at Clair, who smiled back. "She and I have plans for tomorrow. Maybe the next day would be a better day to paint. Since Clair's going into New York to be with her father that day. And I'll be free. Okay?"

"Yes! Her eyes lit up, and she danced up and down on her toes. "Will you bring Winslow too?"

"Of course. He'd be unhappy with me if he thought I visited you without him." Lauren widened her eyes and pursed her lips, Brooke giggled and clasped her hands under her chin. Their conversation seemed to hold Jackson's interest more than Thelma's did.

Brooke threw her dad a petulant glance, then danced off to explore under the mounds of draped furniture.

Thelma left Clair chatting with Jackson and came to Lauren. "Would you like a tour of the house?"

"Oh no! Not now, Thelma." Lauren lowered her voice. "I'm embarrassed just being here. I wouldn't be comfortable going through his house with him here. It's time Clair and I were going anyway."

"Why on earth are you embarrassed?" Thelma frowned. "Jackson would not think a thing about you touring *his* house." Thelma teased her. "He'd be pleased."

Suddenly Lauren felt foolish and miserable. She spoke sharper than necessary. "Clair, we really should be going, Winslow will think I've deserted him."

Thelma glanced at her. An uncertain expression clouded her kind eyes.

Impulsively Lauren hugged her. She didn't want Thelma to think she'd gotten her feelings hurt with her teasing. "Thank you," she whispered. "I'll come with you another time and see the house if you'll ask me again."

"Of course, I will." Thelma brightened.

Clair stood from where she'd been sitting on the arm of a draped chair and they all moved toward the front entry. Thelma had the key in her hand for the yardman. Brooke bounced along in front of the group. She kept glancing back at Lauren, smiling. Her actions made Lauren nervous. She didn't want Jackson thinking there were secrets between her and Brooke.

Whatever went on with the father and daughter, it had nothing to do with Lauren. A slow throb started in her head. She just wanted to get home.

"Um, Lauren, may I speak with you for a moment?" Jackson asked, his expression unreadable.

All faces turned toward her. Thelma stopped speaking mid

sentence, Clair's eyes widened, and Brooke became still for the first time since they'd been there.

"Yes … yes, of course." Suddenly the throbbing in her head picked up the tempo.

"Would you be free to come by the gallery tomorrow, say around three-thirty?"

"I'm afraid I can't tomorrow."

She glanced at Brooke, whose eyes were as round as saucers as she stared at Lauren.

"I already have plans tomorrow, but the next day would be fine. I have only one commitment that day.

Would that work for you?"

Out of the corner of her eye she saw Brooke bouncing on her toes again.

"That'll work fine. Thank you." His gaze lingered.

She hastily turned away from those entrancing gray-green eyes.

While the pounding in her head grew fierce.

CHAPTER 15

rooke

BROOKE HADN'T POUNCED on him about Lauren and the dog the minute they settled in the truck. He breathed a silent thank you. He didn't want to talk about the dog. His thoughts lingered on Lauren's parting smile. Well, almost a smile. Enough of a smile to make his heart beat faster. She'd glanced over her shoulder as she and Clair walked toward her Range Rover and caught him watching her. She quickly looked away, but he'd seen it.

"Dad, why are you smiling?"

Brooke's tone came as an accusation interrupting his thoughts.

"Are you sure I was smiling?" He feigned surprise. Actually, he *had* been smiling without realizing it.

"Yes. Can't you tell when you're smiling?" She narrowed suspicious eyes on him.

"I dunno. Maybe I *can't* tell when I'm smiling." He turned toward her with a big smile.

"Dad—you can too, tell—are you smiling now?" She grinned.

"I think so, but I'm not sure," he said, stretching his smile wider.

Giggling, she twisted and fidgeted with her seat belt.

"Yes, Daddy, you're smiling. Are you teasing me?" She stretched her lips into a smile and felt both sides of her mouth. "You can tell."

"Yes, sweetheart I'm teasing. But sometimes people smile, not realizing it." Jackson glanced sideways. "Does that make sense?"

"Uh-huh." She gazed into his eyes and twirled a strand of blonde hair.

Uh-oh, he knew that look; she prepared to pounce.

"Why did you ask Lauren to come see you at the gallery?" Her eyes narrowed again.

"I want to talk with her about something very important. I asked her to come at three-thirty so you could be there too."

Brooke ran her hand up and down the strap of her seat belt. "Is it about a dog like Winslow?"

"That's exactly what it's about. Matt told me that Lauren rescued Winslow. I'd like to know where she got him and what we'll need to do to find you a dog similar to Winslow." He glanced at her again and the look on her face cut his heart as surely as a knife would have.

Brooke's eyes widened, her face mirrored a happiness that only an innocent child could express.

He'd withheld that happiness because a dog represented an inconvenient responsibility. Lauren Ashby, not him, could take credit for the indescribable look of joy on Brooke's face.

He could have wept.

Jackson blinked and turned his gaze away as he breathed an apology to Jenna. He'd tell Brooke about moving to the house as soon as they'd talked with Lauren about the dog. He reached his hand to her small shoulder and gently squeezed it. She had to know how much he loved her. He had so much making up to do —and a dog to find.

* * *

MATT'S CAR already sat in his parking place when Jackson swung his truck into its slot at the gallery. He'd gotten around early and expected to be the first one there.

Matt looked up from his computer. "You're early. Where's Sunny Girl?"

"Aunt Willa offered to take her to school. What are you doing here at this hour?"

"I wanted to get some things together before I go over to Mrs. Parker's. We've made good headway. I've always liked Ally's grandmother. She really has a nice collection. I may try to sell a couple of pieces for her." He glanced briefly at Jackson and headed to the client office.

Something had him wound up tight. Jackson grinned, shaking his head. Matt seemed almost nervous. Mrs. Parker could be dominating. But Matt usually got along great with the senior crowd. Ally would know if a problem threatened.

The phone rang and Jackson glanced at caller ID.

"Good morning, Ally. My thoughts must have winged your way."

"Hmm, I'm flattered to be on your mind so early. Anything in particular?"

"That *thing* we talked about, are you making any progress?' Jackson lowered his voice.

"Jackson, this is just our third meeting. I can't start snooping into Matt's personal life immediately. Give me some time." Ally's laughter sounded carefree. "And it looks like this project may take longer than we first expected."

"Why? Is there a problem with your grandmother?"

"Heavens no, Gram loves Matt. She may be guilty of dragging this out. She loves discussing art with him."

"He seems a little nervous this morning, I just thought they might be having a conflict."

"Not in the least, he's relaxed and charming with Gram, and she's always liked Matt." Ally didn't speak for a moment. "We really had a good time, and Matt is fun to be with. The two hours passed rather quickly."

"Well, then let's quit worrying about him. Things have a way of working out."

"Oh, Jackson, I almost forgot what I called for. The other day at the club Myra Whitcomb announced that her niece is back home and looking for a job. She has gallery experience. I told Myra that I thought you and Matt had talked of hiring another person for sales and office work—did I do good mentioning it?"

"Ally, you read my mind. I intended to speak with Matt first chance we had. Could you fill him in about the girl after your meeting this morning? Maybe he can interview her."

"I'll be happy to. I'm glad to help. Got to run, talk with you later, bye."

He sighed, pleased that all seemed to be going well. Good old Matt had worked his charm on Ally's grandmother. She was no different than the other ninety-nine percent of the women in Valley Ridge. They all loved Matt. The only ones who didn't love him were the ones who'd never spent time in his company.

Jackson sobered. Things *do* have a way of working out. He had a flashback of Matt and Lauren huddled at the show, talking and laughing. He'd seen Matt put his arm around Lauren once, their heads close. It had happened just before Lauren and Clair left the show that night. He wondered …had Matt picked Lauren up later? Jackson tried to recall the excuses Matt offered for wanting to celebrate the success of the show at another time.

Jackson's stomach tightened at visions of Lauren and Matt together.

"Jackson, I'm gone. Heading over to Mrs. Parker's. The sooner I get started the sooner we'll finish. And you were right, the earlier the better is her motto."

"Sure. See you later."

"Did I hear Matt leave?" Maggie stepped into the office and slid onto the corner of Matt's desk.

"Yes, you did. He's getting in some time on Mrs. Parker's art collection. She may sell some of it, and Matt's helping her with the project."

Maggie had a way of giving the illusion of her perfect nose actually turning up when she didn't approve of something.

"Is he getting paid for his time or is it just a *favor* for Ally."

Jackson looked up from the latest Art News and shook his head at her. "Maggie, don't be petty. If Matt wants to do a favor for a friend, it's his business."

She glared at Jackson, wiggled off the desk and flounced back to her own office.

He shook his head when Maggie's door closed with a firm sound.

* * *

"HELLO PUMPKIN. How did class go this morning?" Jackson closed his file and followed her toward the break room.

"Fun. Mrs. Jenkins told David Holt if he talked one more time he would have to go to the principal's office. You know what *that* means, Dad?" She watched his face, an excited gleam in her eyes.

"Not sure I do. What does it mean?" He placed her peanut-butter-and-jelly sandwich on the table, and poured her a glass of milk before unwrapping his own sandwich.

"At recess David said it meant the old paddle." Brooke giggled.

"Hmm, what does going to the principal's office, have to do with an old paddle?" He shook his head, playing the confused parent.

"Da-a-a-d, you know." She patted her hip and giggled until Jackson had to remind her to eat.

"I hope you don't talk in class and upset Mrs. Jenkins. You don't, do you?" He had never gotten a note about such behavior.

"No! I always help Mrs. Jenkins, and I never talk without raising my hand." She shook her head vigorously, "I don't want the old paddle."

Brooke was clearly taken with the notion of the paddle. Signs of another giggling fit caused Jackson to grasp at something to get her mind off the incident. "Don't forget we have a meeting with Miss Ashby tomorrow."

She took a big bite and mumbled, "With Lauren?" Her mouth was full as she gazed over her sandwich.

"Uh, yes. With Lauren."

Chewing and smacking she swallowed. "I remember, and I can't wait. She's bringing Winslow."

Winslow got her mind off school real quick.

"Where will we keep my dog, Daddy?" She nibbled around the crusts of her sandwich.

Jackson had wanted to wait until after they talked with Lauren about finding a dog before telling Brooke about the house. He debated all of three seconds before deciding to tell her now.

"I've been thinking. A dog needs room to run and play. It wouldn't be fair to keep him penned up all the time." He glanced up—surprised. Her eyes were round and beginning to tear. "Hey, Pumpkin, what's the matter?"

"You've changed your mind about my dog!" She dropped the sandwich on the plate and crossed her arms, the tears pooled in her amber eyes.

"Whatever made you think I'd changed my mind?"

"Well, have you?"

Jackson lifted his hands in exasperation. "No, I haven't changed my mind. Where did you get that idea?"

Hopefulness crept into her eyes, but doubt lingered.

"We don't have a place for my dog to run. He'll *have* to stay penned in my room," she wailed.

"Come here, Pumpkin." Jackson turned from the table and held out his hands to her. Brooke rose slowly from her chair and stood in front of him, her head hung as she blinked back tears. He took her hands in his. "I've been keeping a secret from you."

Her head came up, interest sparked in her wide eyes as tears clung to her lashes.

"I think your new dog would like living in the country, don't you? How would you like if we moved to the country house? There's lots of room for a dog to run and play out there. What do you think?"

He wasn't braced for the small body that launched itself at him, causing them both to nearly land on the floor. They laughed and held onto each other.

"Daddy! You mean it?" She whirled at the sound of the office door opening. She threw herself at Matt when he stepped into the break room.

"Uncle Matt! Guess what! I *am* getting a dog for real. And guess what else?" Brooke bounced up and down on her toes.

"Well, let me guess—"

Brooke squealed, "We're moving to the country so my dog won't have to stay in my room his *whole* life!"

"My, my, I'd say that will be one lucky little dog."

Matt chatted with Brooke about dog plans while Jackson straightened the break room. They all returned to the office and Jackson relaxed into his chair.

"Time to get back to school, Pumpkin. Come give me a hug first."

She hugged him and Matt before skipping out the door.

"Well, my friend, you're pretty lucky yourself. You know it?" Matt sighed and settled into his chair

"Yes, Matt. I really do know, though I didn't think so not long ago." He had come to feel he couldn't share his new feelings with Matt. How could he be happy again, knowing that something troubled Matt?

If only Ally would hurry and find out the source of that trouble.

CHAPTER 16

 Touch...

MATT STARED at the open file without a clue why he'd pulled it out in the first place. Unable to remember what he needed it for, he sighed and once more replayed the last two hours he'd spent in Ally's company. Laughing about something her grandmother had said, Ally had lightly placed her hand on his arm. It lingered there. Impulsively he'd placed his hand on hers, and she hadn't pulled away. She raised her face to his, her blue eyes betraying her feelings. She had carefully pulled her hand from under his warm caress.

Both sensed the electric current that flared between them. *She couldn't have missed the longing in his eyes.*

He had loved Ally from the first time he and Jackson double-dated one summer when she was home from college. She had been Jackson's date. He no longer remembered the name of the girl he'd taken on that date. But Ally Parker had been in his heart and mind ever since.

It hadn't taken long though to see that no other guy, including him, stood a chance. Nothing had distracted her from Jackson. Even after Jackson and Jenna began dating in college.

Propping his elbows on the desk, Matt dropped his head to his hands and rubbed his weary eyes. "Oh Man, what have you done now?"

"Muttering to yourself?" Jackson entered the office.

"Oh—Jackson. Yeah. I didn't hear you come in." Matt quickly shuffled papers around. "I'm having trouble getting my ducks in a row this morning."

"I hear you. How's the project coming along with Mrs. Parker's collection?" Jackson set his briefcase on the floor next to his desk and glanced at his watch.

"It's fine. I'll finish up in a couple or three weeks. Much sooner than I expected." Matt couldn't look at Jackson. What kind of man harbors feelings for his best friend's girl? Tomorrow he would apologize and make things right with Ally. But even in the throes of misery his traitorous heart soared at the prospect of seeing her again.

"You don't have to rush, you know." Jackson glanced at Matt. "Mornings are usually pretty quiet anyway. Besides, we'll have the new girl here before long. Take your time with Mrs. Parker."

He turned on his computer. "Did you say you had a good interview with the new girl—what was her name?"

"Sonya Weldon. Yes, I liked her. I think she'll be good. I just hope Maggie will be nice and get along for the rest of the summer." He glanced at Jackson. "She can't start until week after next."

"That's okay. It'll be good to have extra help in the gallery since I'm spending more time at the house. Another person here with Maggie should make her happy, too. Anyway we can hope it does."

Matt cleared his throat. "Speaking of the house, have you told Ally about it yet?"

Jackson turned his chair toward him. "No, not yet."

Matt thought he wanted to say more, but Jackson turned back to his computer. Matt cleared his throat again.

"I know it's none of my business, Jackson, but the other day in the bank someone asked me about the work that Claude was doing out there. Word is getting around."

Pushing his hand through his hair Jackson sighed. "I know." He swiveled his chair once more to face Matt. "I'm telling Ally tomorrow evening. We're having dinner at the club."

Their eyes held, Matt said, "Good, she needs to hear it from you."

Jackson nodded. "Yes, I know." He returned to work.

Matt got the feeling that Jackson wanted to confide something. He didn't suspect anything about him and Ally, did he? What was there to suspect? Besides, Ally wouldn't do anything to hurt Jackson. And he hoped he wouldn't either.

The bell jangled, and Brooke rushed in. She brought relief in a welcomed change of subject. He and Jackson didn't share their burdens as they once had.

"Is lunch ready?" Brooke glanced at her dad and headed straight for the break room. The air charged with energy in her wake.

Matt and Jackson looked at each other, raised their brows at the same time and trailed after her.

"I don't usually set lunch out until you get here, Pumpkin. What's the hurry?" Jackson reached into the fridge, pulled out the lasagna Aunt Willa had sent for lunch and stuck it in the convection oven.

Matt arranged their plates, silverware and napkins on the table.

"I need to hurry, Dad! I'm going to stop and watch Lauren paint, and I get to play with Winslow too." She hurried things along by splashing milk into her glass.

Matt and Jackson shared a furtive glance and raised their brows again.

"Where does Lauren paint when you watch her, Brooke?" Jackson asked, setting the lasagna on the table along with a salad.

Brooke swigged her milk and swiped the white moustache with her hand.

Jackson handed her a napkin.

"At the church."

She helped herself to lasagna after blessings were asked on the food.

"Oh, I see. You stop on the way back to school?"

"Uh-huh. Lauren paints real pretty." Brooke skipped the salad and concentrated on the lasagna.

"Brooke, you remember Lauren's coming at three-thirty to talk with us?"

"Uh-huh, I remember—she's bringing Winslow."

Matt wondered at Jackson's expression. He became more and more of a puzzle. He appeared anxious when he mentioned that Lauren would be there at three-thirty.

"You have a meeting with Lauren this afternoon?" Matt asked.

Jackson peered briefly in Matt's direction. "Yes. Here at the gallery. I want to get more information about how she went about rescuing her dog, I may do the same when we're ready to get Brooke's dog."

"*Winslow*, Dad. Lauren rescued Winslow." Brooke corrected with a stern look.

"Sorry, Matt. *Winslow's* not just any dog." He grinned at Matt and forked up a mouthful of salad.

Jackson had a meeting with Lauren about dog adoption? Valley Ridge had an excellent animal rescue facility. Why didn't he just go by there? They could tell him what to do about getting Sunny a dog. They probably had the perfect dog right now.

After Brooke inhaled her food and left in a whirlwind, they

straightened the break room. Jackson fidgeted around his desk, restless and sighing every few minutes.

Matt found himself wishing for a still, quiet place. Maggie saved the day when she returned from lunch and asked him to please come and check her computer, the *ongoing* headache. But for once he gave thanks to have a task to concentrate on. He gave thanks for anything that got him away from Jackson's nervous sighing.

Girls' offices always smell good and the quiet in Maggie's office had never sounded so good, or *peaceful*. Matt relaxed.

Maggie scooted onto the desk and said, "What's the matter with everybody around here?"

"What do you mean?" He opened her computer to probe the depths of technology.

Maggie could be perceptive.

"I don't know ... nobody talks anymore. We used to laugh a lot. I personally sold nine paintings at the show, and we still haven't celebrated. We've always celebrated after a good show."

Maggie knew how to pout too.

"You're right, Maggie, and we need to correct that oversight and celebrate. Let's work on it, okay? Tomorrow we'll plan a gallery celebration. Let's make it a real party, invite the new girl, Sonya." He looked into the unhappy, young face and decided that Maggie should get more credit. She had a good mind. Things needed to be put right. He liked feeling good about himself when he looked in the mirror, not the way he'd felt lately.

"Oh, Matt, that's a super idea. Will Jackson go along do you think?" She frowned.

"Of course he'll go along, why wouldn't he?" He winked at Maggie.

"He's the one that was such a wet blanket after the show, acting like a thunderhead. He even snapped at me." Her eyes widened at the memory.

"Maggie, pay no attention to that. Jackson didn't mean

anything. He's had a lot on his mind lately." Apparently they'd both had a lot on their minds and it was time to put a stop to it.

The wall growing between him and Jackson had to come down. He'd kidded himself, imagining the gaze of affection in Ally's eyes. It hadn't been anything.

She would marry Jackson in the near future, as planned and life would go on.

Ally and Jackson would always be his dearest friends. He'd see to that, if it killed him.

 he Request

LAUREN REMAINED quiet on the ride home from town. Clair glanced sidelong at her occasionally as if she wanted to say something, but hesitated, which wasn't like her. By the third time, Lauren laughed quietly and said, "Clair, do you have something on your mind?"

"Yes, I do. But first, thank you for letting me change your plans today. I'll leave for New York first thing in the morning. It shouldn't interfere with your day. And, I've wanted to ask you something all day, but I feel selfish doing so." She turned slightly in her seat.

"You are the least selfish person I know. What could you possibly ask that would be selfish?" Lauren inclined her head toward Clair, keeping her eyes on the road.

"Drew has asked me to stay in New York the rest of the summer. His company owns the Belmont Hotel. Did you know that?"

"No, I didn't know that."

Clair sighed and leaned her head back against the headrest. "He's given me one of the client suites for the summer. It's rather large. Two bedrooms."

"What are you getting at?"

"Be forewarned. I'm prepared to beg. I'd consider it a huge favor if you'd close your house and come spend the summer with me. We could see plays, visit old friends and plan my wedding—"

"Oh, Clair, I can't do that. Valley Ridge is my home now. I'm still settling in. I have things to do, but I'll come see you often. I have my work, and Winslow loves the country too."

"I'm begging you." Clair spoke softly.

"Please, please don't beg! You know saying no is hard for me. Why don't you come stay in the country? Drew could drive out for the weekends, and after being in the city all week it would be a refreshing change for him."

"It's not Drew I'm worried about." She turned her head on the headrest and looked at Lauren. "He's not the one who's going to be hurt."

"What *are* you talking about? What makes you say that?" Her heart skipped.

"I probably shouldn't say anything, but when did that ever stop me?" She faced straight ahead. "I believe Jackson is deeply attracted to you. He's a nice person and I like him, but I gather he's already made a commitment to Ally Parker. If he's not careful, people will be hurt. I don't want it to be you." Clair twisted in her seat. "And before you ask how I know, Thelma told me in conversation. She expects he and Ally will be married after he moves into the house. She said they've been seeing each other since two or three years after his wife died. Jackson and Ally were childhood friends." Clair gazed out the window. "I think they may have dated a little in college."

"That has nothing to do with me." Lauren reached to squeeze Clair's hand. "You stop worrying about me, and concentrate on enjoying your summer with Drew, and plan on lots of weekends in the country." She forced a cheerful voice, in spite of the lonely ache that crept into her heart.

"If you insist you can't come, then I'll see you here. But you can change your mind anytime." Clair didn't match Lauren's cheerfulness, and she changed the subject.

"What do you suppose Jackson wants to talk with you about tomorrow? What will you do if he asks you to show in the gallery?"

"He doesn't know anything about my painting. I've been very careful to keep it that way. I don't have a clue what he wants, but I'm sure it's something about Brooke. And I agreed to see Jackson because I want to speak with him about her."

Clair mused, "Art lessons? You're fond of that child aren't you?"

"Lessons maybe. I suppose I am fond of her. Something about Brooke reminds me of myself at that age."

"You feel sorry for her, don't you?"

Lauren tapped a thumb on the steering wheel. "No, it's not that. She's a delightful child." She said lightly, "That's all."

Clair sat quiet for a long moment. "Lauren, I don't want you to get hurt, but neither do I want to see Brooke hurt. And don't ask me what I mean, you know what I mean."

The silence thickened as a tiny throb pulsed in her temples. Yes, she did know what Clair meant. But Clair could be wrong this time. "I'm not sure what you mean."

Clair's expression chided her as if she were ten years old and caught telling a fib. "I believe you do know. But I'll refresh your memory." She paused. "How many times have you allowed a friendship to develop, but when the person got too close or too serious, you backed out of the picture and ran off Europe. Or back to the states to work." Clair waited, allowing her words to sink in.

"I don't recall ever having a friendship with a child before—a child is different from adults and especially men. A child doesn't demand changes in your life." Lauren glanced at Clair. "They already have the people in their lives who they depend on and look to for security. They know the one who's *responsible* for them." She took her eyes off the road and gazed at Clair. She raised her brows and returned Lauren's gaze.

"Okay," Clair finally agreed, "that's all true. But as you said, they're different. A child loves unconditionally and from the heart. They don't understand about getting too close."

"I don't plan on getting that close to Brooke. I'll only be her art teacher. I never got that close to any of my teachers." She glanced at Clair to see her brows go up again, lips pursed. "Oh, Clair, you know what I mean. You were different ... you saved my life."

"Who's to say you won't save Brooke's life—that she won't be having this conversation with you in fifteen or twenty years?"

"Clair, my head is killing me. Can we have this discussion another time, please?"

Clair reached over and patted her arm. "Of course we can. Are we almost home? I can't tell since you took the new short cut. I'm making dinner tonight while you lie down and get rid of that headache."

"Yes, we're almost there. Clair, I know I have commitment issues."

"We'll talk later, lets get you home for now."

At least one good thing came of going to Jackson's house yesterday, she learned this new route and it shaved seven minutes off the drive into town.

* * *

LATER WHEN LAUREN WOKE, Clair had set a pretty tray on the back patio table. Tall frosted glasses of iced tea, a light chicken salad, whole-grain crackers and colorful fruit cups greeted her.

"I could get spoiled, Clair. This looks delicious. And my

headache is gone, those aspirin did the trick." Lauren placed her napkin in her lap and waited for Clair to settle into her chair.

"I get those awful headaches too. They can last for days unless I take several aspirin at the onset" She settled at the table. "Before I forget, Matt called while you were asleep. I told him you'd gone to bed with a headache, he said he'd call back in the morning when you were on your feet again."

"Oh, Thank you. I'll call him back."

Clair asked the blessing and then handed the chicken salad to Lauren. "I know it's late to be eating, but you need some food in your stomach."

Lauren's thoughts turned to Matt as she helped herself to the salad. He was a sweet person, and he didn't upset her nerves the way Jackson did.

"This salad looks scrumptious." She set the bowl on the table. "Matt really is nice, isn't he? I do like him a lot."

"Who are you trying convince, me or yourself?" Clair reached for her tea, and taking a long sip, she leaned back in her chair and looked out across the back to the woods where the sun slipped below the horizon.

"This is what's *really* nice." She grinned at Lauren.

* * *

THE NEXT MORNING Lauren stood by Clair's bed, helping her fold and pack her things.

"Be sure to tell your dad hello for me. I'm looking forward to seeing him very soon."

"Of course I will. You know he'll insist you come and spend time with us." Clair stopped packing to look at her. "Lauren, be careful. I can't help but worry about this situation. I want you to be happy, that's all." She closed her bag and tossed a light sweater on top of it.

Lauren didn't want to start that again. "You don't need to

worry. There is no situation." Her anxious mind flashed forward to the meeting with Jackson.

"What do you have planned for today? Will you do some painting? I'll wait and go to New York tomorrow if you'll come with me. What do you say, just a few days?"

"Thank you, but I can't. First I'll get back with Matt and see what's on his mind. And then I'm going to do some landscape painting."

"Until the meeting with Jackson?"

"Yes, until the meeting." She didn't make eye contact. Clair could read things that weren't even there.

They carried Clair's bags to the lease car. Lauren hugged her before she slid behind the wheel. Clair reminded her that she'd be back in five days. Her suite at the Belmont wouldn't be available until the following week, and rather than stay with her dad the whole time, she wanted to spend some time with Lauren. Besides, she'd promised Jackson four paintings for the gallery and she planned to bring those back with her.

The white Lexus LS sedan pulled out of the driveway. Lauren hurried into the house to get Winslow. Her phone rang as she made her way back to the garage, carrying Winslow to avoid his dawdling.

Glancing at the screen, she pressed accept. "Hello, Matt. I was just about to call you."

"Can you talk for a minute?" he asked.

"Sure, I can talk. I'm headed into town." She deposited Winslow in the front seat and touched the garage door opener.

"Would you be free for lunch today?"

He sounded anxious, not like Matt.

"I told Brooke I'd be painting at that little church on The Avenue at twelve-thirty. She loves to see Winslow." She sensed Matt's anticipation. "But I have to run to the bookstore around nine-thirty? They have big comfy chairs, drinks and sandwiches. We could sit and talk."

"Sounds perfect. I'll meet you there, okay?"

"Great. How did you know I needed a visit with a friend right now?" She laughed and ended the call.

Lauren absentmindedly swiped at the smudged screen of her phone. She liked Matt and she knew he liked her, maybe their paths were meant to do more than just cross. She sighed. But if that was true, why did she anxiously anticipate the time she would see Jackson again?

CHAPTER 18

irst Meeting

JACKSON CHECKED HIS WATCH. Three forty-five. He wasn't the one late for a change. He liked Lauren for that.

Matt shut his computer down and stood. "Jackson, I think I'll cut out early, okay?"

"No problem, Maggie's here." Someone entered the show room. Maggie's stilts sounded on the marble floor as she left her office to greet them. No, he didn't worry about their clients with Maggie around. In business matters she interacted well with people.

Minutes later Maggie appeared at the office door.

"Jackson, Miss Ashby to see you."

"Come in, Lauren. I see you have your buddy." He grinned. "I'll get Brooke and we can go where it's more private to talk." He headed to the break room and seconds later Brooke came skipping out. Jackson followed close behind her. Lauren set Winslow on the floor and handed Brooke his leash and continued chatting with Matt.

Jackson heard Lauren say something to Matt about how she'd enjoyed their visit earlier.

"You two had lunch today?" Jackson's envious mind immediately played a video of them together.

Matt said, "Actually we had a sandwich at the bookstore. I would never have thought of eating there if Lauren hadn't suggested it."

"I didn't know you *could* eat there. I'll have to tell Ally." Jackson glanced at Lauren. "Are we ready?"

She smiled and nodded.

"Brooke, come along."

Jackson chatted with Lauren as they walked the length of the gallery to the large quiet office at the back of the showroom. He sat in his chair behind the desk and indicated a chair in front of the desk for Lauren. Brooke stood at his side with Winslow in her arms, waiting to introduce them.

Jackson smiled at Lauren and turned to Brooke, "So, this is Mr. Winslow that I've heard so much about?" He ran his hand over Winslow's head "You're a good little fellow, aren't you?"

Brooke giggled and leaned on Jackson. "Dad, he's happy to meet you, look at his tail!"

"I think you're right, Pumpkin, he's sure happy about something isn't he?" He took Winslow onto his lap, while Brooke hung an arm around Jackson's neck and wallowed in his lap with Winslow. Jackson glanced at Lauren over Brooke's head to find her watching them. Her head tilted to one side, her soft expression made her even prettier. She smiled, but when he let his eyes linger on hers, she lowered her gaze to Brooke and Winslow.

Lauren laughed when Winslow gave Brooke kisses on her face, "You have to watch him, Brooke. He gets carried away when he's excited."

"I like Winslow's kisses." Brooke giggled, putting her face close to Winslow's again.

"Matt tells me that Winslow's a rescue dog. Brooke wants a dog and we'd like to do the same for her." He glanced fondly at Brooke who listened while he explained to Lauren what they had in mind.

"Dad, we want a dog just like Winslow, don't we?" Brooke looked at Lauren as if placing an order.

"I think Matt may have misunderstood about Winslow. I did rescue him, but not from an agency or animal shelter. I found him at the cemetery where my parents grave sites are." Her hands were folded in her lap where she occasionally toyed with the ring on her finger. "He found me, actually. I was putting fresh flowers on their gravesites, when he crawled to my side and turned his little face up to me." She paused at the memory. "He was starved and dirty. It broke my heart so, that I had to do something. I carried him to a veterinarian who checked him over and did everything that needed to be done and Winslow's been with me ever since."

She smiled at Brooke. "I think it was meant to be."

Brooke came to stand beside her. "Did you have Winslow with you that morning when I saw you the first time?" Brooke waited, her eyes large.

"That morning I was painting the church? Yes, Winslow was asleep in the Range Rover." Lauren nodded and smiled.

"No, the *first* time I saw you."

"I don't understand, Brooke. That was the first time when you stopped on your way back to school, don't you remember? You were on your bike."

"No, the first time on the highway when we passed you. I remember. And I remembered your car, too."

Lauren's voice dropped to a whisper, "That was you in the red car?"

"Uh-huh, I had ball practice. We were late and Maggie went real fast and we passed you." Brooke nodded, her eyes wide.

Jackson frowned when Lauren's face froze and her eyes widened. He wasn't sure he'd heard all that Brooke had said. He leaned forward with Winslow still perched on his lap. "What are you girls talking about? Brooke, did you say Maggie drove fast? Were you in the car?" Uneasiness edged his voice.

Brooke turned, caution clouding her eyes. "Yes, sir." She glanced from Lauren to Jackson. "When we practiced that Saturday out of town. It was real early. Maggie had to stop on the way and it made me be late. She *had* to drive fast." Brooke spoke hesitantly, darting a look at him.

Lauren leaned forward in her chair and took Brooke's hand. "Brooke, Winslow looks thirsty. Could you take him and find some water?"

"Oh, sure, we have plenty in the break room." She ran and scooped Winslow from Jackson's lap. Lauren and Jackson sat motionless until Brooke's chatter faded away.

Jackson stood and ran his hands through his hair. He paced a few steps and turned to Lauren. "Tell me what this is all about. What happened?"

Lauren gripped her hands together and stood, as if facing an enemy head-on. White faced, her mouth grim, she faced him. "You allow that person to drive your daughter to ball practice? Don't you know she's not a responsible driver? You put her in charge of your child's safety?"

Her words stunned and condemned.

Jackson stared at her for an eternity before he turned on his heel and paced. He faced her again. "I would *never* knowingly put my daughter in danger. That's absurd. Just tell me what happened."

"That girl, that *Maggie* nearly ran me off the road! And she went around me in a no passing zone, on a curve, with Brooke in the back seat." Lauren jammed her hands into her pockets.

"Why didn't you tell me this when it happened?" Jackson sat heavily in his chair.

"I didn't know you then. How could I have told you? I didn't know Maggie, and I didn't even know it was Brooke at the time. I just got a glimpse of her in a ball cap. I didn't really see her face."

"Of course, you couldn't have known." Jackson stood again and pushed his hands into his pockets and began pacing once more. "Are you a parent, Miss Ashby, are you experienced in raising children?" His jaw hardened, he glared at her. "Well, are you?"

Eyes wide, Lauren marched across the short space, planting herself in his face. "No. I have no children. But *I* do have common sense. *I* would *never* put my child in the hands of an *irresponsible* —" She bit off speaking as if she'd been slapped and stared at Jackson.

Without thought or planning he pulled her into his arms and kissed her. He held her in his arms until Lauren leaned back and they looked into each other's eyes for an endless moment before Lauren pushed away from him.

"Lauren, I'm sorry—"

"Me too. I'll tell Brooke bye and see myself out."

She practically ran from the office.

Jackson slammed his fist into his palm. What had he done? Dazed he sat back in his chair. He couldn't believe what had just happened. Lauren would never speak to him again.

But, she had returned his kiss.

And Maggie. What had that girl been thinking? He would never have dreamed she'd pull a stunt like that. He *had* trusted her with Brooke. There had never been any reason not to. Jackson choked back the anger and fear at what could have happened to Brooke.

He didn't like being made to look like a bad father either. Maggie would answer to him. He would drill the fear into her for driving recklessly with Brooke in the car—Brooke would never be in the car with her again. If not for Matt's friendship with her parents he would go right now and fire her.

He uttered a thankful prayer that Brooke had not been harmed.

Pushing his weary body up from the chair he hoped Brooke hadn't heard their exchange and that she didn't suspect anything. Innocent of any wrongdoing, she would be crushed that something she'd said had upset Lauren. He headed for the break room.

"Dad, Lauren just left. She's going to help us find a dog like Winslow." She grabbed his hand and skipped along beside him as he entered the office.

She'd not heard them. He silently thanked Lauren for sending her from the room.

"I'm sure she'll do all she can to help us, sweetheart. Did you have fun with Winslow?" He looked at her sweet face, and the thought of Maggie endangering her life made him want to go throttle her.

"I love Winslow. He's always fun, and he likes us, Dad. I can tell." She became quiet and pensive. "I wish I could just have Winslow." She turned wide eyes on Jackson.

"That's not possible, Pumpkin. But we'll find another little dog so much like Winslow people will think they are twins. I just bet we do." He raised his brows and nodded.

Brooke giggled and hugged him before he went about straightening his desk. He ignored the awful feeling in his chest and the hollow pit of his stomach. A fierce longing to drive out and walk in the woods filled his chest. He glanced at his watch, too late for that. Storming into Maggie's office and having it out with her wouldn't be good either, not with Brooke here. He needed to cool down before he spoke to her anyway.

He'd looked forward to this meeting with Lauren for the last two days. Thoughts of her had filled his mind constantly, and try as he might he couldn't stop or banish them from his head.

Did Matt have the same feelings for Lauren? Did he think of

her every moment of the day too? He and Lauren had coffee together earlier—did they see each other often?

The load on his heart grew heavier. If Matt had fallen in love with Lauren, then he had no choice but to forget her. But he had to know, one way or the other. That brief moment of holding Lauren in his arms and tasting her sweet lips reminded him that time was running out.

"Brooke, did you remember that I'm having dinner with Ally at the club tonight?" He toyed with a pencil from the stack Brooke had just sharpened for him. He and Matt still used the old-fashioned wood pencils that Jenna had preferred.

"Uh-huh, Aunt Willa's making macaroni and cheese for me, I can't wait." She hummed happily as the pencil sharpener grounded away Matt's pencils.

"Aunt Willa's macaroni is the very best, you lucky duck." He grinned and she nodded, smacking her lips. Thoughts of Willa's macaroni casserole and a crisp salad beat dinner at the club any day of the week. Especially when dinner at the club included telling Ally about the house and moving back to the country. He wished for the courage to tell her he loved her—but not the way she wanted and the way she deserved. That would have to come later.

The bell jangled as Matt entered the office. "Is your meeting over?" He put his arm around Brooke as she bounced to his side.

"Yeah, it didn't take long." Jackson shot him a cynical look. "What are you doing back?" Jackson turned off his computer and swiveled his chair to face Matt where he'd taken a seat at his desk.

"I forgot to grab Mrs. Parker's file. I'm stopping by there in the morning before coming in to work."

Brooke grinned and hung onto Matt. "Lauren's going to help us get a dog just like hers."

"She is? That's great, Sunny. You'll be a good mama to that

dog. Sounds like the meeting went well ... " Matt's cheerfulness faded at Jackson's expression.

"Brooke, could you run make sure the break room is straightened before we leave. Okay, sweet?" As soon as she had skipped from the room Jackson sat forward. "The meeting couldn't have gone any worse. It's a long story, and I can't go into it with Brooke here." He glanced toward the break room. "Maggie's in big trouble. Were you aware that she drives fast and recklessly? And with Brooke in the car with her."

Matt sobered quickly. "No, of course I wasn't aware of such a thing, how do you know that? Did Sunny say something?"

Jackson lowered his voice. "Like I said, it's a long story. I'll tell you tomorrow. Right now I'm dreading dinner with Ally." Jackson gave Matt a weary glance and rubbed his hand over his face. "I have a feeling dinner will go about as good as the meeting with Lauren did."

Matt seemed at a loss. "I'm sorry, pal. Maybe everything will work out better than you fear it will. How do you think Ally will take the news about the move and everything else?"

The sick feeling in Jackson's stomach climbed to his throat. He swallowed. "What do you mean, *everything else?*"

Sometimes Matt knew what was on Jackson's mind before he even told him. But he couldn't know about his feelings for Lauren or his true feelings for Ally. He had barely admitted them to himself.

Matt sighed. "It's none of my business of course, but I assumed marriage to be the main reason for moving back to the house. I imagine everyone will be assuming that you and Ally are finally—"

Jackson groaned and pushed both hands through his hair. "Matt, I'm in trouble. I have to tell someone. You're the only person I can trust." He sat quietly, working up courage. "I love Ally. I always have. But it's not the kind of love to build a marriage and a life on." It felt good to finally be saying it out loud. "I won't do that to Ally."

He glanced briefly at Matt. They were quiet.

Matt must be in shock hearing him say that. Toying with a pencil he continued. "I never thought about it much. Ally's just always been there." He glanced sideways at Matt. "Answer me a personal question."

"Sure. If I can," Matt said.

"Is there anything between you and Lauren?"

"Well, I consider Lauren a good friend."

Jackson studied Matt's face for a moment. "You're sure that's all?"

"Absolutely. I know it for a fact. Why do you ask?"

"I needed to know. After meeting Lauren, I've come to know that I don't love Ally the way she deserves." Jackson hesitated. "I can't stop thinking about Lauren Ashby. I find my thoughts on her all through the day. But we can't even have a civil conversation without arguing."

Matt leaned forward in his chair. "Well let me make it clear. There's absolutely nothing but friendship between Lauren and me."

Jackson's relieved sigh caused Matt to frown, a question in his eyes.

"I kissed Lauren."

"You what!"

Brooke skipped into the office.

"Dad, I put Winslow's water bowl in the dishwasher, and I cleaned up the water on the floor, and wiped the table, and I watered the ivy plant. Is it time to go yet?" She dried her hands on the tail of her school uniform.

"Thank you, Brooke, you're such good help. And yes, it's time to go."

Jackson stood and grabbed Matt's hand with a firm pressure.

His eyes searched Matt's. Understanding and something else, something that Jackson couldn't read, met his gaze.

Matt gripped his hand, smiling from ear to ear. Jackson we need to talk—coffee in the morning?"

"Yeah, that'd be great."

Matt lowered his voice. "You really kissed Lauren?"

Jackson nodded. Relief flowed through his body, Matt wasn't angry. He could breath again. And bask in the memory of Lauren's kiss. The wheels of destiny had just changed course.

No turning back.

CHAPTER 19

 egrets

THE PHONE RANG every thirty minutes. It had done so ever since Lauren got home. She'd emptied an entire box of Kleenex. It rang again. This time it hadn't been thirty minutes.

"I can't talk now, Clair," she moaned as she sank into the corner of the plush sofa. She hugged her knees, resting her forehead on them. Each time she closed her eyes she saw Jackson's face when she accused him of endangering Brooke's life.

Tears welled again.

But then the image would change to him taking her by her shoulders and pulling her into his arms. Or had she imagined he pulled her into his arms? She may have fallen into his arms, because that's where she'd wanted to be. Why did he kiss her like that if he'd asked another woman to marry him? And everyone thought him above that kind of behavior. Poor Ally.

She tormented herself until the house grew dark and cool.

Dragging the afghan from the back of the sofa, she wrapped herself in its woolly comfort and dropped into a fitful sleep.

* * *

A DISTANT RINGING roused her from oblivion. She reached for the phone—but she couldn't shut it off. Finally the fog cleared. The noise came from the door chimes. Lauren threw the afghan back and stumbled toward the door, a key scraping at the lock stopped her in the dark entry.

She stood motionless as the door opened.

Clair stepped inside and gasped, "Lauren? Why on earth are you standing there in the dark? You gave me a scare." She reached for the wall switch, turning on a lamp on the entry table. "What's happened?" She peered closer. "You look just awful." She put her arm around her shoulders. "Come dear, I'll make coffee." Turning on more lights, she herded Lauren toward the kitchen.

"I'd fallen asleep when I heard the door chimes. I started toward the door, but when I heard someone put a key in the lock I stopped ... and you found me standing there." She sat in one of the tall bar chairs at the island. "And don't ask me what's the matter because I don't know."

Clair started the coffee. "I could venture a guess, but you wouldn't like it."

"It doesn't matter. I'm going back to New York with you. Right now. I'll go pack." Lauren stumbled to her feet.

"Hold on, Missy. I've got coffee going. And you haven't told me what's happened yet." Clair pulled a chair out for herself and tapped Lauren's place for her to sit back down. "Now, tell me. Does it have something to do with your meeting with Jackson?" Clair reached for two tall mugs from the tray in the middle of the island bar.

Lauren nodded, not looking up.

"What did he want to talk with you about?" Clair peered at her from under half-lowered lashes.

"I'm not sure. We didn't get that far. I think he wanted to talk about getting a rescue dog for Brooke." Lauren turned her red, swollen eyes toward Clair.

Clair stared. "That's all? That doesn't make sense. Rescuing a dog isn't rocket science. You go to the shelter and pick out a dog. Is that what he told you he wanted to meet with you about? Oh, Lauren dear, he just wanted to be with you and that was an excuse." Clair shook her head.

"No, Clair, Jackson never really said what he wanted. I didn't give him a chance."

An hour later, Lauren had explained what had taken place during the meeting, anyway most of it. She hugged the memory of his kiss to herself, not ready to talk about it with anyone, not even her dearest friend.

"My dear, any parent would be sensitive if someone implied they were doing a poor job of raising their child. What made you do that? You're normally a kindhearted person." Clair spoke softly.

"I don't know why I did that. I simply don't know. I shocked myself. Driving home afterward I couldn't believe what I'd said to him." Fresh tears flowed as she whispered, "It shocked Jackson too."

"Well, what's done is done. Quit thinking about it and stop crying. The question now is what to do next." Clair carried their cups to the dishwasher. "What do you think you should do or what do you *want* to do?"

"I want to pack and go back with you. Right now."

"We can do that. Or you can pretend to be a big girl and go to the gallery in the morning and apologize to Jackson and help him find Brooke a dog."

"Have you lost your mind, Clair?" She mopped her eyes with the soggy ball of tissues as the tears poured once more. "He won't let me do anything for Brooke now. And I don't blame him."

"Well, you should still go and apologize, you were in the wrong. Why not call Matt and test whether he's a real friend or not. Tell him what you did and ask him what he'd do. If Matt is the person I think he is, you'll be glad you called him." Clair gave a big yawn. "I'm going into your guest room now and retire to bed."

Lauren turned, her arms crossed. "Clair, what are you doing here anyway?"

"I called to find out about the meeting with Jackson, I guessed something was up when you didn't answer your phone. I told Dad I'd be back later, and here I am."

Lauren held her arms out. "You! I need a hug."

They shared a long comforting hug.

"Now, you need to put an icepack on those eyes or you'll look really cute tomorrow when you eat crow for Jackson." Clair laughed and shoes in hand she padded to her bedroom.

Lauren's cell phone lay on the bed beside her. She picked it up several times and put it down. Matt should still be up, ten-twenty wasn't late. Grabbing the phone, she tapped in his number before she had time to back out.

He answered on the second ring. "Hello, Lauren, you were just on my mind."

"Really? What were you thinking about me?" An image of Jackson warning Matt what a nosy, opinionated, and hateful person she was, flashed across her vision.

"Oh, about what a pleasant time we had at the bookstore this morning."

"Was that only this morning?" She listened to Matt's reassuring chuckle. "It feels like days ago." She pinched her lip, working up courage. "Matt, I need your advice."

"For what it's worth, it's all yours."

She gripped the phone in a tight clench. "I said some awful

things to Jackson this afternoon at the gallery. I think I made him very angry." She heard a heavy sigh on the other end. "Has he said anything to you about it?" She held her breath.

"Lauren, you and Jackson need to talk. He's not so much angry as he is hurt."

"Did he say anything … ?"

"He didn't have a chance to talk about what happened, Brooke was there, he couldn't talk." Matt hesitated for a moment. "You two need to have lunch, go for a walk or something and talk. Jackson is a great dad, I know that much."

"Oh, I know he is too. I should go and apologize. Do you think? I mean, I know I owe him an apology, but do you think he'd listen?"

"I have no doubt he would listen. Give him a call. He should be getting home about now. He and Ally had dinner. Suggest a walk in the new park. He appreciates the open air … and good company."

"Thanks, Matt. Clair was right, as usual. She told me to call you." She thanked Matt and ended the call.

Now to summon the courage to call Jackson, so without further thought, she tapped in the private number Matt had given her and held her breath. Her fingers ached from the death grip on her phone as she counted three rings.

"Hello."

"Hello, Jackson, this is Lauren. I called to apologize for my mouth; sometimes it goes off without permission. I'm following up on its behalf." His deep chuckle brought instant relief and her fingers relaxed.

"I accept your apology and offer mine in return. I took offense too quickly. No harm done."

"Thank you. But the fault was all mine. I'd like to apologize in person, a walk in the park or coffee … that is if you'd like?" He might never want to see her face again.

"That would be great. Is the choice mine?" He laughed, "I'd like a walk in the park if that's okay with you?"

"That's perfect with me. Well, sorry I called so late."

"Oh no, I'd just walked in. Your timing couldn't have been better. What time tomorrow?"

"I'm free all day, so, whatever time is best for you."

"Um, what about two-o'clock?"

"Perfect time for an afternoon break. I'll be there. Well ... good night, see you tomorrow." They ended the call. She would pretend the kiss had never happened. She jumped off the bed and hurried to Clair's room and knocked softly on the door.

Clair mumbled, "Yes?"

Lauren opened the door, crossing the dark room she plopped onto the empty side of the bed. "Clair, you were so right. I talked with Matt, and he told me to call Jackson and I did and he—"

"Why are you whispering?" Clair touched the light switch on the bedside lamp and sat up, plumping her pillows behind her. "Okay, now."

"Well, Jackson couldn't have been kinder, he didn't make me suffer or feel awful. He even tried to take part of the blame."

"Wonderful. So, no hard feelings? You'll continue to be friends with Brooke? That's good, but the main thing is that you and Matt have taken a step closer to a deeper friendship."

Lauren plumped the pillows and propped herself next to Clair. "What do you mean, a deeper friendship with Matt?"

"He will naturally appreciate that you respect and like him enough to turn to him for advice. That's flattering to anyone." Clair glanced at Lauren. "What? What does that look mean?"

"I *already* like and respect Matt a lot. But that's all. I first thought it might be more, but it isn't, not for me."

"Matt's a good person, and he'd make a good husband. Do I need to remind you that another birthday is coming up? And before you jump on me, remember, you were the one who said you planned to settle down by the time you turned thirty?" Clair straightened and smoothed the covers over her lap. "Remember?"

"Yes! Yes, I remember. And I still have several more years, don't rush me." Lauren sighed and toyed with the tie on her pajamas for several quiet moments before she jumped up. "I'm going to bed. Good-night, see you in the morning." She glanced back as she reached the door.

A smile teased Clair's face.

"Now what?"

"Oh, nothing, just thinking how a few words spoken by the right person turned a horrible evening of tears and recrimina- tions into hope and happiness. You better think twice about Matt." She smiled and adjusted her pillows, reached for the light and scooted down in the bed.

Lauren huffed, "Good night Clair." But she stepped lightly and twirled the ribbon ties of her pajamas on the way back to her room.

Comfortable in her bed, she replayed every word of her conversation with Jackson over and over. In a few hours she would be strolling in the open air with him. Clair had been right, a few words spoken by the right person turned tears and regrets into hope and happiness. Clair just had the wrong person in mind. But perhaps she did, too.

When she spoke with Jackson he had just come from having dinner with the woman he would soon marry. What kind of man would treat his fianceé that way, and be two-faced with another woman?

Once again her tears flowed freely.

Feeling for the box of Kleenex on her night table, she dragged it onto the bed next to her pillow and pulled out a fist full of tissues.

pologies

THE LAST PERSON in the world he would have guessed to be calling at eleven o'clock at night would have been Lauren Ashby. Excitement *and* dread spiked his heart rate when he heard her voice. Had she remembered another criticism to hurl at his head? Jackson's weariness fell away the instant Lauren apologized. Her soft voice turned his knees weak.

She wasn't angry with him about the kiss.

And he had an invite to walk tomorrow, just the two of them. He drew the first easy breath he'd taken all evening since she pushed away from his embrace and rushed out of the office.

Jackson slipped off his shirt and tossed it into his laundry hamper. There'd be no sleep tonight.

How could a day that began ordinary and normal turn into one of the worst he'd had since Jenna died? And now draw to an end as one of the happiest he could remember in a long time?

Jackson placed his phone on the bedside table. When he told

Matt that he didn't love Ally the way she thought he did and that he had feelings for Lauren, he'd expected shock or disapproval. But there'd been only surprise and something Jackson couldn't put his finger on. Whatever the reason, Jackson had been thankful for his friend's understanding. With Matt's goodwill and Lauren's apology, Jackson saw light at the end of a long dark tunnel.

* * *

HE ENTERED the kitchen next morning to find his aunt busying about.

"Morning, Jackson. You're up early. There's leftover casserole. Do you want to take it for lunch today?"

"Yes, I'm a little early and yes, the casserole sounds great." Aunt Willa could read him like a book. And since he didn't care to be read this morning, he carefully avoided eye contact. "Matt and I are meeting early for a business chat before the others get there."

"Shall I take Brooke to school?"

"That would be nice, if you don't mind, please." He accepted the large foil wrapped dish and kissed her on the forehead before hurrying away.

Jackson arrived at the gallery to the aroma of coffee as he entered the office. He went straight through to the breakroom and put the casserole in the fridge, as Matt poured coffee into two mugs and placed them on the table. Jackson doctored his with half and half and blinked at the first hot mouth full.

"Have you thought about what I told you, about Ally? Do you think I'm a heel, or worse?" His eyes searched Matt's.

"Is that what you thought I'd think?" Matt returned Jackson's intent gaze. "I don't judge you, Jackson. Matters of the heart are not always conveniently tied up in neat packages. I appreciate your concern for Ally's happiness." He crossed his ankle to rest on the top of his knee "I know I would hate to wake up one day and discover I'd married the wrong person out of convenience or because everyone expected it." He traced his thumb along the handle of his cup. "Actually, I admire your courage. Did you tell her how you feel?" Matt lowered his eyes to his cup.

Jackson relaxed a little. "I didn't go into that last night. I plan to soon though. I don't want to hurt Ally. I thought it best to break the news about the house first." He glanced up. "Surprisingly, it didn't upset her." He went to the coffee maker and refreshed his cup and waved the pot at Matt, who held his cup out for a warm-up. "She and her parents have thought for years that I should sell the house. I guess I expected more of a reaction."

Matt glanced at him. "Did you get the feeling that she might assume marriage is the next step since you're moving back to your house?"

"Oh, I'm not sure. I couldn't tell. She seemed ... different. But maybe I'm being paranoid. I'll talk with her soon, but the time has to be right." He glanced at his watch.

"Lauren called me right after I got home last night. We're meeting this afternoon, at the park."

"Um, you'll enjoy that, nice walking trails there. And Lauren's easy to talk to."

"Maybe for you, but every time I've been around her something goes wrong, and I end up looking like a fool, or worse, a bad father."

Matt grinned. "But you managed to get her in your arms long enough for a kiss. You must have done something right."

Jackson pushed his hand through his hair and chuckled. "Yeah, but that just happened. I didn't plan it."

They'd been talking close to an hour when the back entry bell jangled. They raised their brows at each other.

"Maggie, early?" said Matt.

Jackson frowned and pushed out of his chair. "I'm having a word with that young lady."

Matt clapped his hand on Jackson's shoulder and followed him from the break room.

"Don't be too hard on her, Brooke wasn't harmed. Her dad is a friend—Brooke will be that age one day." Matt's voice rose as Jackson's long stride carried him toward Maggie's office.

Forty minutes later, Jackson returned to the office and shook his head at Matt. "Were we ever that young and that full of ourselves?" He perched on the edge of Matt's desk.

"We were. Did you do any good? Will she think twice before doing that again? What all did she promise if you wouldn't tell her dad?" Matt leaned back in his chair, smiling.

"The talk about her driving didn't take long. I let her know she wouldn't be driving Brooke to practice anymore and if I ever hear of her driving recklessly again, I *will* tell her dad." Jackson fiddled with a pencil. "Maggie swore that was the first and only time she ever did that. And, she's put out with you because you were supposed to help her plan a gallery party." Jackson sat on the corner of his desk. "I see why she's good in sales, pity the poor man who falls under her spell." They both laughed at the idea.

"I'd forgotten the gallery party, guess I'd better go see what she's got planned."

Alone in the office, Jackson pulled Jenna's old file and found the photo and clipping of *Sara Collins.* He reread the entire thing and sat back in his chair. He wanted so much to see her work. He longed to talk with her about art and painting. He wouldn't mention it though until she confided to him or Matt. Lost in thought he didn't hear Matt return.

"We thrashed that out. Next Saturday evening a dinner party at the club, just our group and any guest each of us wants to invite." Matt walked closer and noticed the old file folder. "You browsing for another artist already? Clair should be bringing us some of her pieces this next week." He reached for the clipping. "Ah, this is an old one, the child prodigy, Miss Sara Collins. I told you Clair knows her, didn't I?" Matt squinted and studied the photo closer. "Hey, that's Clair with ... Sara and her mother ... but that's ... " He lowered the clipping and reached for his magnifier. Studying the clipping intently for several long minutes, he lowered it and frowned at Jackson.

"You knew this?"

Jackson nodded. "I discovered it accidentally several days ago. I didn't say anything, I figure she has her reasons for not talking about it."

"Will you bring it up today when you see her?" Matt still held the clipping; he kept glancing at it.

"No. I won't bring it up. She'll tell us when she's ready. But why do you suppose she hasn't told us?" Jackson shuffled the file into neat order and held his hand out for the clipping, tucking it back into the file.

Matt spoke slowly, shaking his head, "She probably didn't want us pressuring her to show in the gallery. Man, I hate that. And I feel like a fool." Matt began to pace. "It's no wonder she recognized the quality of Jenna's painting, even comparing her brushwork to Sorolla's."

"Yes, my first thought when I realized who she was." Jackson blinked and turned away from Matt. *Sara Collins*, a person worthy of owning Jenna's little painting.

Matt sat in his chair. They were both quiet, each lost in his thoughts.

Maggie stopped in the doorway. "Has something happened? What's wrong?" Her eyes darted from one to the other.

"Absolutely nothing is wrong. We were just worrying about what to wear to the party next week." Matt kept his tone serious.

Jackson joined in the teasing, stroking his chin and pursing his mouth.

"You guys are strange. I'm going to the bank." She rolled her eyes and marched out.

"Sometimes I get the feeling Maggie's the real boss around

here." Matt chuckled and glanced at Jackson. "Penny for your thoughts."

"My thoughts aren't worth a penny, and I'm afraid I won't be either by two o'clock. I'm looking forward to seeing Lauren, but I'm scared too. I'll *need* to walk by then. Matt, do you have lunch plans?"

Matt turned from his computer screen with a glance over his shoulder. "Nah, what's on your mind?"

"If you'd have lunch with Brooke, I could drive out and check on progress at the house. I need to walk off some energy."

Matt grinned at him. "I've never seen you like this before. Go on, take a run out to the house. I'll warm lunch for Sunny."

Jackson pushed his chair to his desk. His thoughts were not on the house.

CHAPTER 21

 onfession

MATT WANDERED BACK to the break room after Jackson left and poured himself another cup of coffee, looking doubtfully at the dark stream. He peered into the cup of opaque brew and tossed it down the drain. His thoughts lingered on the conversation he'd had with Jackson.

He grinned, wishing to be a fly in the park this afternoon. Jackson had wisely chosen to keep busy until time to meet Lauren. Matt hoped they'd smooth things over and get to know each other better this time.

When Jackson told him he didn't love Ally in a romantic way, Matt had to restrain himself from grabbing him in a grateful bear hug. He'd felt like he must be dreaming.

The office doorbell jangled as he rinsed his cup. Sunny Girl must be early. He headed toward the office.

Ally bumped into him coming around the corner. He caught

her hands in a light squeeze and she returned the gesture with a pleasant laugh. "Oh, Matt. Why the hurry?"

He released her hands. "I thought you were Sunny. It's about her lunch time, and I'm in charge today."

She glanced around. "Really, where's Jackson, with a client?" She made herself comfortable in the chair next to Jackson's desk.

Matt took his chair and faced Ally. "No. He ran out to check on things at the house. I'm not sure how long he'll be." He didn't like being evasive.

Learning that Jackson wasn't there, Ally visually relaxed. She set her purse on the corner of Jackson's desk.

"What do you think about him moving back to that house?" she said in a quiet voice. "Why do you think he's doing it?"

Matt prayed she wouldn't question him too much.

"I'm not sure. Maybe he's thinking about Brooke and how good it will be for her?"

"Brooke is a child, she's happy wherever her dad is." Ally frowned. "No, Matt, he wants to live there again, but why now after all these years? He should have sold the thing a year ago when Dad found him a buyer." Ally crossed her legs and settled into the chair.

Matt didn't want to say something he shouldn't, so he changed the subject. "I missed our work session this morning. How is your grandmother?"

"I missed it too, and so did Gram. She's very well. She's pleased with the way you're handling this job for her." Ally smiled at him and tilted her head. "You're one of her favorite people these days." She studied his face for a moment then stood and began to pace. "Has Jackson confided anything to you about his plans?" She turned and gazed into his eyes. "He doesn't talk to me about anything important. But he never has."

Matt wanted to throttle Jackson in that moment. He stood, slid his hands into his pockets and moved to her side. "Ally, you need to talk with Jackson about this. He doesn't want you to be unhappy. Sometimes a thing that seems bad at first can turn around and end up being the best you could wish for." He didn't know what to say, so he spoke from his heart, and she listened as if he made good sense.

She sighed, tucking a strand of glossy hair behind her ear. "You're a good person, Matt. You make me feel better when I'm with you." She turned to him, and he put his arm around her and patted her shoulder. She leaned into the comfort of his arms.

The back entry bell jangled suddenly, startling them when Brooke burst through the door.

"Uncle Matt, there's a gray cat in the parking lot, and I can't catch it. Where's Dad? I need him to help me." She bolted toward the break room and raced back seconds later. "Where's Dad?" She impatiently brushed fly-a-way hair from her flushed face.

"He's not here, Sunny. It's just you and me for lunch today. Your dad had to run an errand. But I don't think he'd help you catch a stray cat, and I'm pretty sure he wouldn't want you trying to either."

Brooke scowled, and slumped out of the office.

Matt turned to Ally, "Care to join us for lunch? We're having something Aunt Willa sent. Jackson couldn't remember what she called it, but he said it tasted good." He grinned and raised his brows.

"Thank you Matt. If Aunt Willa made it, I know it's good, but I'd better run. Would you tell Jackson I stopped by?" She touched Matt's arm and called good-bye to Brooke.

Matt said goodbye, still feeling the warmth of her in his arms as he turned toward the breakroom. He sighed. Back to reality and an unhappy little girl.

"Uncle Matt, couldn't you help me catch the cat?"

"Your dad would have my head. And besides, what would you do with it?"

157

"Keep it."

"I don't know, Sunny, cats and dogs don't always get along. What if your new dog didn't like the cat and tried to hurt it or if the cat scratched your dog? You'd feel bad about that, wouldn't you?"

"Um, yes. But what if they liked each other?"

"We can't take that chance, now can we? Better eat up, lunch break doesn't last long."

"Uncle Matt, what made Ally cry?" Brooke sat at the table swinging her feet.

Surprised by her comment, Matt reached across the table and patted her hand. "Oh honey, Ally wasn't crying. You know how big girls are, they fret about things."

"Fret?" She tested the new word.

The way she glanced at the food said her heart wasn't into lunch.

He felt the same way and considered how he might get her mind on another subject. The new dog should do the trick. "Have you picked a name for your dog?"

"I have to *see* him first to pick a name, don't I?"

"Oh, of course you do." He pinched back a grin.

They spent the rest of lunch period talking about dogs and living in the country. She informed Matt that in the country there'd be room for *lots* of dogs, and she quoted her father. Matt grinned and hoped to be around when Jackson got that piece of news, sure he'd said they'd have *lots of room* for *a* dog.

Brooke picked at her food then rushed back to school. Matt cleaned and straightened the breakroom. Brooke had said she planned to stop and watch Lauren paint again. Matt wished he could watch a Sara Collins painting demo. That would be fun, even for a non-artist like himself.

He picked up the latest Art News and scanned the pages, but Ally occupied ninety percent of his gray matter. Jackson had to do something soon. Matt didn't like telling half-truths and worrying about letting something slip. Jackson had to know the situation wouldn't improve by ignoring it.

When the phone rang he glanced at caller ID—*Ally?* "Hello, Ally … "

"Hi, Matt. Is Jackson back?"

"No, he hasn't made it back, have you tried to call him?" He gripped the phone and hoped she didn't decide to drive out to the house.

"No, I didn't want to speak with him. But I do need to talk. Could you possibly get away? Could we go somewhere that we could talk without interruption?"

"Yes, I'm sure I could since Maggie's here. Where did you have in mind?" He held his breath, then realized that she'd never think of going to the park.

"It doesn't matter. What about the club? There's a nice shade on the veranda at this time of day."

Relief swept over him like a cool breeze. The club, especially the veranda, offered an open, public view. People wouldn't think twice about them sitting there chatting. Paranoia reared its ugly head. Ally just needed a friend to talk to, this didn't classify as a secret meeting.

"That's fine. Yes, now is good with me. Twenty minutes?"

Matt knocked lightly on the doorframe of Maggie's office. "I need to be gone for a bit, Maggie, can you hold down the fort?"

She threw a dazzling smile over her shoulder. "That's what I get paid for, " she said and turned back to work.

At the club Matt saw Ally through the large restaurant windows, seated at a table on the veranda. He motioned to the usher and made his way through the restaurant out to where she sat. Several couples lingered over late lunches. Ally sat near the white rail enclosing the veranda. She smiled when he caught her attention. Matt slowed his step. How beautiful she looked sitting there with the golf greens behind her.

"Matt, thank you for making time for me. I hate being needy, and I'm not normally, you know that don't you?" She wasn't being coy. That wasn't Ally's style.

Ever since that day at her grandmother's when he felt sure she'd seen his feelings for her, there hadn't been a word spoken about it. And except for the incident at the office earlier, there had been no physical contact.

"I confess my thoughts about you have never had anything to do with you being needy." He smiled, motioning the waiter away. "We all need someone to talk to every now and then. That doesn't make a person needy." He hoped she didn't want to talk about things he couldn't talk about. Would he lie for Jackson if it came to that? He prayed not to be tested.

Without preamble or warning, Ally said, "Matt, I don't want to live in Jackson's house. I don't like it, and I don't like being in the country." She moved her purse on the table and toyed with its clasp.

"Have you told Jackson how you feel about any of this, about not wanting to live there?" He studied her face.

"That would be a little presumptuous." She cut her eyes at him. "He hasn't asked me to live there, yet." Ally leaned closer. "I've come to realize something. Ever since he told me about opening the house, I've been terrified that he would ask me to marry him and live there. I've had to be honest with myself. Something I should have done years ago." Her hazel eyes were clear and determined. "I've known for some time, deep down. I had a crush on Jackson from the first grade. And over the years he just became a lovely habit."

Her gaze, wide and direct, she leaned closer. "Matt, I would have already persuaded Jackson to marry me if I'd really loved him in that way. Jackson's just always been a part of my life." She turned puzzled eyes on Matt. "I wasn't devastated when he married Jenna, as everyone thought. I didn't go to Europe to get over Jackson. That trip had been planed for over a year." She sat quietly for a moment. "I just stepped back in after Jenna died."

Matt froze, not sure he'd heard right. He cleared his throat. "What are you saying, Ally?"

"Oh, Matt, please don't think I'm awful. I love Jackson to death. You know I do. I'd fight tigers for him. But, I've come to realize that I'm not *in love* with Jackson." She brushed her hair back, not meeting his gaze.

Matt thought the tightening in his chest might actually stop his breathing. Yet all he managed was a lame, "I'm glad you realized it before it was too late." *Glad?* Could a person suffocate from gladness? He felt as if he might be about to find out.

"Ally, you've got to talk with Jackson, he needs to know how you feel. Will you do that?" He locked his fingers and held them steady on the white tablecloth. "Will you tell him soon?"

Leaning forward again, Ally widened her eyes. "But I can't bear the thought of hurting Jackson."

"Trust me, the sooner the better. If you feel this way, what good will come of waiting? I hate for Jackson to be hurt too, but the sooner you tell him, the better."

"I'm sure you're right, Matt. I'll try. But I'm cowardly." She gave a sarcastic lift of one brow. "I wouldn't still be living with my parents at my age and dating a man for three years if I wasn't a coward, would I?"

He chanced the freedom to hold her hand. "You're no coward, and Jackson will appreciate your honesty." Matt couldn't remember a time in his life he'd ever experienced more happiness than at this moment.

He'd somehow persuade Jackson to wait about talking to Ally and give her time to break up with him first. Which one did the breaking up wouldn't matter to Jackson, but Ally's pride might be hurt if Jackson spoke first.

Matt hoped the relief and happiness he felt wasn't as obvious as it must surely be. Ally wouldn't understand his excitement, not yet. He looked forward to telling her that he had loved her since that weekend many summers ago, when as a college student he'd fallen in love with her and there'd been no one else since.

But, he'd waited all these years. And knowing that Ally would not be marrying Jackson, he could relax and breathe easy.

And wait a while longer.

CHAPTER 22

ood Advice

CLAIR GLANCED up from chopping vegetables when Lauren entered the kitchen. "I hope you haven't had dinner, this salad is growing into a huge one." She laughed and tossed more tomatoes into the large bowl of spring greens.

"Good, I'm starved." Lauren hung her bag on the back of the tall chair close to where Clair worked and slid onto the seat. She helped herself to a slice of the cucumber Clair had started on.

"So, how was your day, Susie homemaker? Did you take your paintings to the gallery?"

Clair smiled and continued chopping. "I had a wonderful day. There really is something about being in the country. I relaxed, read a book, called and extended the contract on my rental car, and I talked on the phone with Drew. He's looking forward to coming out."

"Good. I'm anxious to meet Drew. What about the gallery?"

"I ran by, but Matt and Jackson were both gone, so I didn't leave the paintings. I prefer to deal with one of them. I should have made an appointment. I went to the farmers market and pretended to be in Italy and handpicked these veggies for dinner, like we do there."

Lauren reached for another slice of cucumber. "No doubt the reason I chose to live in Valley Ridge had something to do with the countryside and it's similarity to Italy and France. I knew you'd love it here too."

"Okay, enough about my day. I can see you're bursting at the seams. So, tell me about your day and the visit with Jackson." Clair smiled and kept working.

Picking up the butter knife Clair had set in front of her, Lauren began to spread butter on the four thick slices of French bread spread on a small cookie sheet.

"I visited with Brooke this morning. She's all excited about getting a dog and the move to the country." Lauren sneaked a glance to see Clair's expression. "I asked her if she'd like to take art lessons." Lauren puzzled about how to explain to Clair the child's reaction.

Clair shook the bottled salad dressing in a firm action. "And?"

"At first her eyes lit up, but then she put her face against Winslow and mumbled." Lauren stood and walked around the island to slide the pan into the oven and stood watching over it.

Clair sat the bottle of dressing on the island and stirred the lemonade. "Thanks, I tend to burn it. So, what did she mumble?"

"That she didn't want to take art lessons. When I asked why, she informed me that she was a sports girl, not an artist. Soccer, softball, gymnastics, all that." A glance at the bread and Lauren wandered away from the oven.

Clair's face clouded and her brow puckered. "Sounds like a child parroting words they've heard from an adult." She cut her eyes to Lauren.

Lauren threw herself on Clair in a bear hug. "I knew it! That's exactly the feeling I got." She marched back to her seat. "I brought it up to Jackson. I'm sure he's the one who's convinced Brooke that sports is her thing."

Clair sat next to Lauren. "But why would he do that? He loves art. What would be his motive for pushing his daughter into sports?"

"I have no idea why." They sat side-by-side lost in thought for a moment.

Clair jumped at the smell of well-done garlic toast and hurried to pull it from the oven. "Well, aside from the disappointment of the art lessons, how did your apology go with Jackson? Did you two manage not to argue?" Clair laughed, teasing, but sobered quickly at the look on Lauren's face.

Lauren stood and began to pace, twisting her ring. "There's no way Jackson and I could have anything between us. I admit I'm attracted to him, more than I've ever been to any man." Back and forth she paced, wanting to tell Clair how he'd made her feel when he'd kissed her the day before. But she didn't. "Why does he make me act like a crazy person?"

"So, you did argue?" Clair stared, incredulously. "What ever did you find to argue about?"

Lauren stopped pacing and crossed her arms. "I told him I thought Brooke might feel pushed into sports."

Clair groaned and rolled her eyes.

"What? What did I say wrong? If he is doing it, he needs to think about it. I've seen Brooke's interest in art."

"Did you explain that to Jackson?"

"I didn't get a chance. He got all huffy, asking me how I knew so much about child psychology and one thing led to another. We'd been at the park for an hour when I brought it up, so we said goodbye and parted."

"What? You enjoyed each others company and conversation for an hour and still managed to get into an argument?" Clair reached out and took Lauren's hand. "In all the years we've been friends, I've never known you to be quarrelsome or argumentative. What is this with you and Jackson?"

"I don't know—what about him? He's so sensitive."

"You attacked his parenting. Again. What do you expect? Parents' don't appreciate that. I have no children, but I know that much. Just let someone hint at something about me, and you can see Dad bristle." Clair chuckled.

Lauren sighed. "You're right, I guess. Anyway, I've decided to come spend the summer with you after all. It'll be fun and since Brooke doesn't want to take lessons there's no reason I can't take some time off."

Ice clinked as Clair filled their glasses and poured the lemonade. Handing Lauren hers she said, "No, you are not coming with me until you really make peace with Jackson. I agree it's probably best to get away from him. But maybe I haven't been right after all." Clair sipped her drink and studied Lauren. "I'm starting to think you pick arguments with Jackson as a way of keeping him at arms distance. You admit you are attracted to him."

"Oh, please—"

Clair silenced her with a hand in the air. "Let me finish. You're afraid of Jackson even though you're drawn to him. Jackson comes with the responsibilities of a child. It's easy to tell him how to raise his daughter when you bear no responsibility." Clair glanced at Lauren. "But Jackson is a package deal, you get him you get his daughter." She said softly, "Keep him offended, and you're in no danger of getting the package."

Tears threatened as Lauren swirled her lemonade. "All of a sudden I'm not hungry." She headed toward her room. From her side vision she saw Clair pull the big salad bowl toward her and pick up a fork.

Lauren flopped on her bed. What Clair had said might be partly true. In each instance, she'd been the one who started the argument. What else could it be? Jackson's bewildered expression flashed across her vision. They had been laughing and enjoying the conversation when out of the blue she hit him with her opinion on Brooke's choice of activities. He'd stammered that he never pushed Brooke into anything, except fishing, maybe. He admitted he wanted her to enjoy fishing with him.

Lauren put her hands on each side of her head and squeezed. Why *had* she done that? Jackson would probably hang up on her if she called to apologize again. Maybe Matt could help. Matt, she wondered vaguely why he had wanted to talk the other day. He'd sounded like he had something on his mind. He never mentioned anything in particular when they met at the bookstore.

Scooting off the bed she grabbed her lemonade from the night table and went back to the kitchen and hugged Clair. "I'm sorry, and thank you for letting me be me without getting offended." She slipped onto the chair. "Hand me that fork."

Reaching for the silverware, Clair pushed the salad bowl closer to Lauren and munched a mouth full and swallowed. "I feel deliciously uncivilized when I eat from the salad bowl."

"Me too, it taste better, doesn't it?" They laughed and forked mouthfuls until Clair pushed away from the bowl and clattered her fork on the granite bar.

"I'm full."

"And I'm not as hungry as I thought either." Lauren peered briefly at Clair. "Jackson and I did have a good time until I started … until the argument. We walked and walked and then sat in the swings." She laughed and pushed the salad bowl to the center of the island. Reaching for the lemonade she refilled her glass and indicated more to Clair.

Clair nodded, holding her glass out. "What did you talk about?"

"Everything, but mostly art and travel. He's never traveled much, except with his parents as a child." Lauren leaned down and picked Winslow up as he ambled in from his doggie bed. "Hello, little pal." She hugged him close.

Clair sobered. "Have you decided what you're going to do about Jackson?"

"Do about him? What do you mean? I can't *do* anything about Jackson except stay away from him." Fluffing Winslow's top hair, Lauren smiled recalling Jackson's expression when she'd said he might be pushing Brooke into sports.

"Would you care to share what's so amusing?"

"Oh, just remembering how Jackson looked when I said what I did about Brooke and her sports."

Clair's eyes widened and her mouth gaped, she sputtered.

"Oh, Clair, I wasn't amused because I hurt his feelings. I'm not cruel. I was remembering the way he looked like a child defending himself." She became serious. "What can I do? I can't seem to help myself when I'm with him."

"Face your fears, as you should have long ago. And then you could get on with a happy, normal, committed life—like the rest of us." Clair grinned and started cleaning up the kitchen. "I liked your mother, as you know. But I didn't agree with her about a lot of things. Childhood trauma needs to be dealt with. And when it's not, it gives the past power to hurt." Clair spoke softly. "I know a good doctor who would listen and could still help. It's not too late to get professional help."

As she placed their glasses in the dishwasher, Lauren choked back the old panic. Dredging up the past just made it worse. Her mother had drilled that theory into Lauren deep and solid. No, whatever Clair thought, Lauren's past was not the problem.

She and Jackson were just not meant to be. She relived his embrace and the feel of his lips on hers, her hands slowed in their task.

"You're awfully quiet," Clair said.

Sighing, Lauren closed the dishwasher and set it to wash later. "Oh, I was just thinking." She cleared her thoughts of the man she daydreamed about. "You know, Clair, talking to you does as much good as any doctor could." Lauren had never told

Clair the extent of her mother's resistance to talk about things that hurt.

"Not really, Lauren. An impartial, experienced person knows best how to guide the injured through murky waters." Clair smiled at Lauren. "Think about it."

With the kitchen back in order, and Winslow stationed at the sunroom door, where he stared out for hours at a time in hoping to spot a squirrel, Clair suggested a movie. Ten minutes into a black and white John Wayne, the phone rang. Lauren glanced at it and then to Clair.

"It's Matt." She jumped up from the sofa and walked toward the kitchen. "Hello." She smiled and listened for a moment before looking at her watch. "Sure, I'd be happy to. I'll be ready, bye."

Replacing the phone, she wandered back to the den and sat on the sofa next to Clair. Tucking her feet under her on the warm sofa, she waited while Clair muted the sound.

"Matt asked me to take a drive with him. I think he has something on his mind."

Clair brightened. "Um, nice. Unless, horrors, you're afraid he's getting serious."

Lauren rolled her eyes. "I'm not afraid of anything about Matt. I just hope he's not unhappy with me because I upset Jackson. He sounded like he did the other day when we met at the bookstore. Like he wanted to talk, but we didn't talk about anything in particular." She frowned. "I can't possibly think what could be troubling him."

Clair pulled a face. "Maybe he lost his nerve that day and wants to give it a second try, you suppose?" For once Clair didn't have an answer.

"I'd better get ready, he said he'd be here in twenty minutes."

"Twenty minutes!" Clair threw a pillow at her. "Never let a man think you can be ready for *anything* in twenty minutes."

Lauren laughed and tossed the pillow back at her.

"Something tells me my appearance won't matter to Matt."

She headed to her room to change and grab a sweater. A ball of nerves gathered in her stomach. She liked Matt and hoped his best friend wouldn't have a negative bearing on their friendship. Had Jackson told Matt about their argument?

Lauren brushed her hair and grabbed a sweater. No, it wasn't the past or Matt she was afraid of—it was the future and Jackson Montgomery she feared.

CHAPTER 23

rust

Matt's hands never sweated. Not in high school before a big game or before college exams, not even on first dates. Not when he, Jackson, and Jenna had signed the contract to build the gallery. And that had been a big deal, enough to make a man sweat. But those were all things he'd had some control over. He clenched his warm hands and hoped he hadn't done the wrong thing in calling Lauren. His gut feeling told him he could confide in her.

A newcomer, and one he hadn't known long, still he sensed he could trust her. If he didn't chicken out again.

Lauren had proven herself when she didn't contradict Jackson about where they first met. He pressed the button on the polished oak door and listened to the muffled bell chimes. His gaze wandered to the neat landscaping around the house.

"Hello Matt. Come in." Clair greeted him with a warm smile.

"Hi, Clair."

Winslow bounced to the door to greet Matt. "He remembers you." Clair laughed.

"Yeah we're buddies aren't we, Winslow." He knelt and scratched Winslow under the chin. After a few minutes he stood and pushed his hands into the pockets of his navy Dockers. "I thought you'd left for New York. Are you bringing us some of your work this week?"

"Oh, my plans change on short notice. I do have four paintings for the gallery. I'll call first and make an appointment."

"Great. Jackson and I are both excited to have you showing with us."

Lauren entered the foyer, sweater in hand. "Hi, Matt. Is it cool out?"

"A little, but it feels good. I have the top down, but I can put it up if you like. This is the best time of day to drive with the top down."

"The top down is fine. See you later Clair."

"Have fun, you two." Clair grinned at her and closed the door.

Matt opened the car door for Lauren and she slid onto the leather seat.

"Are we driving any place special?" she asked when he got in on the other side.

"There's a place just outside of town that I go to when I need to think and can't take the quiet at home. It's a nice place to sit and talk." He pulled out of the driveway. They were quiet on the drive into Valley Ridge.

Going through town, Lauren leaned closer to Matt to be heard over the traffic noise. "Your call surprised me. Um, did Jackson say anything about us meeting today?"

Matt leaned in too. "He mentioned it this morning, but I'd forgotten. How did that go?"

"Oh, we had a good time. I took your advice and suggested a walk in the park—Matt, did you see who that was back there?"

"No, I didn't see anyone. Who was it?"

"Ally. She was getting out of her car."

"Oh really? I didn't see her. Where?" Matt frowned.

"At the pastry shop."

Matt hoped Ally hadn't seen them. She might wonder if they were dating. He didn't want Ally to think that. He pulled into the private parking lot of his favorite supper club at the edge of town.

Lauren flipped the visor down and glanced in the mirror. She ran her fingers through her hair and put the visor up. Stepping out of the car when Matt opened her door, she said, "I like this place. It's charming. With an old world feel."

"I'm glad you like it. I come here a lot." They strolled in and Matt nodded to the usher and guided her to an outside patio that overlooked a small lake with colorful umbrellas and canoes dotting the shoreline. Matt chose a table that set just beyond reach of the main light. The rim light from the restaurant cast a soft, subdued glow on their table. The horizon glowed golden-orange with the last rays of sun.

Matt pulled a chair out for her. "I hope you don't mind sitting outdoors."

"Not at all. I like it."

He pulled his chair out and sat across the small table from Lauren. "I want to talk, and I like it here farther from the crowd." Matt hesitated. He felt at a loss how to start. "Lauren, may I ask you to keep our conversation in confidence?"

"Yes, of course."

"Thanks. I thought I could." He sat stiffly in the chair and looked across the lake for several moments. "I don't really know where to start." Leaning back in the bentwood chair, he said, "You can tell me it's none of my business at any time, and I'll take you home." He crossed his arms and studied her. "Are you aware that Jackson is very fond of you?"

"What?" Lauren croaked, cleared her throat and said, "Why do you say that? What would Jackson think of you telling me this?"

"First, he confided his feelings to me." Matt saw the warm flush touch her face. "And yes, he would have my head. He talked to me in confidence." He chuckled nervously. "Jackson and Ally are my two closest friends. I know them both well, and I don't casually break a confidence. I do so now only because I'm afraid they're in danger of making a mistake." Matt glanced again to the lake. "One they may both regret for a lifetime." He hesitated. "If they go through with it, I know I'll regret it the rest of my life."

"Can you share with me this mistake you think they're about to make?"

Matt hesitated. "Jackson and Ally love each other dearly. But they've both discovered recently that their love is not the kind of love to base a marriage on." He watched her reaction.

She looked down for a moment and then glanced back to Matt. "But if they both know this, why on earth would they go ahead with such a marriage?"

"Because neither one knows how the other feels. They each came to me in confidence. I worry they'll go ahead with the marriage rather than risk hurting one another."

"I see. Why are you telling me this?"

Matt glanced across the lake and back. "I've wondered how you feel about Jackson. I thought if you returned his feelings, even a little, it might give him the courage to speak with Ally."

"Matt, please." Lauren adjusted her sweater on her shoulders. "My feelings have nothing to do with this. It's not courage that Jackson needs. Even if he thought I was crazy about him. And after today ... anyway, he would still be afraid of hurting Ally. As far as he knows, she's expecting to marry him soon."

"True." Matt exhaled wearily. "Maybe I thought it would give me courage." He looked across the table and frowned. "What did you mean, "after today?""

She reached to touch his hand. "Oh, never mind that. I believe you have courage. Could you not tell Ally about Jackson?"

"I can't, except as a last resort. It would bother her that Jackson confided in me before he spoke to her. Jackson has to tell her."

"We need Clair here. She's good at working things out to everyone's satisfaction."

"I really like your friend. You've known Clair a long time haven't you?"

"Since I was eight-years old." Lauren propped her chin in her hand and gazed across the lake, a soft smile on her lips. She turned to Matt. "How did you know I'd known Clair a long time?"

Matt thought quickly. Lauren had never told him how long she'd known Clair. Suddenly he wasn't up to keeping any more secrets. "I know that Clair mentored you from an early age. I know that you paint under the name of Sara Collins." Matt studied her face in the soft light.

She lowered her gaze.

"I hope you don't mind that I know that about you. I confess to being dumbfounded when I learned of it."

Lauren raised her face and smiled, placing her chin in her hand again. "I don't mind, it's common knowledge. I've never kept it a secret."

"I don't know why I never put it together before. How did you choose that name?" he asked.

"I didn't choose it. My agent did. He advised my mother that I should use a pseudonym. I started doing so at the age of fifteen. I believe he thought it would give me a little privacy. It's part of my mother's maiden name, Elizabeth Sara Collins. My agent liked the last two names. Does Jackson know?" she asked.

Matt grinned. "You'll have to ask him." He motioned for the waiter. When he arrived, Matt asked him to surprise them with something delicious and light. He leaned his forearms on the table, and clasped his hands and studied her for several moments. "I'm curious, Lauren. Jackson says you two argue every time you get together. I find you so easy to talk to, and Jackson hates confrontation. So how do you even manage to get an argument going?"

She heaved a sigh, a sound that came from the bottom of her soul. "It's my fault. I don't know why I argue with Jackson. It just happens. We argued today." She glanced at Matt for his reaction. "Clair says I run from commitment. Maybe she's right. But just between you and me, I do like Jackson." She studied her nails. "I like him a lot."

Their waiter set two desserts on the table with coffee for Matt and the hot tea that Lauren ordered.

"Panna cotta. Oh, it looks *so* good." Lauren was glad for the diversion. She turned the plate, admiring the chef's artistry.

"It's Italian, yes?" Matt raised his brows.

"Yes, everyone in Italy eats it. The name literally means cooked cream."

After they finished dessert they talked and had several refills of coffee and tea until the night air grew cool.

Lauren slipped her arms into her light sweater. "You seem to have it all figured out, Matt. You're settled and happy with your choices in life, as I thought I was. But lately I've been questioning … do you ever question things?"

"You've heard of living a life of quiet desperation?" Matt needed to share his secret. "That is the state of my life—quiet desperation."

"*You*? But, I don't understand. You have a wonderful life."

"Lauren, I have been quietly and completely in love with Ally Parker since I first met her, at the tender age of twenty-one."

"Oh, Matt . . . I'm sorry. She reached across the white table-cloth and touched his hand. She hesitated briefly, then stood and dragged her chair around next to his.

Matt laughed when he realized her intent to offer comfort.

Lauren leaned her head on Matt's shoulder, he put his arm around her and she patted his arm as they sat in the dim light looking out over the lake and the darkening sky. Thankful for this new friend, gratitude swelled his heart. He suspected if she and Jackson could really get to know each other ... there had to be a way for that to happen.

CHAPTER 24

rustrated

OUTSIDE THE PARK GROUNDS, Jackson had said a curt good-bye and watched Lauren climb into her Range Rover and drive away without a glance back.

He'd watched, hoping to catch her eye, why he didn't know. He pushed his hands through his hair and got into his truck. Come on man and stop being a fool, give up. He started the truck and headed for the country road. He regretted the day Lauren Ashby stepped onto his property. She'd called him a bad father. Irresponsible. And now he's guilty of pushing Brooke into sports, imposing his will over hers. *Where* had Lauren come up with that notion? Thoughts of her festered like a thorn in his side. Immediately after turning onto the private drive, tension drained from his shoulders, he breathed easier. He glanced through the woods to the lake—his escape. The water was up after the last rain. Good, the new lawn would thrive. The entry gate stood open. Disappointment rose at the sight of Thelma's

Cadillac. He loved Thelma, but he didn't want to talk, not today. He needed to be alone to walk, kick things and mutter to himself. He didn't feel like conversation or civil manners. Thelma started toward him, waving her arm the minute she saw his truck.

"You're just the person we need to see. I suggested doing away with those old stone benches in the back garden, but Claude likes them." She looked up at Jackson with her hand shielding her eyes.

"I have to go with Claude on the benches. They've been here ever since I have." Jackson laughed and hugged Thelma.

"I'm not surprised. What are you doing back out here?" she asked. "Claude said you were out earlier today. Are you getting anxious?"

"Yes, I guess I am. Everything looks great." Jackson strolled around nodding in approval.

"What does Ally think about you moving back to the house?" Thelma walked beside him, glancing up every now and then like she had something on her mind.

"We haven't talked about it much. Have you heard something that I haven't?" Jackson stopped and looked down at Thelma.

"No. Not really."

"Thelma, that makes no sense. Either you have, or you haven't. Which is it?"

"Jackson, all I get is beauty shop gossip."

Being evasive wasn't like Thelma.

"Since I don't hang out at the beauty shop, maybe you should tell me what you've heard." Jackson stuck his hand in the air and waved across the yard to Claude.

"Adel Parker is openly campaigning for a match between Ally and Matt. She thinks her only granddaughter has wasted enough time on you. Her words, not mine." Thelma looked up to see how Jackson took the gossip.

Jackson threw his head back and laughed, then grabbed Thelma in a bear hug. "And what do you think, Thelma?"

"Honestly? I tend to agree with her. You need to marry that girl or let her off the hook."

"Thelma, I care deeply for Ally. I would hurt anybody that tried to hurt her, so how can I be the one to do the hurting?" Jackson pleaded for Thelma to understand.

And she did.

She laced her arm through Jackson's and they continued walking. "Sometimes we flatter ourselves, believing we're far more important than we are. When Jenna died, you suffered and thought you'd die too. But you didn't, you're strong and you survived." She patted his arm. "And you've made a happy home for Brooke. Ally is a strong, intelligent woman. Things work out, life goes on."

"I should have known Dad's old truck headed this way for a reason. I needed you to talk to me." Jackson walked with his head down, both hands in his pockets.

"You're always free to tell me when I'm off base. But while I'm at it, I like Lauren Ashby. And I think she likes you, Jackson. I couldn't help but notice the glances that passed between the two of you here the other day. You'd have an edge, you know."

"What do you mean, I'd have an edge?"

"You wouldn't have to sell *her* on living in this house. She already loves it, along with your daughter."

Jackson chuckled. "Yeah, the house or Brooke either one would have a better chance with her than I would."

Thelma laughed with Jackson, then sobered and slowed her step. "One more thing, Jackson. Adel Parker is a very shrewd woman. She doesn't spout off without thinking. In the forty years I've known her, she usually get's her way once she sets a course."

"Thank you, Thelma. I've known Ally's grandmother all my life too. I wasn't teasing about needing to talk with you. You've been a huge help. I'm going to speak with Claude, then head back to town."

"Okay. I'll say bye for now. I need to run to the house and check on the inside progress."

After letting Claude know he really liked the way the grounds were shaping up, and reminding him of something he forgot earlier, Jackson climbed back in the truck and headed for town.

How could a person get to be his age and still be so blind? He must truly be a selfish person, seeing only what mattered to him.

The signs were all there. He thumped the steering wheel. Yes, ever since he'd told Matt that he had feelings for Lauren and that he loved Ally like a friend, Matt had been happy. For the first in a long time he'd noticed Matt whistling as he walked to his car. Jackson remembered the first time it happened, he'd puzzled over the change in Matt. He'd even intended to mention it to Ally. But she'd been busy lately too. Jackson, you blind fool.

CHAPTER 25

Secrets

THE AROMA DRIFTING into Lauren's bedroom teased her senses and nudged her awake. Always it had been a toss-up as to which she liked best, the smell or the taste of coffee. She threw back the covers and grabbed a light robe. She enjoyed both.

"Did you crack my door on purpose?" She accused Clair. "You know I can't resist the smell of fresh coffee." Lauren sagged onto a bar chair and reached for the steaming cup that Clair pushed in front of her.

"I waited up half the night for you to get home." Clair refilled her own cup and scooted back on her chair. "I'm dying to know what Matt had on his mind. So, was it romantic, business or otherwise?" Clair watched her over the rim of her cup.

"Romantic." Lauren sat with her shoulders hunched and her hair wild around her face.

Clair nearly dropped her cup on the granite counter, causing a sharp ping on contact. She leaned in, her arms on the counter. "Really? You don't look too excited about it. What happened?"

"Everything is a mess. And you can give up on Matt and me. Oops, I promised Matt I'd not repeat anything."

"Oh, that doesn't count with me," Clair said matter-of-factly.

"And why not?"

"I don't live here. I don't know these people. And who would I talk to about it anyway?"

"I guess you're right. And I know you wouldn't repeat anything. The thing is, Matt loves Ally Parker and has for years."

Lauren leaned back in her chair, pulled her feet up and hooked her heels on the edge of her seat. She wrapped her arms around her knees and recalled poor Matt's misery.

"Um, does Jackson know this?"

"No! Of course not." Lauren widened her eyes and spoke sharply. "And you can't say anything either."

"Sorry!—cut my tongue out—so what's to be done?"

Clair, ever the problem solver stepped up ready to tackle Matt's problem head-on.

"I assume that Ally isn't aware of Matt's feelings for her?" Clair ventured.

Lauren shook her head. "No, but Matt confided that a small incident happened recently, causing him to believe that Ally knows how he feels and that she cares for him, too. Nothing's been said, but they're working on a project that throws them together a lot."

Lauren pushed her hair back, put her face in her hands and groaned, mumbling through her fingers. "Why does it have to be so complicated?"

"I don't think *It* is the complication. People complicate—by not being honest and facing things head on."

Lauren lowered her hands from her face and gazed at Clair for a second before she rolled her eyes, and covered her face again.

Clair laughed and went to get the bread and began to prepare toast. "You don't like to hear that, but it's true. What does Matt plan to do? Suffer quietly? Let Ally and Jackson end up married and living—how? Regretful for fifty or sixty years?" Clair stuck the bake-sheet in the oven and stood guard over it. "And all because ... why?"

"Everything is not as cut and dried as you manage to see it, Clair. People don't want to hurt those they love. Ally loves Jackson, and so does Matt. They can't bear to hurt him."

Lauren's nerves failed her when she opened her mouth to tell Clair the part about Jackson's feelings for her. She still couldn't talk about that, not yet.

"Lauren, remember that first year that you spent the summer with us at the beach house in Connecticut?" Clair pulled the toast from the oven and stacked it on a plate.

"Of course I remember. I was ten years old, and I had a blast. We painted on the beach every day." Lauren smiled at the memories.

"The first time you stepped on a sand burr you thought you would surely die. You hobbled around half the day not letting me pull it, *because it would hurt!*"

"And it did hurt." Lauren laughed.

"Yes, of course it did. All of three minutes, compared to half-a-day of misery and tears." Clair dribbled honey on a piece of toast and took a bite, her eyes on Lauren.

"This is not quite the same. Really, Clair."

"I know it's not, and I'm not making light of the situation. But the principle is the same. Pull the sticker and get on with the day."

"Clair, Clair." Lauren shook her head and reached for the toast.

They ate silently until Clair spoke again.

"What's funny is right away I saw that Jackson wasn't mad about Ally. She acted possessive of him, but that's different from love. I got a clear impression that Jackson perked up when you showed up." Clair turned a firm expression on Lauren. "If Ally and Matt really love Jackson, they should be honest and tell him the truth."

Lauren placed her half eaten toast on her napkin and cleared her throat. "You're exactly right, and I suggested that to Matt last night. But I don't know if he'll do it or not." She'd lost her appetite.

Winslow wandered in from the sunroom. "Hey, little sleepy head." She lifted him up to her lap. "Are you ready for your breakfast?"

Clair's phone rang. She answered it and strolled away from the kitchen, laughing and chatting.

Lauren thought about all that she and Matt had talked about last night. One thing was sure. She had no part of the situation going on between the three close friends. She didn't want to think about Jackson, either. The best thing for her to do would be to bury herself in work, and put distance between herself and Jackson Montgomery.

She could be strong in that conviction, when not in his presence.

With Winslow fed, she begin straightening the kitchen when her phone rang. At a glance, a smile spread across her face. Thelma. "Good morning, Thelma."

"Am I too early? I forget most people don't start the day as early as I do."

"Oh, no. Clair and I have been up for hours. What's on your mind? Not another house, I hope." She laughed, remembering how she'd barked at Thelma that she didn't want to see any more houses."

"Not another house." Thelma laughed too. "I'm going out to Jackson's place and wondered if you'd like to ride out with me. You never really got to see the house. I'll be going out around two o'clock."

"Could I get back with you in a little bit? I'm not sure if Clair and I have plans today. And I'd rather not go if Jackson will be there."

Thelma hesitated. "I can never say for sure if he'll be there or not. Sometimes he comes out on the spur of the moment. I think he's getting anxious to be finished with the work." After a long pause she said, "Lauren, I wish you and Jackson could meet on a common ground and get to know each other."

"I don't know if there is a common ground for us." Lauren's head began to ache. She recognized the starting of one of her headaches. "I'll get back with you. No, on second thought I'd better just say we can't make it today. I'm sorry, but thank you for asking." They chatted for several moments and ended the call. She hurried to her bedroom and fell on her bed. Why were people pushing her at Jackson? First Matt and now Thelma.

Clair knocked lightly on her open door. "You okay?"

"Uh-huh, but my head is starting to ache." She rolled on her back and pressed the pillow over her head. "Maybe I should stay in bed today"

"I can't hear you." Clair stepped into the room and pulled the pillow away from Lauren's face. "Come with me to deliver my paintings to the gallery. I called, and Matt said to bring them on, he would be there."

"Clair, I think I'll stay home today, go without me."

"I think you should get up and 'get back on the horse', so to speak."

Lauren sat up and gazed at Clair. "Where in the world did you get that?"

Clair plopped on the bed. "In that movie I watched last night. This guy told his young son to get back on the horse after the child fell off. The dad said it would be better if he got right back on, that if he waited, he might never get back on again." Clair smiled and studied her nails.

"And how does that apply to me?"

"Well, you argued with Jackson, now you walk into the gallery like nothing had happened. He'll be relieved and glad it's over. He won't have to deal with something he doesn't have a clue how to deal with anyway. And you can let go of that headache."

"That's scary. You almost make sense."

"Just don't analyze it too much." Clair rose from the bed and padded to the door.

Lauren closed her door and ambled to the shower. She wanted to take offense about the headache remark, but Clair was right. She turned on the brass handles of the shower and held her hands in the thunder of warm water.

She closed her eyes and breathed deep. Would Jackson be glad to see her? She wasn't certain he would be, but if it turns out he was—she would know it.

And if she had to bite her tongue till she tasted blood, she would not argue.

 onflict

BY THE TIME Jackson got back to town he'd practically memorized the conversation with Lauren. He determined to figure out what had made Lauren think he pushed Brooke into sports. He really didn't even care about sports, except for fishing. Brooke had come to him and asked about playing soccer.

He knocked lightly on Aunt Willa's open door. She laid her book down. "What's up?" She glanced at her clock and back to him. "Is it time for you to be home already?"

"Yeah, well I've been out to the house. Do you have a minute to talk?" Jackson leaned against the doorframe.

"I'd love a talk. Let's have one small cup of fresh coffee." Already on her feet, she took the lead going downstairs.

Lowering himself onto the tall bar chair, Jackson crossed his arms and leaned on the granite counter. He didn't want coffee, but it made his aunt happy to do things for him. He watched her start the coffee and then set a picture-perfect chocolate pie in front of him.

Jackson raised his brows at the pie.

"We're adults, we can have a tiny piece of pie before dinner," she declared and sliced into the pie. "Come on, what's bothering you?"

"I don't even know where to start. I worry if Brooke is doing well, if she's really happy? And I wonder if it's the right thing to move back to the house." He took the coffee and the sliver of pie Aunt Willa pushed across to him.

Aunt Willa looked surprised.

"I believe Brooke is happy. What makes you think she might not be?"

"She's eight years old. What makes little girls happy? Oh, she's excited about the dog." He grinned at his aunt. "I'm taking her to the rescue facility this weekend to look at dogs. I haven't told her yet."

"Best not, you wouldn't get a moments rest. Most children are happy if the home is happy. Brooke takes her cue from you Jackson. Are you happy?"

"As much as I expect to be. But do you think I push Brooke, like in soccer? I want her to get exercise and all that, but do you think she's happy playing sports?" A frown puckered his brow.

"Sometimes she's whiny about practice but that's normal with all kids. What brought this on anyway?" Aunt Willa cradled her steaming cup.

"Oh, I just want Brooke to always follow her heart in whatever she chooses." Maybe he was taking Lauren's opinion about the sports thing too seriously. But what made her think that in the first place?

"Have you sat down with Brooke and talked with her about this?"

He slowly shook his head. "No. I haven't. Lauren said something about it. She thinks maybe Brooke feels pushed into playing sports." He glanced at his aunt's troubled face.

"Did you ask her what made her think that?"

"No, we can't seem to engage in normal, constructive conversation."

He glanced at his aunt when she chuckled and covered her mouth with her napkin.

He grinned. "We've never had a conversation that didn't end in an argument. It's the strangest thing. I hate it, because I like Lauren." He gazed into his aunt's eyes. "I like her a lot."

"I had guessed as much. I like her too."

"But we react like oil and water. She must not feel the same about me." He took a bite of pie. "This is the best one you've made so far."

Aunt Willa laughed lightly. "You say that about every pie I make."

"Because it's true about every pie you make." He grinned.

"Back to this arguing thing with Lauren. Who usually starts the argument?"

"At the risk of sounding like a man—she does." He raked his fingers through his hair, leaned back in his chair and crossed his arms, ready to defend his position. He watched his aunt's habit of tilting her head back slightly and laughing as if laughter was a pleasure that she took time to enjoy.

"I believe you, dear. You've never been one to argue and grumble. But how does Lauren get you to argue with her?"

Jackson scrunched his face. "It's always about Brooke. She's oddly protective of her. She's quick to criticize my parenting. When Lauren starts in about something, I get angry and just want to end it."

"You never stand your ground and make her understand your thoughts on the matter? Well, that's a fault on your part Jackson. Don't let that girl get away with anything. Make her explain herself."

"You don't understand—"

"Don't give me that. Understand or not, you have to stand your ground, find out where she's coming from."

"Yes, ma'am." Jackson stood and walked around the serving island and hugged his aunt. "What would Brooke and I do without you?"

"Speaking of ... I ran into Thelma the other day, and she tells me you're getting a housekeeper. Is there something you need to tell me? Am I not still capable of keeping a house?"

"You're one of the most capable people I know, and I want to keep it that way. The new housekeeper is part-time only until you're ready for her full-time. The country house is twice the size of this place. There's no sense in you running yourself ragged keeping up with all that." He squeezed her in a big hug. "I'm standing my ground on this, okay?"

"Put that way, I'll agree. See how easy it is? Remember that next time Miss Lauren tries to argue."

Jackson mimicked his aunt by putting his head back and laughing. "Somehow, I don't think it'll be the same." He started to move away when Aunt Willa caught his arm.

"One more thing, Jackson. About moving to the house. Have you and Ally made plans or talked about the move?"

His aunt couldn't have helped but hear his weary sigh. He sat back down on the bar chair and crossed his arms, shoulders slumped.

"We've spoken very little about it." Jackson remembered the beauty-shop gossip that Thelma had shared with him. "Have you heard anything that I need to know?"

"I've heard something. Whether you need to know it or not, I'm not sure. Adel Parker makes no secret about how she feels about Ally having to live in your house."

"*Having* to live in my house? What do you mean? He frowned again.

"Well, if you two get married ... I mean, why are you redoing the house and yard if you don't plan on living there?"

Jackson stood and quietly and paced the length of the island for several minutes. He glanced at Aunt Willa, should he confide in her. She would be closed-mouth when it came to family.

"I do plan to live there. But I haven't asked Ally to live there with me as my wife." He turned his back to his aunt and stood looking out to the small patio and pool area.

Aunt Willa came to stand beside him and rubbed his back.

"Jackson, dear, I wish I could help and tell you what to do, but you have to figure this out on your own." She gently nudged him. "I'll support you and stand beside you whatever you decide, you know that."

He leaned his head against hers. "I know you will, and I'm glad you're here."

"Whatever, you'll have to decide before too long. I understand from Thelma that the house should be ready for you in a few more weeks. She said the yard is as beautiful as it was when your mother and Claude Sr. kept it."

"You haven't been out to see it yet?" Surprise tinged his voice.

"No, I want to wait and see it as it looked when I lived there before." She smiled and patted his arm. "I can't help but be concerned about Ally. She's a sweet person. I've always liked her. But my concern is that you both do what's best for each of you."

"I'm concerned also. I love Ally, and I always will. But it get's complicated. I'll talk with her soon, so stop worrying."

"Jackson, promise me you won't do anything out of a sense of obligation or because others expect you to or even out of guilt. You know what I mean?"

"I know what you mean. And I promise not to do anything for any of those reasons."

"Good." She turned and went to check the ham in the oven. "Dinner will be ready in a short time."

"Smells good. Aunt Willa, I don't know what all you've heard at the beauty shop, but I'm talking with Matt first thing in the morning to settle some things."

"I think that's wise." Her knowing eyes were kind.

He didn't know if it was wise or not. He headed back upstairs.

Depending on Matt, tomorrow he would either have his old friend back or the wall between them would reach even higher.

 utterflies

BY THE TIME she and Clair headed to the gallery, the butterflies in her stomach were going crazy. Torn between hoping Jackson would be there and praying that he wouldn't be, Lauren had dressed with care, just in case. Her long sleeveless summer white dress, belted at the waist with a narrow brown leather belt, moved softly against her ankles. The belt matched her leather sandals. No bling today, even though Clair believed it inspired courage.

Arriving at the gallery, they left the paintings in the car for the guys to collect later. The cool interior struck Lauren as always, elegant and restful. She experienced the same impression each time she stepped through the door.

Matt walked briskly toward them. "Good morning, ladies. You both look pretty as springtime."

They smiled, murmuring thanks.

Matt looked cheerful and excited.

Clair glanced around the display wall. "Matt, the four canvases I promised are in the back of my car."

"Great! I'll tell Jackson you're here and we'll bring them in." He hurried to the office at the back of the gallery.

Lauren's breathing quickened and a nerve throbbed in her temple. *Stop it.* Clair's words sounded in her head. *Act as if nothing had happened.* The guys were headed toward them. Clair threw her a supporting glance.

Jackson slowed his step as they approached, allowing Matt to reach them first. "Clair, if you'll give me your keys, Jackson and I will get the paintings."

"Good morning, girls." Jackson smiled at Clair and glanced furtively at Lauren. "As you can guess, we're anxious. We've waited a long time for this day."

Matt jangled Clair's keys and they moved toward the door.

Clair pressed Lauren's arm, and widened her eyes and smiled. "You're doing good. Keep smiling."

"I can't stop, my lips are frozen," she muttered.

Clair nodded approvingly and turned to study a painting. "Your work would look good in here. And the gallery is so close to you too."

"Clair, please, don't start—" The door opened as the guys returned. Deep in conversation they chuckled now and then as they carried the precious cargo.

Matt nodded for the girls to follow as he and Jackson continued on toward the back. In the large office they carefully leaned the wrapped paintings against the wall.

Jackson went to the built-in refrigerator that matched the rich paneling and brought out a bottle of pink sparkling mineral water. Placing it on a tray with four crystal glasses, he set the tray on the credenza at the end wall. He poured the pink water, waved for everyone to gather around and passed each of them a tall glass.

"I propose a toast to Clair Weston, our new exciting addition to Montgomery Fine Art. May our association be a long, joyous and fruitful one." A round of ayes and clinking crystal followed.

Matt spoke next. "May this long association be solid in friendship as well as in commerce." More ayes followed.

Clair's laughter sounded as light and pleasant as the tinkling crystal. "Thank you, Jackson and Matt. I look forward to working with you both."

Amidst the excitement, Lauren forgot about her throbbing head, and the butterflies had settled peacefully.

Everyone fell quiet at the same moment that Jackson cleared his throat and spoke. "Lauren, would you possibly be free on Saturday morning?" He hurried on. "Brooke and I are going to the animal shelter and we'd like it if you could go with us." He glanced at Matt and Clair. They'd stopped talking and stood listening. Jackson glared at Matt until he and Clair turned away, smiling at each other.

"Yes, I'd love to go. Is Brooke beside herself with excitement?" Lauren kept a straight face at Jackson's stunned expression. He pushed his hand through his hair and maneuvered his back to Clair and Matt.

"I haven't said anything to her yet. I wouldn't get a moment's peace from now until then. I'll tell her Saturday morning at breakfast. Otherwise she wouldn't go to bed at all Friday night.

"Oh, yes, good thinking." Lauren nodded and pursed her lips.

Jackson concentrated so intently on Lauren's face, that without realizing it, he mimicked her actions. She struggled against a smile.

Matt turned. "Hey, people, we haven't unveiled our new paintings. Line up over there" He motioned to the front of the long desk. "And I'll open them one at a time." The three of them shuffled into line, waiting as Matt carefully removed the brown paper from each of the canvases.

Lauren clasped her hands. "That's our café—our table!" She ran and kneeled before the last painting, pointing out the table where they always sat. Suddenly she looked up at Clair. "You painted me at our table—I love it!"

Clair grinned and nodded, sipping her water.

Jackson hurried across to kneel beside her to study the painting. "It *is* you, and a good likeness too."

Matt looked at Clair from where he'd knelt at the painting also. "These are great paintings. They won't last long once our clients get a look at them."

Clair murmured her thanks.

Lauren strolled across the room to stand beside her. "You didn't even give me a hint you were painting that. I'm going to buy it for myself."

"No, don't. I have another one for you. I'll show you later." Clair had a pleased expression. "But I'm glad you like it."

Clair slipped her arm through Lauren's and they strolled to where the guys still discussed the other paintings. "I hate to be a party pooper, but I'm starved. Lunch is my treat at the club. You guys can discuss my work this afternoon while I'm home taking my nap."

Matt gathered the brown wrapping paper, and with parting glances at the paintings, they moved from the office.

The girls drove Clair's rental to the club. Going on ahead, they left the guys to take care of business details before joining them. Lauren checked her watch. It felt like it should be one o'clock. The silver watch read eleven thirty-five. She shifted in her seat and adjusted the seatbelt. "That went well, don't you think?"

Clair smiled, not taking her eyes off the road. "Yes, it did. Jackson and Matt will be a dream-team to work with." She peeked sideways at Lauren. "Now I can't wait for them to discover Sara Collins."

Lauren gave a soft chuckle and toyed with her watch. "Matt knows."

"What! You didn't tell me. How? Did you tell him?" Clair threw a quick glance at Lauren.

"He found an old newspaper clipping from somewhere."

"Does Jackson know?"

"I asked Matt if Jackson knew, he said I'd have to ask him, of course I won't."

"You should tell him anyway. Did I hear Jackson inviting you to go somewhere?"

"Yes, you did. He's taking Brooke to the shelter on Saturday to look for a puppy, and I'm going with them." Lauren hesitated. "Clair, thank you for advising me about the argument with Jackson. He is relieved it's over and so am I."

"Good, I'm glad it worked out. Just think, you've been together over an hour and no biting each other." Clair grinned at her.

"Don't jinx it. We still have to get through lunch." Carefree laughter filled the car. It felt good to be happy again.

They found front row parking at the club since they arrived earlier than the regular lunch crowd. Clair scrambled for sweaters, reminding Lauren of how cool restaurants can be.

They'd barely gotten seated when Ally Parker came in with another woman. Clair leaned, nudging Lauren.

"Isn't that Jackson's good friend with that woman?" Clair smiled and settled her sweater on her shoulders.

"Yes it is. Should we ask them to join us, since the guys will be here shortly?"

In a low voice and sounding as if her lips weren't moving, Clair said, "I'd wait and let Jackson do whatever he wants." She glanced at Lauren. "What?"

"You sounded funny—oh, here come the guys."

Suddenly, under cover of the white tablecloth, Clair gripped Lauren's arm and in the same tight-lipped voice hissed, "Stop looking at Ally."

Lauren smiled as Matt pulled the chair out next to hers and Jackson sat next to Clair.

This was one time she needn't worry about picking an argument with Jackson. Clair's grip had paralyzed her from saying anything that might once more make the claw grab her.

Leaning back comfortably in her chair, Clair touched Jackson's arm and ask him to order for her. Whatever he had, she'd take the same.

Lauren leaned closer to Matt and asked what he recommended.

"My favorite is the Caesar Steak salad. The steak is consistently good and the salad is always fresh." He raised his eyes in question to Lauren.

"Hmm, sounds perfect." She closed her menu and relaxed, looking forward to lunch.

Jackson chimed in, agreeing that the Caesar Steak was what he nearly always ordered. Clair smiled and nodded.

After the waiter served their salads and freshened their tea, Matt turned the conversation to the painting of Lauren at the outdoor café. Quizzing Clair about the café and the location and how she'd found it, talk soon turned to travel. Matt revealed a desire to travel, but Jackson stood firm that he preferred being on home soil. Lunch was a fun and lively occasion. But talking ceased when Ally approached the table and smiled at everyone. Jackson and Matt rose from their chairs, greeting her.

"Hello, Matt, Jackson. I didn't know you guys were having lunch here today." She glanced at Matt several times.

Jackson pushed his hands into his pockets. "Why didn't you join us, I didn't know you were here. Where were you sitting?" He glanced in the direction to which she vaguely motioned.

"I'm with another party, in fact she's waiting for me. I'd better go." She smiled and nodded at Clair and Lauren and gave a quick glance at Matt. Jackson walked out with her. He returned to the table in a few minutes.

"I hate that I didn't see her." Jackson aimed a troubled look at Matt.

"Yes, they could have joined us if we'd known. But Ally understands about business."

Lauren dared a glance at Clair, who smiled serenely back at her.

Clair took a sip of water and said, "Speaking of business, we'd better let you guys get back to yours." She prepared to stand.

As they walked out of the club, Jackson fell into step beside Lauren. "Shall Brooke and I come by for you Saturday morning?"

"That won't be necessary. I'll drive in and meet you at the shelter. What time do you think?" She watched him bite his lip and calculate.

"Can you be there around ten-thirty?"

"Sure. I'll see you then." She smiled and placed her hand in the one he held out to her. His grip lingered.

"Deal. Until Saturday then."

When she turned to say goodbye to Matt, he gave her a private, wary smile. He reminded her of Winslow tilting his head at her with that same look. Matt had observed the lingering hand shake. In the car, she got the same smile from Clair. Lauren sighed. "What?"

"Nothing. Nothing at all." Clair mocked and pulled out of the parking lot.

Lauren rolled her eyes and rested her head on the headrest. On the drive home, events of the day went round-and-round in her mind.

"You're awfully quiet." Clair glanced over when she didn't say anything.

Lauren looked straight ahead. "I'm scared."

"Scared? Like how?"

"Like I'm walking on tip-toe through quicksand. Like one false step, one tiny misjudgment, and I'm lost, sucked down forever."

"Goodness, that's dark. Exactly what does it mean?" Clair asked.

Lauren's eyes were large, her voice quiet.

"That's why I'm scared. I'm not sure what it means."

CHAPTER 28

 onfrontation

JACKSON COULD HARDLY WAIT to get back to the gallery and really study Clair's paintings. He knew of at least two of their collectors who would break their necks to get there for the first look.

"Well, what do you think?" Matt grinned at Jackson. "Are they as good as you expected?"

The four large canvases propped against the wall depicted a series of sidewalk café scenes with people lounging at small tables. The glow of late afternoon light dappled the narrow, sienna and ocher-tinted streets, while powerful, compelling, vibrant colors infused life into each canvas. Executed with confident strokes, placing bold color expertly alongside soft muted warm and cool hues. Each canvas shimmered in harmony, enticing the viewer, drawing them into the scene.

Jackson's eyes moved from one canvas to the other. A new sensation stirred in his being. He longed to walk those narrow streets, to sit under the striped umbrellas and join in spirit with those happy people.

Matt laughed and tapped him on the shoulder. "I can take your stunned silence for an answer?"

"Stunned is the word," Jackson muttered and turned to Matt. "I'm about to change my mind about being a homebody. This makes me want to travel. I want to be there, in that place."

Matt knelt beside Jackson where he sat for a closer look. "Me too. Let's plan on it. We deserve a vacation. Next spring?"

"No, not next spring, this fall." He turned to Matt with a steady gaze. "Lets see if Ally and Lauren would go with us this fall."

Matt's face flushed, he stood abruptly, and turning his back to Jackson, walked to the desk.

Jackson stood and approached him. "I intended to speak with you this morning about Ally. I didn't know Clair planned on bringing the paintings today. We need to talk."

"You're right. We do need to talk—"

Maggie knocked on the open door and walked in.

"Hey guys, a woman just called and asked if—wow! Where did you get *those*?" Maggie clipped across the room. Hands on her hips she studied Clair's paintings.

Matt and Jackson followed and stood gazing with her. Maggie walked slowly past each of the canvases.

"These are great. I'll have no trouble selling this work." She read the name aloud, "C. A. Weston. Who is this artist?"

Matt walked over and put his arm around Maggie's shoulder. "C.A. Weston is that pretty red-head that you were rude to the night of the show."

Maggie drew back to look at Matt, not bothering to deny she'd been rude. "*She* painted these?"

"Yes, she did. Clair Weston."

Maggie leaned in for a closer look at the one with Lauren seated at a table under a red and white-stripped umbrella, a breeze caught her hair away from her face, her smile captured in a carefree moment.

Maggie turned back to the guys. "I know who would buy this one. Mrs. Ray Franklin. She loves this kind of scene with figurative work."

Jackson walked over, picked up the painting with Lauren in it and moved it down the wall apart from the others. "This one is already sold."

Matt gave Jackson a sharp look. He stepped to Maggie and put his hand on her shoulder. "I believe you had a question?"

"Oh, yes." She pulled her eyes away from Jackson. "Some woman called and asked if we do appraisals, and if not, could you recommend someone. I said I'd get back with her."

"We can recommend someone. I'll get a phone number to you later. Jackson and I need some private time to discuss some business. Can you pretend that we're not in the gallery and give us a little time in here?"

She gave his chest a playful tap. "You got it. You're not here until you show your faces again." She gave the paintings another look and hurried out, closing the door behind her.

Matt took a seat behind the desk and watched Jackson pace the length of the long desk. After three or four minutes he spoke. "You said you'd planned to speak with me this morning? What about?" He toyed with a silver letter opener they kept on the desk.

"I told you, about Ally. But I don't really know where to start." Jackson ventured a glance at Matt.

Matt tilted his head and raised his brows. "Try starting with the trip to Italy this fall. I'm curious which one of the girls you plan to be with."

"I'd rather start with the one you should be with. I think it's time you admit your feelings for Ally." Jackson gazed at Matt. He didn't remember a time that there had ever been an awkward moment between him and Matt. He didn't like it, and was determined not to leave the office until they'd settled it, one way or another. Not even if it meant ordering in pizza.

Matt laid the letter opener on the desk and stood. He took his turn at pacing. His face flushed. Jackson sensed that Matt didn't want him to see his expression. They were speaking of Ally. Matt groped for footing on new ground.

"Has Ally said anything?" Matt asked, his back half turned from Jackson.

"No, she hasn't said anything. But I'm not blind. At least not anymore."

Matt glanced at him, a question in his eyes.

"Look, I've confided my true feelings about Ally and about Lauren. You're free to do the same." Jackson hesitated briefly. "Ally has been quiet lately when we're together. I get the feeling she wants to talk about something, but she never does." Jackson gave Matt time to say something, but when he didn't, he continued. "I've been open and honest with you, Matt. I need you to do the same with me."

Matt walked back to the desk and sat back down. "I feel like such a heel. But I've never let Ally know how I feel about her. I wouldn't have when I thought you were going to ask her to marry you. But recently, since we've been together a lot ... "

"Well, it's time you let me know your feelings." Jackson pushed his hand through his hair and hardened his voice "Matt, tell me if you care for Ally, or not, just tell me." Matt's fear of confessing his love for Ally had reached new heights of frustration for Jackson. He'd already guessed that Matt cared, but Matt had to admit it, to say it out loud and make it real.

Matt's voice lowered and grew even quieter. "I do care for Ally. I have since the first day I met her."

Jackson leaned forward, his elbows on the tops of his knees. He dropped his head into his hands.

Matt stood and hurried around the desk. "I'm sorry, Jackson." Alarm raised the volume of his voice. "But I'm glad to finally say it. I love Ally Parker. Believe me, I've tried not to. But you did tell me that you cared for Ally as a friend only." He pushed his hands in his pockets.

Jackson raised his head and stood, smiling. "Matt, I'm happy to hear that you love Ally. I thought I was the only blind fool, but you've been just as blind as I have. Why didn't you say something years ago?" Jackson grabbed Matt in a bear hug. They laughed, hugged and parted, then gripped hands in a firm handshake until both could speak again.

"What now? Will you talk to Ally?" Matt gazed at Jackson.

Jackson took a deep breath and crossed his arms. "You need to talk with Ally. Tell her how you feel and see if she feels the same about you. We'll see what happens from there." Jackson sighed. "Knowing that you love her may encourage her to come talk with me."

Matt began to pace. "But suppose she's hesitant to say anything for fear of hurting you? She'll worry about that." Matt rubbed his chin. "Remember, she doesn't *know* how you feel. She may be expecting you to ask her to marry you. Everyone else seems to think that's the next move, she may also."

"Yes, you're right. And above all I don't want to hurt Ally." Jackson suddenly needed a cup of hot coffee. He stepped behind the desk and beeped Maggie on the intercom.

"Yes, sir?"

"Maggie, would you do us a big favor and make a pot of coffee?"

"Coming right up."

Matt smiled at Jackson. "She's been awfully nice ever since you threatened to fire her over her driving."

"We'd better enjoy it, it won't last long."

The moment of lighthearted laughter gave some relief from the tension in the room.

"So I have your permission to confide my feelings to Ally?"

Jackson shook his head. "You don't need my permission, but

you certainly have it. I hate to think of all the years you've lost because of me. Just think, you and Ally could have had half-grown children by now if you'd only spoken up years ago."

Matt's color rose, but he laughed, taking a seat in one of the chairs in front of the desk. "It wouldn't have done any good then. She had eyes only for you."

"But what about the years after Jenna and I married? Why didn't you pursue her then?"

"If you'll remember, she left for Europe right after you married. Everybody assumed she escaped there to nurse a broken heart. She stayed away almost two years. And when she did come back her grandmother fixed her up with that guy, the son of a friend of the family. Rumors of an engagement came to me through my mother." Matt sighed. "I gave up hope. And when Jenna passed away, Ally still hadn't married, but she got back with you."

They fell silent for several minutes.

"I'd forgotten all that. But honestly, Ally's main interest in me was just to satisfy her need to fix something. I became her project from grade school on." Laughter greeted Maggie when she tapped on the door and walked in balancing a tray.

Jackson hurried to take the tray. "Thank you, Maggie. This will keep us going for awhile."

She glanced from one to the other, obviously happy that they both looked pleased about things.

After she'd gone, Jackson poured steaming coffee into the two tall mugs. Maggie had remembered his half-and-half and she'd added a small plate of chocolate cookies.

Matt accepted the mug of coffee and reached for a cookie. "I'll talk with Ally tomorrow. We're having lunch after work at her grandmothers. I'll play it by ear and see how far I can go. I can't tell her that I've loved her for twenty years. I think it's too early for that."

"Too *early*? After twenty years? She might be flattered,

you know."

"You know what I mean." Matt laughed. "But about you and Lauren—she tells me you argue every time you're together."

"*We* don't argue, she argues. But she's agreed to go to the animal shelter with Brooke and me on Saturday. I'm hopeful." Jackson thoughtfully munched a cookie.

Matt turned to Jackson his expression puzzled. "Why do you suppose she starts an argument every time you're together?"

"I've thought about it." Jackson shook his head. "And I can't figure it out. I've even wondered if Clair could help me understand what's going on."

"If anyone should know what makes Lauren Ashby tick, it would be Clair. She's known her since she was eight years old."

"How do you know that?" Jackson asked.

"Lauren told me so."

Jackson studied Matt's face. "How did you stand to see Ally with me all this time and not go crazy thinking about it? I'm jealous of the times you've had coffee with Lauren."

Matt smiled before his gaze turned serious. "I won't deny it has been difficult."

Jackson sighed. "I wish I had known."

"The timing wasn't right until now. Everything has its time. Maybe it had to be this way, for all of us."

Suddenly a flash of insight turned Jackson to the painting of Lauren, and he knew.

Fear drove Lauren's actions.

Not physical fear. Think, Jackson, you're afraid too, and why? Heart and soul you've been captured by the person in the painting with the carefree smile. *She feels the same about you.* But for some reason her fear of captivity is unreasonably rooted. The constant arguing, keeping him at arms length, is her safety barrier.

Could Clair help him understand Lauren's fear?

He had to know or risk losing her.

CHAPTER 29

he House

DROPPING her bag onto the island bar, Lauren said, "I should have gone and toured Jackson's house with Thelma instead of going with you." She went to the sink and ran a glass of water.

"Why?" Clair slid onto a bar chair. "We had a good time at lunch." She held up her shopping bag. "And I found that book I've been wanting."

"Lunch with the guys *was* fun. And your paintings impressed them—and me too." She sipped her water and peered at Clair over the rim of the glass. "But now I'm committed to an outing with Jackson."

"You didn't have to say yes. I'll bet money that Jackson keeps the painting with you in it for himself." Clair laughed and looked at her.

Lauren felt the blood rush to her face. "Why would he do that?"

"Oh, let me think—maybe because he *likes* it?" They stared, each daring a further comment.

Lauren set the glass in the sink, grabbed her bag and headed to her room. She quietly shut the door and leaned against it. She had agreed to go with Jackson and Brooke to the animal shelter on Saturday. Panic rose in her throat squeezing her breath to a faint gasp. She straightened her back and took a deep deliberate breath. What *was* the matter with that man? Practically engaged, and yet he'd told Matt he had feelings for her. He'd made a pass, kissing her. Lauren jumped when Clair tapped lightly on the door. She hurriedly moved across the room.

"Yes?"

Clair opened the door a foot and popped her head in.

"It's still early. Why don't we drive out and see if we can catch Thelma at the house. I'd like to see the yard now that it's restored."

Lauren glanced at her watch. "It's three-thirty. Thelma will be gone by the time we could get there."

"Maybe not, but it won't matter. We can still see the yard. And I want to check out the lake. I may drive out and paint tomorrow."

"It would be nice to get out and walk a bit. Let me change into my grungies first." She'd mended the tear in the seat of her old jeans and they were as good as new.

"Yes, I'm changing too. Oh, and Winslow's awake. I hear him slurping water." Clair grinned and with her bags in hand, she strolled to her room.

Lauren hurried out to the sunroom. Winslow finished a long, noisy drink after sleeping all afternoon. "Hey guy, you want to take a run to the country?" She carried him back to her room, plopping him on the bed. She changed into the old jeans and boots, remembering the first time she'd gone to the house.

Clair thumped on Lauren's door when she passed, announcing she'd be ready whenever. She grabbed two bottles of water from the fridge as Lauren entered the kitchen with Winslow in her arms.

"You did mean grungies, didn't you." Clair raised her brows.

Lauren looked down and laughed. "These are my favorites. They've just been laundered to death."

Raising the garage door, Lauren insisted they take her vehicle. "We may decide to drive over to the lake."

They had never gone the back way to the house before. The landscape looked different.

"Help me watch for the turn-off."

"What's the name of the road we turn onto?" Clair asked.

"I don't remember. Just watch for it." They drove quietly for a few minutes. Lauren's thoughts turned to Clair's painting from that morning. "I hate that I didn't get to see the rest of your paintings this morning."

"You'll see them."

"Well, of course I will, but I wanted to see them today. And you said you had a painting for me? Where is it? When do I get to see it?"

"Keep your eyes on the road, please." Clair motioned her to look ahead. "It's in my room. You can have it when we get back if you like."

"If I like. Are you crazy? Now I'll be anxious to get back to the house."

Clair laughed. "You may not like it at all. I painted it several years ago."

"You know I'll love it."

Lauren sensed that Clair had something on her mind; she recognized the signs. She waited and drove on in silence.

"Have you thought anymore about talking to my doctor friend?" Clair tilted her head to read Lauren's expression.

Lauren nearly jerked the car off her side of the road.

"Thought anymore about it! I haven't thought about it at all. What brought that up? Sometimes, Clair, you worry me."

"I brought it up because Jackson is serious about you. I can see it, so can everyone else." Her fingers tapped a rhythm on her seatbelt. "I don't know what he's going to do about Ally Parker—that's beside the point."

Lauren's knuckles turned white from her grip on the steering wheel. "What does Jackson have to do with me talking to your doctor, anyway?"

"I don't want to wake up one morning and learn that you have taken flight to France. I went ahead and made you an appointment with Dr. Brickman. I knew if I didn't, you never would."

"I can't believe you did that!" She shot past the turn too fast to make it and slowed to look for a turn-around. "You truly amaze me, Clair."

"I know. And I'm sorry to spring it on you. That special painting is waiting for you, does that earn me redemption points?"

"That might be the only thing that does." Lauren grudgingly admitted.

She slowed, making the turn. Thelma's white Cadillac came down the drive toward them, she stopped and Lauren pulled up beside the Cadillac and put her window down.

"Hi, Thelma, we decided to run out and see if you'd still be here. I figured you'd be gone."

"When I'm out here I slow down and enjoy the break. I don't get in a hurry to get back to town. I'll follow you back to the house."

Lauren drove slowly up the drive and passed through the gate. Neither she nor Clair could believe the transformation that had taken place.

"Whoever is in charge of the work must be a magician." Clair breathed reverently.

Thelma joined them once they'd parked. They strolled to stand at the front of the house. Lauren glanced to the woods at the right where she had first stumbled onto the property and fell in love with the house. A new iron fence stood along that side, blocking entry from the woods. She grinned and pushing her hands deep into her pockets, she surveyed the house.

"I knew it would be wonderful once restored, but it's even more magnificent than I imagined."

"Yes. Magnificent." Thelma glanced at her. "Do you want to go inside?"

"Yes, I do. I'm glad Jackson's not here." Lauren smiled at Thelma. "Call me silly, but I'll be more comfortable looking at it without him around."

Thelma touched Lauren's arm, and slowed her step.

"I can't promise that Jackson won't show up. He's anxious for the work to be finished, and he drives out almost every evening." She had stopped and half turned back. "So if it really matters, you may not—" they turned at the same time to see Jackson's white truck coming up the drive. A small head bobbed on the seat next to him.

Lauren planted her feet and took a deep breath, caught again. They all three waited as Jackson and Brooke came toward them from the far side of the house where he'd parked. Brooke launched into a run when she saw Winslow in Lauren's arms.

"Winslow!" She landed against Lauren, reaching for the wiggling little body.

Laughing, they got him on the ground and untangled his leash.

"Dad didn't tell me you'd be here."

"Your dad didn't know. A spur of the moment idea struck Clair. She wanted to come see the yard."

Jackson reached them and hugged Thelma, and nodded in their direction. "Hi Lauren, Clair. You girls out for some fresh air?"

Clair smiled. "Yes, I twisted Lauren's arm. I love your lake."

"Thanks, that's one of my favorite places to spend time." He watched Brooke run after Winslow, the leash stretched full length. Then turning to Lauren, he said, "Looks like Winslow can put her through her paces." He smiled and watched them a moment longer. "Have you seen inside the house?" he asked.

"Um, no, not really." Lauren glanced after Clair as she meandered across the yard toward Claude Jr.

"Thelma, are you coming with us?" he asked

"Sure." She gave him a funny look, and glanced away, an amused quirk touched her mouth.

Folded and stacked on the floor, the furniture drapes had been removed to reveal beautiful period pieces decorating the spacious great room. The cabbage rose rug, cleaned and freshened, looked lovelier than ever.

They strolled through the rooms with Thelma pointing out unique features in each room until her cell phone rang. Squinting at it from arms length, she said, "It's Claude." With a glance at Jackson she moved several yards away.

Jackson took the lead, strolling into a large library study at the back of the house. Huge windows from floor to raised ceiling looked out over a beautiful garden view.

"How could anyone ever leave this wonderful room?"

Jackson smiled. "Yes, it was my mother's favorite room above any other in the house—"

"Jackson, I hate to interrupt." Thelma stepped into the room. "But Claude needs to see you about something, can you speak with him?"

"Of course. Tell him I'll be right there. Lauren, go ahead and look around." He headed outside with Thelma on his heels explaining something.

Lauren stood at the windows allowing her gaze to roam the gardens. She became aware of muted sounds that drifted from above. But everyone except her had gone outside.

Her curiosity piqued; she climbed the wide stairway that was carpeted with a runner in the same pattern as the rug in the great room. She stepped onto a large open landing that also served as a gallery. Other rooms branched off from the landing. The doors to the rooms were open, all except one. Pausing, she listened. The faint sounds led her to the closed door. This room would be above the study that she and Jackson had been in downstairs.

Lauren listened at the door for a moment before quietly turning the knob. The heavy door opened without a sound.

Brooke stood before a large easel with a half-finished canvas on it. She clutched Winslow on her hip and lightly dragged a brush over the dried canvas, talking to Winslow while she pretended to paint.

Lauren's breath released. "Oh, Brooke, I thought you and Winslow were outside."

"I came inside to look for you and Dad." Brooke shifted Winslow higher on her hip and quickly laid the brush down, stepping away from the easel.

Lauren glanced around. She was in Jenna's studio. The room had been left undisturbed, as if the artist had just stepped out. A vase of dried daffodils stood on a draped prop stand. Lauren's throat squeezed tight as she recognized the colorless still life setup.

"Brooke, sweetheart, let's go downstairs and find Clair. Hurry!"

"But I want to stay. I want this to be my room."

Jackson and the others voices drifted up from downstairs. Lauren didn't want to be caught in here. "Please, Brooke, hurry!"

"Dad said I could pick any room I wanted, and I like this one. Winslow does too."

Lauren pulled her out of the room and barely made it away from the door before the others reached the top of the stairs.

Brooke struggled to keep her hold on Winslow as she staggered toward her father.

"Dad, I've picked my room." She pointed to the closed door. Jackson glanced at the door and then to Lauren, where she stood rooted to the floor. Pushing his hands through his hair, he lowered his gaze.

Thelma's eyes widened with concern.

Lauren wished she could drop through the floor. He *knew* she'd been in there; had she intruded on Jenna's space?

CHAPTER 30

$\mathcal{B}$rooke's Room

JACKSON GLANCED AT BROOKE, and a frown pinched his brow as he glanced at the closed door.

Thelma hurried to put her arm around Brooke. "Don't you think Winslow would be happier outside, dear?"

"No, ma'am. He's happier with me." She shifted him to her other side and Winslow scrabbled to hang onto her small shoulders. Brooke giggled and said, "Dad, look, Winslow's hugging me!"

"Brooke, let's go downstairs—" Thelma tried again. She looked at Jackson when he touched her arm.

"It's okay, Thelma. I did tell Brooke that she could choose whichever room she wanted. If you'd like to finish showing Clair the rest of the house, maybe Lauren would like to see Brooke's new room."

He saw the cautious glance Thelma directed at Lauren before guiding Clair toward the other rooms.

The three of them were left standing alone in the upper gallery. Jackson tentatively looked at Lauren. "Would you like to see Brooke's new room?"

"Yes, Jackson, I would."

His heart skipped. He liked the way she said his name. "Come on Brooke, let's have a look."

"Thank you, Daddy. I *told* Lauren you said I could pick any room I wanted."

"You were right, I did. But first, Pumpkin, take pity on poor Winslow and put him down. He looks uncomfortable hanging there like that."

Brooke giggled as Lauren reached for Winslow. Between the two they got him safely on the floor. As soon as Brooke's arms were free, she skipped to the door, turned the knob and pushed the door back.

It was the first time he'd been in Jenna's studio since her death. A quick intake of breath shuddered his body. He steadied his nerves. He respected that Lauren hung back as Brooke touched everything and asked him a hundred questions. Rubbing his hand over his face and pushing it across to the back of his neck, Jackson lowered his eyes to the floor and said, "I'll have Thelma find someone to pack everything and store it in the attic."

Brooke turned large, stricken eyes on him. "No! Daddy, no! Don't move anything!"

His head jerked up. "But Pumpkin, where would you put your bed, and all the other furniture in your bedroom?"

Lauren looked from one to the other, her eyes widened. When he glanced at her, she looked as if she wanted to say something, but she looked away.

Brooke picked up a wide, soft watercolor brush and tickled it back and forth across her mouth, her eyes mere slits as she watched him. Stopping the brush motion, she took her mother's determined stance. "I don't want my bed in here. Put it in another room."

Jackson continued to push his hands through his hair and cast a bewildered look at Lauren. She lowered her eyes and gave him the hint of a smile before turning her back.

"Well, I guess we could manage that."

Brooke's body relaxed. She smiled, closed her eyes and dragged the soft brush across them several times before placing it back in the jug with the other brushes.

"Which room do you want your bed in?"

"I don't care." She gave a careless shrug and moved about the room, humming.

In that moment Brooke quietly took possession of her mother's studio. Jackson ached with love and gratitude for this daughter Jenna had given him. It would have broken his heart to dismantle the studio, as he had expected to do. Crossing the room to where Brooke posed the arms of a wooden manikin, Jackson sat on a stool next to her. "Pumpkin, I'm glad you want to keep the studio, but why do you want to keep it?"

Concern widened her eyes. "You won't move anything away while I'm at school, will you?"

Jackson drew back. "Of course not. I just wanted to know why you like the studio so much. Did you know this was where your mom worked when you were a baby?"

"Yes. I know. Did she let me stay with her when she painted?" Brooke watched his face.

Jackson delved deep for the answer she wanted. "Your Mom never took a step without you. Sometimes when I got home in the evenings you were both still in your pajamas and you would have so much paint on you, I thought you had taken up painting too!"

Brooke giggled and threw her arms around him. "I love you Dad, thank you for letting me have my room."

"You still haven't told me why you like this room so much."

"Lauren said she would give me art lessons. I want to take

lessons and use these brushes." She feathered her hand across the tops of a pottery jar full of brushes.

Lauren turned from the window, brushing at her eyes. "But Brooke, you told me you didn't want to take lessons, remember?"

"Uh-huh. I remember." She ducked her head.

"I'm glad you've changed your mind. But why?"

Her head still down. She mumbled, "I didn't want to make Daddy cry."

Jackson and Lauren looked at each other. "Why would your art lessons make me cry, Brooke? I'd be happy for you, sweetheart."

"You used to cry when you looked at Mommy's paintings. I didn't want to make you cry like Mommy did."

Jackson pulled her to him, hugging and kissing her until she giggled wildly, scrambling to get away from him. Winslow ran across the room when Brooke squealed. She grabbed him up and waddled from the room with her burden, chattering and laughing, she thumped downstairs.

"This is the first time I've been here since Jenna ... I didn't know if I could ever walk into this room again." Jackson's voice broke. "I didn't know if I could handle it. I wouldn't have attempted without you and Brooke."

"Jackson, you handled it very well. And even though you have reason to believe otherwise, I think you are a wonderful father." Lauren felt the warmth rising in her face as tears filled her eyes. She turned to leave.

"Lauren." He reached her at the door and took her shoulders. "You know how I feel about you, don't you?" He shook his head. "How could you not know?" He searched her face.

"Yes, I know." She lowered her head for a moment. Then looked up into his eyes. "Jackson ... I'm not good at relationships. I can be a great friend, but I'm not sure about anything more."

"What better way to start than with a great friendship. My

parents were great friends, and they had a long, happy life together."

Lauren laughed softly. He pulled her close in a tight embrace and closed his eyes. *She would love him.* As if she read his mind, she raised her face.

He kissed her and whispered, "I love you, Lauren."

"I love you too, Jackson, but I'm scared."

"I know. Me too. But we'll work it out together."

"Are you sure?"

"I'm sure. I promise."

They stood quietly holding each other until Lauren looked up and said, "It's getting late, the others will wonder if we've killed each other."

They laughed and shared another kiss before heading downstairs.

"Dad, look what Claude made for me. A swing and it fits me perfect."

Jackson went to check out the swing while Lauren joined the girls on the patio.

"Hey, that is a neat swing. Is it strong enough to hold me too?" He inspected the handiwork. "Don't forget to thank Claude. This is a nice swing."

"I'll do it right now." She flew across the yard.

In a few minutes he strolled back to where the girls were. Thelma and Clair stood from the white wrought iron lawn chairs that Claude had set up on the stone terrace. Thelma patted her hair and tugged at her belt, trying to act casual. But Jackson saw her curiosity. Clair reminded Lauren that they only had a salad at lunch.

"Would you girls let me take you to dinner?"

Brooke had come running back in time to hear the invitation and tugged on his arm.

"Yes, you too, Pumpkin."

"No, Dad, Aunt Willa's making fried chicken tonight. The way I like it."

"Oops, I'm sorry ladies, we'll make it another time." Jackson sent a warm glance in Lauren's direction. He walked along with them as they sauntered toward their cars.

Brooke walked beside Lauren. "Will you still give me art lessons?"

"Of course I will." She glanced at Jackson before continuing. "We'll have fun. And you have a wonderful studio to work in. What about planning your lesson schedule next week?"

"Okay." She hugged Lauren and handed her Winslow's leash before skipping off to the new swing.

Jackson said goodbye to the girls. His gaze lingered on Lauren for a moment before he returned to the house.

He went to Jenna's studio. In the quiet room he closed his eyes and heard Jenna's laughter. He saw her at the easel, with him at the window reading and sharing the latest gossip from Art Talk News while she painted. Jackson rubbed his hand over his eyes. He walked to the easel and studied the canvas propped there. The last one, she had not been able to finish.

He didn't know that Brooke had entered the room until her small hand found his, and in a soft voice she asked, "Daddy, are you going to cry again?"

He lifted her up. "No, sweetheart, I'm not going to cry. Mommy wants us to be happy.

CHAPTER 31

Matt's Choice

MATT STRAIGHTENED his desk and gathered the things he'd need while at Mrs. Parker's. Closing his briefcase, he hurried to the door. He hoped not to run into Jackson. He didn't feel like talking this morning. He and Ally were having lunch after they finished work at her grandmother's. Anxiety gripped a relentless fist around his chest, forcing a deep breath every few minutes.

Anticipating Ally's greeting, he blinked in disappointment when her mother answered the door. "Good morning, Mrs. Parker." He liked Carol Parker. Tall and attractive, it was easy to see where Ally got her looks. "You look like you're set for a game of golf this morning."

"Morning Matt. Yes, I'm on my way. I just ran something by for Ally and her grandmother. They're in the den, expecting you, I believe."

"Thank you. Have a good game." He found his way into the spacious den that overlooked a great stone patio.

"Good morning, ladies. Have you got my work laid out for me?" He smiled at Adel Parker; she beamed, wishing him a good morning in return.

Ally barely looked up as she mumbled good morning and repositioned one of the paintings that leaned against various pieces of furniture. She busied about placing each canvas in order of importance, she'd take several steps back, view the lineup, frown and rearrange the order.

Matt stepped to her side, sliding his hands into his pockets. "Has she decided to sell all of those too?"

"Maybe." Ally moved away, putting distance between them.

He took the few steps to her side. "Is something wrong?"

She gave him a cool gaze and turned away. "Of course not. What could be wrong?"

"Well I don't know—that's why I asked. You don't seem your cheerful self." He began to imagine things. Had Jackson said something, had he told her he didn't love her? "Have you spoken with Jackson?"

Ally jerked around. "No. Why do you ask?" Concern gathered in her eyes.

"I just wondered if something was bothering you. I'd like to help if I can."

They turned when her grandmother stepped briskly into the room. She carried a large tray with pastries artfully arranged next to a teapot. A trail of fragrant steam drifted from its spout.

"Ally, Matt, take time for a cup of tea before you get started. I have several phone calls to return that can't wait. I won't be too long, though." She settled the tray on the large sofa table and left the room as briskly as she'd entered.

Ally made her way to the table and poured hot tea into the thin china mugs.

Matt followed her, accepting the tea. "These pastries look delicious. Did you make them?" He teased, reaching for one.

"No. I didn't make them, but they are very good. I picked them up the other evening at that new bakery on Main Street." She glanced at him and back to the tray. "I saw you and Lauren Ashby together while I was there." She didn't look up as she put sugar in her tea.

Matt frowned trying to remember where she would have seen them. "You saw us? Oh, yes, I remember now, Lauren said she saw you."

"She did see me. I was getting out of my car when you went by. You had the top down on your car." She stirred her tea. "I didn't know two people could sit that close in a car with a console between them."

He placed his pastry on a napkin and along with his tea, set them on the table. He touched Ally's arm. "I want to talk with you, Ally. That's the reason I asked you to have lunch with me at The Colony instead of here today."

Shrugging from his touch, she carried her tea to the large windows and stood quietly looking out for a moment. "I can probably guess what you want to talk about. It's her, isn't it? You're in love with her." She glanced over her shoulder and said, "I'm sorry Matt. It's none of my business."

Matt walked up behind her. "If you mean Lauren, no I'm not in love with her." He placed his hands on Ally's shoulders and stood close. They looked out over the patio and gardens. "Ally, I'm in love with you."

She stood still as if she hadn't heard.

He was about to repeat the words when she set her tea on a nearby table and turned to face him.

"You love me?" Her hands hung at her sides. Her anxious gaze searched his eyes.

"I love you." He gently shook her shoulders.

Slowly a smile spread to Ally's mouth. She lowered her head, causing her hair to swing forward. "I've always liked you, Matt." She spoke without looking at him. "And when I saw her in the car with you, and then again at the club the other day, I just thought, well, you know." She glanced up and said, "Over the past month, I've become very fond of you. I envied Lauren."

Matt offered his hands and she placed hers in them. He pulled her into his arms and she raised her lips to his—just as Adel Parker breezed in.

Adel stopped. "Excuse me, children," she said, and backed out of the room, closing the door.

They hugged and laughed before returning to the interrupted kiss. "Will your grandmother have me hanged for this?" he asked afterwards.

"My grandmother loves you. I suspect she'll be very happy." Ally wrapped her arms around Matt and pressed her head against his chest. "This feels so right, Matt. I've been very foolish."

"Yes, it does feel right." He caressed her hair. "I'm afraid I've been foolish too. Let's finish the work here and go have lunch. We have to decide what to do next." They parted with a tender look. Ally crossed the room, opened the door to the den and shaking her head and raising her voice, she said, "My grand-mother; the matchmaker."

Adel Parker breezed into the room, a big smile on her face. "I heard that, my dear."

Ally laughed and hugged her grandmother. "I intended that you should. Come and tell us which of these paintings you want to sell."

"I really don't care. I need to get rid of most of this artwork. My dear, take any or all of it you want. I have a meeting at my club. I'll leave you two to work this out. I'm suddenly tired of it." She smiled and patted her hair before strolling out of the room.

Ally looked at Matt, they raised their brows at one another and laughed.

Matt glanced at the doorway. "She doesn't care what we sell? What came over her?" he asked.

"I'd guess she thinks she's gotten her way again. Grandmother will now be on to other challenges bigger than you and I and her art collection." Ally waved her hand. "Don't ask me to explain. We haven't the time."

Laughing, Matt glanced at his watch and got to work. They finished cataloging in record time; time to take an early lunch. They arrived at The Colony, a private sports club and restaurant, before the lunch crowd began to filter in. Matt guided Ally to his favorite table.

"I like this place, but I've not been here much." Ally's languid gaze moved appreciatively around the clubroom. Done in rich leather and plush carpeting. Large paintings decorated the walls, while warm light made the spacious room feel cozy.

"It's one of my homes away from home." Matt pulled Ally's chair out and then settled into his own. He waved the server away, indicating they'd order later.

"Ally, do you want to speak to Jackson first or would you rather I talk with him?" Matt reached and covered her hand with his.

"I feel that I should tell Jackson. I don't want to hurt him. I have to make him understand that I love him dearly. He's my oldest and dearest friend." She sighed.

Matt bit his tongue to keep from blurting out that Jackson felt the same way she did. But he couldn't share that confidence. It had to be done this way.

"May I tell you something that might make it easier to tell Jackson about us?" Matt asked.

"Of course. Anything. I don't know where to even start." Her eyes clung to his, hopeful.

"I've learned that Lauren is attracted to Jackson. But she's under the assumption that you and Jackson are practically engaged." He watched her reaction.

"Oh, my goodness!" Ally looked stunned. "Lauren is attracted to Jackson? And I was worried about you!" Laughter bubbled up as Ally leaned back against her chair, her hand going to her face. "What tangled webs we weave ... " She checked her laughter. "But how can we let Jackson know how she feels without seeming to push her at him?"

Matt swallowed. Guilt lodged in his throat like a physical object, knowing already that Jackson cared for Lauren and that Lauren returned the feeling. It was his turn to sigh. Friendship could be a headache.

"The sooner we tell Jackson about our feelings for each other, the better. And when Lauren learns there's no engagement between you and Jackson ... well, you know. She and Sunny Girl are good friends already."

"Good friends, with a young child? How odd."

"Sunny wants her to go with them to the animal shelter. She's looking for a dog to adopt. Lauren adopted the little dog she has."

"How did Brooke and Lauren get to know each other in the first place?" Ally asked, amused.

"Lauren's an artist. She's been doing a series of watercolor sketches of the old church building just down from the gallery." Matt nodded to the waiter that they were ready to order. "Sunny stopped to watch her paint one day. That's how they met."

"What does Jackson think about Brooke inviting her to go with them to the shelter?"

"Oh ... you know Jackson, whatever makes Sunny happy." He grinned.

"Yes, that's true. He spoils her." Ally was thoughtful for a moment. "Matt, as soon as I get home I'll call Jackson. I'll talk with him this evening. I promise."

"Good. I think that's for the best. Will you let me know how it goes? And if you need anything, call me."

"Yes, I will, and thank you." She sighed. "I'll be a nervous wreck until after I've spoken with Jackson."

Matt gazed at her for a second. "Look at it this way. Whatever happens, it will be better than a situation you might regret from now on. The person we spend our life with should inspire us, be a part of our heart and soul."

Ally gazed across the table, a tender expression in her hazel eyes. "I understand that now, Matt. Thank you for showing me. I value Jackson's friendship very much, and I'd rather live my life alone than to have his friendship turn to resentment and bitterness over the years."

Matt reached and took her hand. "You won't lose his friendship." His gaze never wavered. "And you won't have to live your life alone."

Not if he had anything to say about it.

CHAPTER 32

*L*ove Spoken

As they followed Thelma's car down the drive, Clair smiled. "Did you and Jackson stay upstairs to argue?"

"No, we didn't argue. Clair, I think I'm in trouble. Jackson told me he loves me." Lauren turned wide eyes toward Clair. "I told him that I love him too."

"Oh ... *Ohh*. I see. Shall I hide your car keys in case you decide to bolt?"

"Don't tease. Just tell me when that appointment is with Dr. Brickman."

Clair took a deep breath and her eyes grew round. "I have the appointment date at home."

Lauren rolled her head gently from side to side. "I have to take something for my head and go to bed as soon as I get home."

Clair studied her for a moment. "I'm sorry, dear. We'll have a light supper after you're feeling better."

"No, you go ahead and have dinner. I may not eat tonight." She prayed Clair wouldn't grill her about what exactly did happen upstairs. She didn't want to discuss it. Maybe tomorrow. She began to hum softly, unaware, until Clair looked sharply in her direction. She stopped and turned the cool air vent into her face.

Clair put her hand on Lauren's arm. "Everything will be okay. I don't understand Jackson, but I do think he'll do what's right."

"Of course. I know that. I'm just being stupid." She gripped the steering wheel and looked straight ahead.

"You are incapable of being stupid." Clair glanced at her. "But you are capable and very likely to get a speeding ticket if you don't slow down."

"Oh, this thing should have come with wings. It wants to fly." Lauren took her eyes off the road for a second. "Thank you for spending so much of your time with me, Clair," she said, touching Clair's arm. "I've heard you making excuses to Drew. He'll hate me for taking you away from him so much."

Clair laid her head back on the headrest. "One of the many things I love about Drew is his ability to entertain himself when I'm busy." They rode in silence for a short time. "He knows how important you are to me. I told him you come first."

"Clair! Please tell me you're teasing! You didn't really say that to him, did you? He hates me already! And I don't blame him."

"Oh, calm down. I told him that before he even asked me to marry him." She closed her eyes and smiled. "That's one advantage to waiting until my age to get married, nobody gets rattled as easily as when they're twenty."

Lauren tightened and loosened her hands on the steering wheel several times and glanced at Clair. "When I'm near Jackson I forget all about Ally. But I don't know what's happening there. Jackson never mentions her." She sighed. "I don't understand why he says he loves me and yet he's still ... " She sighed again. "Would you get me Dr. Brickman's number as soon as we get home?"

"Yes, I'll get it first thing. Trust Jackson, he'll do the right thing where Ally is concerned. I've come to believe that, don't you?"

"I'm trying to, but in the meantime I seem to be getting in deeper."

They drove in silence for several minutes.

Clair slipped her feet out of her loafers, pulling one foot up under her. "Let's talk about the dinner party tomorrow evening. What do you plan to wear?"

"Oh, no! I completely forgot about that. Well, I'm not going." They were turning into Lauren's driveway. She pushed the button to the garage door.

"How could you forget? The guys just invited us. You should have made an excuse not to go right then if you didn't want to go."

"If you'll remember, I was being agreeable and getting along with Jackson."

"Still, that's no reason to break the commitment. Besides, it'll be fun."

Lauren fumbled about unlocking the kitchen door. "Clair, if I ever wanted to get on a plane and fly away to the ends of the earth as you accuse me of doing, it's right now. How can I endure an evening of chatting with the woman who still thinks she's going to marry the man who's messed my head up until I can't think." She blinked hard holding back the tears that threatened.

Clair placed her arm around Lauren's shoulders.

"Come on. Take something for that headache and hug Winslow. You'll feel better. Perhaps Jackson and Ally's situation has changed by now, you may find out tomorrow while you're looking for a dog—or afterwards." She leaned her head against Lauren's. "And we don't have to go to the dinner party if you don't want to."

"Good. I don't want to."

"You may not want to now, but you never know, tomorrow is another day." Clair set her bag on the island when her phone rang. Glancing at it, she smiled at Lauren and whispered, "It's Drew."

Lauren checked on Winslow. He looked up and wagged his tail, waiting. She scooped him up and held her face against his. Hugging him did make her feel better. She wandered back into the kitchen.

"My dear, it looks like the party wasn't meant for us. Drew needs me to be in New York tomorrow evening. His family is gathering for a dinner party and he really wants me to be there."

"Of course he would want you there." Lauren slid onto a bar chair and sat Winslow in her lap. "What time will you leave?"

Clair pulled out a chair too. "We can have coffee in the morning before I head out. What time are you meeting Brooke and Jackson at the shelter?"

"Around ten-thirty, but coffee first would be great. How long will you be in New York?"

"If my suite is ready, I may go ahead and get moved in. There's a bedroom for you too, you know." Clair glanced at her. "Dad's been asking about you."

Lauren sighed. "Maybe I can have lunch with him when I go in to see Dr. Brickman."

"Oh, I'll get that appointment card before I forget." She slipped off the chair and hurried to her room, returning she handed Lauren a card she'd jotted a date on. "By the way, how is your head feeling?"

Lauren glanced at the card before answering. "Actually, not so bad." She studied the card again. "Dr. Caroline Brickman?" She raised her brow at Clair.

"Yes. I've known her for years. I think you'll like her."

She was still studying the card when the door chimes sounded. She and Clair glanced at each other. "I'm not expecting anyone, were you?" Clair shook her head and headed to her room.

On her way to the door, Lauren checked to see what day her appointment fell on the following week. She opened the door, surprised, she said, "Matt. Come in. What are you up to?"

"I hoped to catch you not busy—have I?"

"You have. I'm never too busy for a friend." She smiled, motioning him inside.

"Could we go someplace to talk?" he asked.

"It's pleasant on the patio this time of day, would that work? With a glass of iced tea?"

"That sounds perfect." Matt followed her through to the kitchen where she fixed two glasses of tea.

Lauren led the way toward the French doors that opened to the patio. She motioned to the large comfortable Adirondack chairs. The last thread of sun lingered on the horizon, and a soft breeze stirred the air.

"I shouldn't have just dropped by, but I wanted you to know that Ally is with Jackson this evening. They're talking." He took a drink of tea. "I told Ally of my feelings for her."

A shiver of dread, happiness, fear and doubt all suddenly washed over Lauren. She drew a shaky breath and reached for her tea. "And she feels the same? Will everything be okay?"

"Yes, to both questions. We had lunch after leaving her grandmother's." Matt gave a rueful grin. "This morning her grandmother walked in as Ally and I embraced and were about to steal a kiss."

Lauren widened her eyes. "Oh—what did she say?"

"She said, 'Excuse me, children', and backed out, closing the door." Their laughter carried into the night air.

"I'm glad you were home, Lauren. You're easy to talk to."

"I'm glad you think so. But you seem nervous. Ally won't back out or anything, will she?"

Matt grinned. "I hoped my nerves didn't show. No, she won't back out—I don't think so anyway," he added dryly. "But I'm nervous for her." Matt drank more tea and looked thoughtful. "She dreads telling Jackson. She's worried about hurting him. She still thinks Jackson was about to ask her to marry him and go live in the country."

"Yes, I know. But if she does tell Jackson how she really feels about him and living in the country, do you think she'll go ahead and tell him about you?" Lauren asked.

"About me, I'm not sure." He tilted his head, a quizzical expression in his eyes and his mouth twisted to one side. "I hope she does, but she may lose her courage when it comes to that."

They both turned as Clair stepped to the patio door and waved. "Hi, Matt! Lauren your phone rang and rang but I couldn't find it in time to answer it."

"That's okay. I'll return the call later, thanks, Clair."

"I looked at caller ID when I found it. It was Jackson."

"Thanks, Clair."

Matt frowned and checked his phone. "If they've finished their talk, I wonder why Ally hasn't called? I guess I should be going."

Lauren walked with him to the door. "She'll be calling any minute now, I'm sure."

"I'd feel better if she already had." He raised an eyebrow and stepped outside.

After Matt had gone, Lauren crossed her arms and stood in the foyer for a moment, thoughtful. If Ally had lost courage and chose to stay with Jackson, what would Jackson do?

She glanced at her phone, ran her thumb over the smudged screen and laid it aside. She'd return Jackson's call later. The possibility that Ally had changed her mind loomed real—if that was the case, Lauren didn't want to know.

Not just yet.

CHAPTER 33

 he Outing

LIGHTS SHOWN from the kitchen windows when Jackson pulled into the driveway. Aunt Willa must be warming her bedtime milk. He hurried his step. He needed to talk and was glad he'd caught her in the kitchen where they did their best talking.

"Hi, Aunt Willa. Is Brooke in bed?" He collapsed onto the tall leather bar chair.

"I believe she is. Her friend Emily called and invited her to spend the day with her tomorrow. She spent an hour gathering her *stuff*, as she calls it, to take to Emily's." Removing the pan of milk from the stove, Aunt Willa poured some into a mug and dragged out the bar stool she kept on the backside of the island and sat across from Jackson.

"Oh, I forgot to remind you, I'm taking her to the animal shelter in the morning. Lauren's going with us."

"She'll love that—I mean Brooke will." Aunt Willa grinned.

"No problem, I'll call Emily's mother and explain. Would you like some warm milk?"

Jackson shook his head, ignoring her humor.

She watched him over her mug. "Where do you plan to keep the new dog?"

"It'll probably be in the house, no matter what I say."

Aunt Willa nodded. "Uh-huh, count on it."

"Yeah." He grinned and traced a pattern in the granite counter top, falling quiet for a moment. Glancing up he said, "I did something today that I'm both happy and sad about."

"Oh? What's that?"

"I had a long talk with Ally this evening. I believe we understand each other for the first time, ever." He smiled. "I feel like I've had a load lifted from my back."

"Sounds serious. What brought about this talk?"

He smiled at her expression. "You knew Ally and Matt were working on her grandmother's art collection?

"Yes, Thelma mentioned it."

Mrs. Parker decided to catalogue all of the canvases and sell several pieces. Matt offered to oversee the project, to help Ally with it. It seems after spending all that time together, Matt and Ally have fallen for each other."

"Oh, I see. And you're pleased about this?"

"Yes, I'm glad for them. But sad they didn't get together years ago. Matt confided to me that he's loved Ally for years. All these years she thought she loved me, but she—we both realized it was not the kind of love to build a solid marriage on." He gazed at his aunt. "It scares me that we might not have realized it until too late." He sat quietly fingering his truck key.

His aunt came around the island and hugged him.

"I'm glad for you and Ally, and Matt. You three will remain friends?" She tilted her head to look into his eyes.

"Oh yes, we'll always be friends, the best of friends." He stood and walked to look out over the lighted back patio, his hands in his pockets.

She walked over to stand with him. "Then what's the matter?"

"You've probably guessed by now how I feel about Lauren."

"Probably." She stood quietly beside him.

"I tried to call her, but she didn't answer. I've worried that she thought I was two-timing Ally behind her back. I've been anxious for her to know there's no longer, actually never had been, anything but friendship between Ally and me."

"So call her again. Girls get busy, you know."

He looked down at his aunt. Suddenly he pulled his hands out of his pockets and hugged her. "I have a better idea. I'm going to see her."

"It's after nine o'clock, Jackson. Are you sure?" She sounded worried but when he glanced back, a wide smile lit her face.

"See you at breakfast." The door closed quietly.

The Dodge knew the way to Old Elm Street. He'd never been to Lauren's house, but he knew the place well.

A short time later standing on the wide porch, he swallowed nervously, misgivings arose about ringing her doorbell at this hour. But since he'd been foolish this far, he pushed the brass button.

Lauren opened the door. "Jackson … ?"

"Forgive me for just showing up. I tried to call." He took in her pink robe, the damp hair pulled up in a messy tumble on top of her head. "Were you ready for bed?" He ran his hand through his hair. "Just forget I was here. We can talk tomorrow." He'd half turned.

"No, no." She laughed, motioning him in. "You surprised me. Clair and I were just watching TV." She led him into the kitchen. "Would you like something … tea ?"

"Tea would be good."

Clair strolled into the room. "Hi, Jackson. How are you this evening?" She scooted onto one of the bar chairs and motioned to Lauren that she'd have tea also.

"Well, I was doing fine until I got this great idea of dropping in unannounced. I know it wasn't a very thoughtful thing to do."

"You're talking to a couple of New Yorkers. We stay up late. Don't let the robes fool you. We wouldn't be going to bed for hours." She took the tea Lauren handed her. "But, if you two will excuse me, I've got a good western going."

After handing Jackson his tea, Lauren fussed with her hair. At a loss for words, she asked, "Would you like to sit outside?"

"Sounds nice. If you'd like to."

"I always like the outdoors." She led him to the patio to the same chairs she and Matt vacated only an hour ago.

Hesitantly he said, "I couldn't wait until tomorrow to tell you something and Brooke will be with us in the morning. I might not get a chance."

"Yes, I understand." She looked at him then leaned her head back against the chair.

"Ally and I had a long talk this evening." He gazed at her profile, willing her to look at him. As if she sensed it, she turned to face him. "Lauren, I hated for you to think I was attracted to you behind Ally's back."

"I confess I wondered. I'd heard that you and Ally were expected to marry, then when you kissed me, what else could I think?" She hugged her knees up, drawing her feet to the chair and tucking her robe around them.

"Of course you would think that. I hated it, but there was nothing I could do until I talked with her. I do love Ally. But I'm not in love with her. I never have been."

"You told her that?"

"Yes. But funny thing, she's had the same thoughts about us lately that I've had. Ally told me she 'loved me to death' but that she wasn't in love with me." He chuckled and leaned his head back against his chair and still looking at her he said, "Ally also told me that she's fallen in love with Matt. She sees the difference in her feelings for Matt and what they'd been for me."

"I'm so glad for Matt and Ally. That took courage. Are you happy for them?"

Face to face their eyes intent, he said, "Words can't express my happiness. They're perfect for each other." He sighed. "Ally and I were never suited, except as friends."

Jackson stood and reached his hand out to Lauren. She gazed up at him for a long moment before placing her hand in his. He pulled her to her feet and held her close. She wrapped her arms around him, her face pressed to his chest. With his mouth against her hair he whispered, "I love you, Lauren Ashby."

"I love you too, Jackson Montgomery." She raised her face. His lips met hers for a long tender kiss.

Afterwards, he studied her face and said, "Will you go to the house with Brooke and me tomorrow? I want to show you everything, inside and out."

"Yes I'd love to. You already know how I feel about your house."

He did know, and it pleased him immensely.

"I'd better get going. We have a busy day ahead of us. You might say a little prayer that we get lucky and find Winslow's twin." Then wryly, he added, "Or at least one that's a tiny bit like him." He liked the sound of her soft laughter. Tucking her arm through his they walked across the patio. "Can I get to my truck through there?" He motioned to the side gate that led from the patio.

"Yes, I'll walk around with you."

"Are you sure Brooke and I can't pick you up in the morning?" He kissed her.

Lauren smiled after the kiss. "Nope, that isn't necessary. I'll drive in."

As they reached his truck Jackson held her in a tight embrace.

"I never dreamed, or hoped to ever feel this way again. Hmm, I guess there's something to be said for catching a trespasser."

Lauren tilted her head back and looked at him with a raised brow. "Am I forgiven?"

"Forgiven." Their laughter mingled to drift softly upon the evening air.

Her expression turned serious, she said, "Jackson, I've *never* felt this way before."

Pressing his face against her hair, he whispered, "I like to think you were waiting for me."

He watched her enter the house before driving away. The Dodge headed toward the country house. He needed to say goodbye to the old days, one more time, alone.

The morning would mark the beginning of his new life.

CHAPTER 34

he Date

THEY'D LINGERED way too long over breakfast and now Clair hurriedly stacked things by the back door. "Just put it there on those books." She directed Lauren about the shopping bag she held in her hand.

"You should still have plenty of time, Clair. What time is the dinner, anyway?"

"Not until seven, but I have to get to the hairdressers and do a little shopping. I'll be down to the wire, I'm sure."

They each got an armload of the stack and headed to the rental car parked in the garage.

"Have fun today, dear, and call me when the dust settles." Clair grinned and hugged her.

"You've got to stop watching those old westerns. When did you start that anyway?" Lauren laughed.

"Drew taught me about westerns. He loves them and now I do too. We may honeymoon in Wyoming." She motioned for Lauren to press the garage door opener and waited for the door to rise. "Don't forget—call me." She slid behind the wheel and backed out, headed for New York.

Since the housekeeper had arrived moments before and would watch over Winslow, Lauren opened the sunroom door so he'd have the run of the house.

Her nerves were on edge at spending the day with Jackson and Brooke. She touched her fingertips to her lips, remembering the night before. She loved Jackson, but relying on another person for happiness and in return being a source of their happiness raised a scary, new feeling. She glanced at her phone when it rang.

"Hello, Matt, how are you?"

"I'm great. Have you spoken with Jackson?"

"He came by last evening shortly after you left." She laughed. "We talked. I understand that you and Ally are as happy as can be."

"Happy as can be, yes. I meant to call earlier and let you know why she hadn't called yesterday. She got a phone call just as she and Jackson finished talking. Her father had an emergency and she rushed to the hospital to be with him."

"Oh, I'm sorry about her dad. Is he okay?" She threw her bag on her shoulder and headed for the Range Rover.

"He's fine now. His ulcer decided to act up. You haven't forgotten the dinner party? I hope not."

"Will it be awkward for you guys ... and Ally, with me there? Clair can't make it. She just left for New York."

"I don't think it'll be awkward. We know how things stand and that's all that matters at present. Are you at home?" he asked.

"Well, actually I'm on my way to meet Jackson and Brooke. This is the big day at the shelter."

"Oh, yes of course. I forgot. Well, good luck and happy dog hunting. I'm expecting to see you tonight."

She and Ally had to face each other sooner or later. She

supposed tonight would be as good a time as any. Her mind turned to what she'd wear as she drove into town.

The shelter, a modern facility, was located at the edge of town next to a pet store, a hardware store and a sprawling nursery. All three businesses looked busy and crowded. The crowds strolled about and wandered the sidewalk plant sale at the nursery. She didn't see Jackson's truck. Since they'd agreed to meet at the main entrance, she parked and headed that way.

As Lauren approached the entry Brooke spotted her and ran dodging through the crowd, as excited as if it was Christmas morning. They met and hugged, Brooke chattering and giggling and not making any sense at all.

"Slow down, I can't understand you." Lauren laughed, as she slid her arm around Brooke's small shoulders.

"Dad tricked me. He didn't tell me we were coming to get a dog until this morning."

"He knew you'd be too excited to sleep last night. Wasn't it a nice surprise though?" Lauren smiled, enjoying her excitement.

"Yes! Yes! I can't wait!" Brooke hopped from one foot to the other.

Jackson strolled up, his hands in his pockets. He gave Lauren a private, tender look and crossed his arms.

"We wouldn't let the hunt begin until you got here. Are we ready to go inside?"

Bouncing on her toes, Brooke grabbed his hand. "Yes Daddy, I can't wait!"

Jackson knelt to her level and placed his hands on her shoulders. "Brooke. Owning a dog is serious business and you must choose carefully, understand?"

Brooke quieted, her eyes wide. "Yes, Sir, I understand."

As they were about to enter the shelter someone called to Jackson. He turned and for a moment searched the crowd before waving. He watched a man his own age hurry across the street. "Ryan Mann?" he muttered. "Hey, Ryan, you rascal. Where did you come from? You haven't moved back have you?" They pumped hands.

"No, just here for the weekend. Getting the old home place ready to sell."

Jackson turned to Lauren and Brooke and introduced them to his old high school friend who had moved away after college.

"Have you got a minute, Jackson? I'd like you to meet my wife and son."

Jackson glanced at Lauren. "Do you girls want to go on in, and I'll catch you later?"

Lauren looked to Brooke's anxious face. "We'll do that. I have my phone if you can't find us."

He touched her hand, his eyes apologizing for the interruption. "I'll find you."

Lauren clasped Brooke's hand and they entered the shelter. They loved all the dogs. After a very short time Lauren saw signs of a problem. Brooke's eyes got wider each time they passed a crate, and she kept glancing up at Lauren.

Finally her step dragged to a stop. She leaned against Lauren. "What happens to the dogs that nobody wants?" She blinked back tears. Lauren understood because she felt the same way.

"Sweetheart, the people here at the shelter work really hard to find homes for all the dogs. And that's why you and your Dad are here. So you can share your home with a lucky little dog."

"But what about the unlucky ones? Dad said we had room at the country house for lots of dogs. Why can't we take more than one?"

"Are you sure that's what he said? A lot of dogs would be a full time job just caring for them. That's why so many people work here. Your dad doesn't have time to care for a lot of dogs." Lauren gently turned Brooke back toward to the crates. "Come on, let's look for a puppy like Winslow."

Brooke crossed her arms and trudged along. A small dog

remarkably similar to Winslow in color and markings barked as they walked up to his crate.

Lauren knelt to the little dog and stroked his face and talked to him. He tilted his head in a questioning posture, making her laugh and think of Winslow. "Brooke, look at this puppy. He's very much like Winslow." She touched his nose through the crate. "You're a sweet little guy." She turned to Brooke, "Isn't he cute—Brooke? Brooke!"

Lauren jumped to her feet, searching the crowd of faces. She ran a short distance down first one aisle and then another. "Brooke!" Frantic, she hurried down the middle aisle. "Brooke!" Her breath came in shallow burst. "Brooke—Brooke!"

Her heart began to thunder and people stared as she ran wildly through the isles.

Voices from long ago rose up—*Irresponsible, Irresponsible! You irresponsible girl!*

Hands reached out—she shook them off, screaming Brooke's name until suddenly Jackson had her in his arms, speaking her name. He held her tight until she could breathe again. He walked her outside to a bench. The white-hot sun beat down, closing in, blinding, as the pounding in her head drowned all other sounds. Jackson's voice sounded distant.

"What happened, Lauren?" He wiped her tears with his hand, and pushed her hair away from her hot face. "Tell me what happened, where's Brooke?"

"I don't know," she whispered, "Brooke's gone." She pressed her fingers to her temples. *Irresponsible girl. You were supposed to watch ...* "I searched, but I couldn't find her." Her head roared with sounds, as she pressed hard against her temples.

Jackson hugged her. "I'm sure she just wandered off. Stay here, I'll go find her. Will you stay here, Lauren? Don't move. I won't be long."

* * *

HOW LONG HAD she been sitting on the bench? She wiped the dampness from her hot face and pushed her hair back. Her body sweltered. *She'd lost Brooke, and now Jackson was gone.*

Her purse lay beside her in the unbearable glare of the sun. Lauren fumbled through its contents until her fingers closed around her keys. She made her way to the Range Rover.

In a fog and willing herself not to be sick, she drove until the open country spread out before her.

With no destination in mind she drove toward New York City —where she belonged.

The Belmont was a huge hotel. It would be a safe place to rest until she could get rid of the pain and fog that clouded her head. Lauren handed her keys to the valet and made her way to the front desk. She watched her hand sign the register. Sara Collins. Lauren smiled, how odd to observe oneself apart from oneself.

The elevator hummed to the seventh floor. Room 710. She unlocked the door and staggered inside.

Dazed by an excruciating headache, she scattered the contents of her bag on the bed. Finding the green bottle of tablets, she shook five into her hand and stumbled to the bathroom. Running a glass of tap water, she washed down the small tablets and forced her legs to carry her across the room where she fell onto the wide plush bed. Crawling to the middle of it, she huddled, her eyes closed tightly, and waited for the room to gradually stop spinning.

Fully clothed, she drifted into a deep sleep.

 evastated

JACKSON GOT Brooke home as quickly as possible where Aunt Willa took charge, asking no questions.

He hurried to his office and searched Clair's file for her phone number. His heart pounded a nervous rhythm. He couldn't remember ever being more scared than when he'd frantically searched the shelter for Brooke. Finding Clair's number, he jotted it on the back of a card.

Clair was his only hope. If Lauren went to her, she might have had time to get there. He gripped the phone.

Please, dear God, let her answer.

"Hello."

Relief slumped his shoulders. "Clair, I'm sorry to bother you, but could I speak to Lauren?" He tried to sound casual while holding his breath at the same time.

"Lauren? She's not here. Isn't she supposed to be with you? She was leaving to meet you right after I left. You haven't seen her?" Clair's voice sharpened.

"Yes, I have seen her, we met as planned. But something happened, I'm not sure what, but she left while I was trying to find Brooke. I thought she might be with you."

"You were trying to find Brooke? Didn't she go to the shelter with you? You're not making sense."

"It's a long story. I'm not sure what happened, but Brooke is okay." He took a deep breath. "Lauren just took off. I went to her house as soon as I found Brooke and knew that she was okay, but the housekeeper hasn't seen or heard from her either."

"Did you talk with Matt?"

"He'd not heard from her since they spoke earlier in the morning." He gave a deep sigh. "I don't know of anywhere else that she would have gone."

"No, me either. Let me do some checking around. I have an idea. I'll call you back one way or the other. I'm sure she's okay."

"Thank you, Clair. I'll have my phone. I love Lauren, and I want to understand what's going on."

"Good. That's the first step. Try not to worry, Jackson, and I'll call you later."

Jackson sat heavily in his chair. He could breath easier with Clair knowing what had happened. What *had* happened? In the state he'd found Lauren, he could only imagine the worst. He'd pretended calm, afraid of upsetting her even more. He'd hurried back to the shelter and searched for Brooke and found her wandering along, probably looking for Lauren at that point. Her arms crossed, head down and tears streaking her face. He'd grabbed her in a bear hug and hurried out to reassure Lauren that Brooke was okay, only to find Lauren and her Range Rover no where in sight—he'd not been gone more than ten minutes.

Jackson had explained to Brooke while driving her back to Aunt Willa, that Lauren had left. Thinking of Brooke, he reached for his phone and tapped a number. "Aunt Willa, is Brooke okay?"

"She finally cried herself to sleep. What in the world

happened, Jackson? Did you and Lauren have words in front of her? I've never seen her so completely distraught."

"No, Lauren and I didn't do anything. I'm sorry I haven't had time to fill you in. I wasn't even in the shelter with them. I ran into Ryan Mann, and we walked across the street. Ryan wanted me to meet his wife and son. I knew Brooke could hardly wait to see the dogs, so I told them to go on in. When I got there a short time later, Brooke had disappeared. I found Lauren hysterical, crying and screaming Brooke's name. That's all I know."

"Brooke couldn't tell you anything?"

"No. By the time I found Brooke and got back to where I'd left Lauren, she had taken off." Jackson groaned. "Brooke seemed to think she'd done something to cause Lauren to leave. She became upset and cried so hard I couldn't get anything out of her. I can't imagine those two getting upset with each other."

"Brooke is safe, so don't worry about her. And you'll find Lauren. I'm sure she's okay too."

He thanked his aunt and ended the call. In the middle of pacing the office, he suddenly slipped his phone into his back pocket and grabbed his keys. He had to walk or explode while waiting to hear from Clair. He headed the Dodge toward Old Elm Road, not worrying about a speeding ticket as he pushed the limit. A walk around the lake might ease the stress and allow his frenzied mind to sort things out.

He parked on the north side of the lake. The woods were quiet and still as he changed from loafers to the tall rubber boots. He patted his pocket, reassured his phone was there. Seconds later it begin ringing. His heart raced when he looked at caller ID.

"Lauren! Oh, Lauren, where are you? Are you okay?"

"I'm fine. I'm with Clair. She said you found Brooke and she's okay?"

"Yes, Brooke's fine. I've been so worried about you. When I

came back to the bench and you were gone I nearly went crazy with worry." He slumped to the ground. Relief weakened his knees. Leaning against the truck tire, he rolled his head back, closed his eyes and squeezed back hot tears.

"Jackson, I feel like such a fool. I just panicked when I looked up and didn't see Brooke anywhere. I don't know why I reacted so frantically."

"It doesn't matter now, you're both okay and that's all that counts."

"I apologize for worrying you. But, Jackson, there's a little dog at the shelter that's perfect for Brooke. I wish you'd go back and see about getting him. You could surprise her with the puppy."

"That's a great idea. How will I know which one it is?"

"When you enter the shelter at the very front, turn to your left and go a short distance. He's in about the seventh or eighth crate. You'll know when you see him. He looks so much like Winslow, it's amazing."

"I'll head back to the shelter right now. But do you think Brooke might be disappointed if she doesn't get to pick her own dog?" Jackson slid into the truck as he spoke.

"Brooke doesn't need to go back to the shelter. Her tender little heart broke when she saw so many dogs, and she couldn't rescue them all. I think that's why she walked away."

"Yes, I can see that happening. Brooke does have a tender heart. Thank you, Lauren. I'm headed that way right now."

"When you get there and if you're not sure just send me a picture, and I'll tell you if you've got the right one. I have to go now."

"Lauren, I'm glad you called, I was worried. I'll send you a picture. I love you." He heard her long sigh.

"I love you too."

"And Brooke? He laughed.

"Yes, and Brooke. And your house, don't forget."

He laughed. "Oh, yes, the house, the main reason you love me." They shared a laugh, but he detected a note of sadness. "When will I see you again?"

"Tonight. I'll be home for the dinner party."

Jackson swallowed, stammering, "You will? That's great ... are you sure?"

"I'm sure."

"I insist on picking you up this time."

"Oh no, I'll drive in. I may do a little shopping here first, then I'll head that way."

"You're sure? Then ... I'll see you later. Please be careful." He ended the call. Something didn't fit. Lauren acted as if nothing had happened. He recalled the way her body shook and the frantic screaming for Brooke.

Driving back to the shelter he kept going over their conversation. Lauren's cheerfulness had been forced. He parked the truck in front of the shelter and had just stepped out when his phone rang. It was Clair. "Hello."

"I heard Lauren tell you she would be at the party, but I'm afraid she won't be." Clair sighed and paused a moment. "She's at the Belmont, the hotel where I'm living and she needs to stay here for the night. My doctor gave her something to help her rest. She wouldn't take anything though until she spoke to you about the little dog. I hope you're able to get him."

"Thank you, Clair. I wondered about her driving back this evening. I'm glad she's with you. I'm on my way to get the puppy now. Will you keep me informed?"

"I will." She lowered her voice. "And let's get together one day next week. I need to tell you something that concerns Lauren."

"Yes, lets do that. Just tell me when, and I'll be there. And thank you again, Clair."

Back in town, he entered the shelter and turned to the left, counting crates—the seventh one. Sure enough the little fellow looked up with a face like Winslow's, all except the blue eyes. Jackson knelt in front of the crate and pulled out his phone camera. He spoke quietly to the puppy as he took pictures. But the whole time, Clair's voice resonated in his head.

She had *something* to tell him that concerned Lauren.

CHAPTER 36

leeing

LAUREN ENDED the call and sat with the phone in her hand for a moment before breathing a long sigh and tossing it next to the pillow. She turned to Clair. "How did you know I'd be here?" Propped against a stack of pillows, she wore the pale blue loaner pajamas that Clair had brought down from her suite.

Clair walked across the room and sat on the side of the bed. "Well, why wouldn't I guess you'd stay at the best hotel in New York?" She smiled. "Besides, the Belmont will be my home when I'm in New York from now on."

Her tone became accusatory.

"I don't understand why you didn't let me know you were here. You have a room in my suite, too. And it's ready for you." She smoothed the linens. "The doctor wants you to stay here tonight. I let Jackson know not to expect you for the party."

"But I'm fine."

"The doctor said rest. We'll get you moved tomorrow. But for now, I'm going to get dressed and have dinner with my sweetheart." She stood and patted Lauren's arm. "If you need anything, call me. Otherwise, I'll see you in the morning. Good night."

"Good night, Clair. Thank you for everything. Sorry you had to break into my room, I zonked out as soon as I got inside. And it is a relief not to be going to that dinner party." She settled into the bed, her eyelids heavy.

"Oh, that's okay, and I didn't break in. There's perks to marrying the hotel owner. But it would have been easier if I had thought earlier to look for Sara Collins." They shared a laugh before Clair closed the door behind her.

Lauren barely remembered signing in. Why had she used her work name? She never used it for anything except signing her work. She puzzled over it until she fell into a deep sleep.

Early the next morning her phone rang, but she'd awakened hours before. "Good morning, Clair."

"Let's have breakfast in my suite. Tell me when you're ready to come up, and I'll order."

"I'll be there in thirty minutes. I may look rather limp. It's the best I can do with the same clothes from yesterday." She laughed.

"We can do something about your clothes. It's suite A-39, Top floor. I'll order right now. You sound better after a good nights sleep."

"I feel better. I'll be there shortly." Lauren took the toiletries she'd ordered from room service and went to the bathroom. She brushed her teeth and pulled her dark hair into a ponytail. A good nights sleep had helped. But making a decision, a hard one, was what really made her feel better.

She was back on track.

Always, she'd been careful not to get involved in a situation that she knew instinctively could shatter the calm ordered convenience of the life she'd chosen long ago to live. The move to Valley Ridge had been a mistake. She had based the move from New York to the country on the memories of a four-year old child. She could barely recall the large house in the country and the man who had carried her high on his shoulders. He'd carried her among the apple trees, amidst sweet smells and laughter, memories for a lifetime.

Lauren studied her reflection in the bathroom mirror. The move hadn't been for a place. She had spent her life trying to recapture a memory, a feeling. A feeling she had longed for since the day her father died. She shook her head. Foolish woman.

Now the people she loved dearly would be hurt. Her eyes squeezed tight against sudden tears, she turned from the mirror.

* * *

TAPPING LIGHTLY on the door of suite A-39 Lauren shifted her purse higher on her shoulder and swallowed at the wave of anxiety that rose from her stomach to settle in her throat.

Clair opened the door. "Come in, breakfast will be here shortly. You don't look *so* bad. No one would even know you had a rough day yesterday." She led the way to a large sitting area. A table was prepared with a white cloth, waiting delivery of their breakfast.

Lauren smiled. "Thanks, that makes me feel better. This is a lovely suite." She meandered outdoors. "Oh, you have a nice large terrace."

"Yes, it is. Would you rather breakfast out there?" Clair glanced at her and then made the decision herself. "Let's do, it's much nicer outdoors."

Room service knocked, and Clair hurried to open the door. A server pushed the draped serving cart into the room.

"Set us up on the terrace, please."

He rolled the cart out to the terrace and draped the table that sat under the wide, green umbrella. Omelets, toast, Danish rolls and orange juice, plus a pot of steaming coffee completed the set up.

"Oh, this looks good." Lauren smiled at Clair.

"Yes, doesn't it? I'm going to be spoiled so rotten, Drew may just have to throw me in the trash." They shared the first relaxed laughter since Clair had left Lauren's house the day before. Clair gave thanks for the food. Then, intent on spreading the napkin in her lap, she glanced up quickly and back to her silver before she spoke. "I just had a thought. While you're already in the city, why not speak to Dr. Brickman? It could save you an extra trip."

"Well, in the first place, my appointment is for next week."

"But Caroline's a good friend. She would work you in if I asked her to." Clair poured their coffee. "Besides, I'm anxious for you to meet her."

"Clair, I hope you won't be upset with me, but … I … I've decided to take the cowards way out, again. I'm going back to Italy for six months or a year. I haven't gotten much work done lately. Looking at houses and getting settled into the cottage has taken a lot of time." She couldn't look at Clair.

Clair set her cup down and leaned back in her chair.

"Lauren, please don't do this. You've got to face reality sooner or later and sooner would be better."

Tension hung in the air as sparrows chirped and flitted in the trees that grew in huge pots sitting about the terrace. Faint sounds drifted up from the street some thirty-odd floors below.

Neither one spoke for a long time.

Lauren raised her face to gaze at Clair. "Please don't lecture me. I've waited too long to change now. I've faced the fact that I've been trying to turn an old memory into reality—and that can't be done. I don't want to hurt Jackson and Brooke any more than I have. It's not too late to stop this with Jackson, not if I leave now."

"You won't go see Dr. Brickman?" Clair leveled a steady gaze across the table.

"You didn't even hear me. I don't need Dr. Brickman if I leave Valley Ridge and get back to work."

"Well, I guess you're right. And if you want to live that way, it's your business." Clair began to eat like the discussion was finished.

"I used to be happy with my life. You know I was."

"Tell me something, Lauren. If you were happy with your life the way it was, why did you move to the country in the first place? Why were you trying to turn an old memory into reality?" Clair chewed, swallowed and sipped orange juice in rapid order.

Lauren had never witnessed Clair angry or losing her cool. "I don't mean to upset you. I just need you to understand."

Clair touched her napkin to her lips. "I certainly wish I could understand. But think about what I said and ask yourself why you moved to the country in the first place, *if* you were happy."

"I know one thing. I wasn't as unhappy as I am now. And that's why I have to leave."

"What about Jackson. What will you tell him and when?" Clair sat back in her chair, a resigned expression on her face.

"I'm going to write him a letter. I think that would be better for both of us." Lauren frowned at Clair's gaze. They stared, neither one saying a word.

"*A letter*? You're going to tell him in a letter?" Clair ducked her head and studied her perfect nails. "Do you remember that I had a painting for you?" Clair glanced up and laid her napkin on the table and prepared to stand.

"Yes. You were about to give it to me the other evening, but we got sidetracked and you never did."

"I brought it with me. I wanted to be with you when I gave it to you. I didn't leave it in case you found it after I'd gone. Stay here, I'll get it."

This pleasant turn in the conversation encouraged Lauren to breath easier. Clair appeared ready to drop the lecture. She would eventually see this was the best for all concerned.

Clair returned with a medium size canvas in her hands. It faced her body. She held it up and studied it for a moment before asking, "Are you ready?"

Lauren smiled and sat on the edge of her chair. "Of course I'm ready, show me."

Clair turned the painting.

Lauren stared at it for a long time before she raised her eyes to Clair's and brushed at the tears that started without warning. "Those were truly some of the happiest days of my life." Lauren stood and took the few steps to Clair. Taking the canvas in her hands, she said, "When did you do this? I never suspected."

"I started it one of the days we painted on the beach. I believe I worked on it about three days total before getting sidetracked. I finished the background from memory a couple of months ago."

"I had my tenth birthday that summer. The summer I learned about sand burrs." They laughed, remembering her misery over the burrs.

They continued to study the painting of a young girl on a beach. Dressed in white shorts and a baggy white shirt with sleeves rolled up past her elbows, she stood at a child's easel. Clair had captured the day—clear blue water, warm sun, and the little artist with a serious expression. As the child painted, the ocean breeze teased the long dark ponytail that glistened with golden highlights.

Lauren sighed. "You loaned me your shirt. I loved wearing it."

"Yes. I remember giving it to you for a smock."

"I kept it until it became threads. I can still feel the breeze and hear the waves lapping."

"Well, It's an old memory, a good memory. Take it with you. Since you insist on hanging onto the bad memories at least you'll have this good one too."

Lauren put her arm around Clair and hugged her. "Thank you, so much. I love it."

"You're welcome, dear."

"Clair, please try to see—"

"It's okay, Lauren, I don't understand, but I don't have to." She waved her hand in dismissal. "We each have to do what we think best. When do you plan on leaving?" At the table once more, Clair refreshed their coffee.

"Today. I called Mrs. Wilkes yesterday after you left, and asked if she could take care of Winslow until I got home. I called her again this morning and made arrangements for her to keep him until I send for him. She seemed happy to do that."

Clair's cup wobbled and clattered as she dropped it back on the saucer. "Today? How can you even be *ready* to leave today?"

"I'll ask Thelma to ship—"

"Lauren—please! Take at least a week or two and re-think this. I have a feeling you'll regret it, maybe not next week or next month, but the time will come when you will.

"You may be right. But as you just said, we have to do what we think is best, and I think this is best for the long term." She stood. "Thank you for breakfast. I'm going to head on to the airport." She picked up the canvas. "May I leave this in your safekeeping a while longer?"

"Yes, of course I'll keep it. What about clothes, shoes? Take some of my things. I need them out of my closet anyway." Clair had stood also.

"I have plenty of clothes at the villa. I'll be okay once I get back to Italy." She went to hug Clair. "I'm assuming I may stay at the villa in my old room?"

"Of course, silly girl. You have your key. I'll run out frequently and check on things in Valley Ridge. I've grown very fond of that little town."

"I know. So did I. You'll be going out now and then to restock the gallery, so feel free to stay at the house."

"Thank you, I will. By the way, did Jackson tell you that Brooke thinks she upset you and caused you to run away?" Clair peered at her. "You might want to write her a letter too," she added, her voice laced with sarcasm.

Lauren felt the blood drain from her face, her knees weakened. "He told you that? Well, it *was* because of Brooke. I just lost it when I thought something had happened to her. But it wasn't her fault ... I ... I can't explain what happened."

"Oh, you know how children are, *sometimes they get an idea stuck in their head ...* " She glanced sidelong at Lauren to drive her point home. They walked to the door. Clair hugged her tight. "You know I love you."

"Yes. I know. I love you, too. Thank you for everything," she whispered before hurrying away to the elevator. She didn't want Clair to see that her chest had tightened until she could hardly breath.

Alone in the elevator she gulped air. She fought back tears, struggling to swallow sobs that lodged in her throat. Sounds, harsh and strangled, rose from deep within.

Several floors later an older woman got on the elevator. Lauren couldn't control the heaving. The woman glanced at her several times before asking if she was okay. Lauren nodded and got off at the next floor. She worked her way to the ground floor and hurried to the front desk and asked the concierge to have the valet bring her vehicle around.

She had booked her flight first thing that morning after awaking. She didn't want Jackson trying to stop her, knowing that Clair would call him immediately. Departure was eleven forty-five.

Questions and accusations dogged her thoughts. She hummed a mindless medley of tunes to drown out the noise. But it didn't work this time. Questions hammered away in her head. What had she done to Brooke? Who would explain to her? How could she forget the only man she had ever truly loved?

The voice from her heart told her it would be impossible. But the voice in her head whispered that she didn't have a choice.

 ew Puppy

JACKSON PAID the fees and made a sizable donation to the shelter and stuck his wallet back in his pocket. The plan was to present the puppy to Brooke first thing the next morning. Explaining the situation to the lady in charge at the shelter, he persuaded her to allow him to pick the puppy up the next morning, even though it was Sunday. A worker would meet him there.

He promised to be waiting at the door at seven o'clock sharp. With Brooke's puppy safely on hold, he headed home to spend some time with her before dressing to attend the dinner party alone. It was going to be a long evening.

Next morning as he had promised the shelter, he arrived on time ready to take possession of Winslow's look-a-like. Setting in the truck with the puppy on his lap, Jackson wished he had thought to buy a crate. "I don't think the seatbelt will work for you." The puppy looked up at Jackson and tilted his head first one way and then another as if also considering the situation.

They managed to get home without a problem. Opening the kitchen door Jackson hesitated, listening for sounds of his aunt or Brooke. Halfway up the stairs he heard the murmuring of voices. Quietly he moved toward Brooke's bedroom, he hesitated outside the door, their voices carried in low conversation.

"But it *was* my fault Aunt Willa." Brooke sounded close to tears. "I left when Lauren started talking to the puppy that looked like Winslow. She said we couldn't have but one dog. But Dad said we had room for lots of dogs. She wouldn't believe me. I walked away and that's why Lauren got mad and left too." Brooke sat in the middle of her bed twisting a corner of her blanket.

"Brooke, Lauren didn't get mad. She became worried when she couldn't find—"

"Are you girls ready for a surprise?" Jackson backed into the room, talking over his shoulder as he went. They looked at each other, and Brooke brushed her hand across her eyes and lowered her head.

"You better tell me if you want to see my surprise."

"I'm ready for a surprise if Brooke is," Aunt Willa said.

Brooke hung her head even lower and her hands grew still in her lap.

"Well you can show me, Jackson. Brooke doesn't have to look. She can shut her eyes, or turn her head away."

"Good idea. Is your head turned, Pumpkin?" He peeped to see her head drop still lower, her chin almost on her chest.

"Okay, Aunt Willa, hold out your hands." He kept his gaze on Brooke as he placed the black and white fur ball into his aunt's hands. Aunt Willa held the puppy in her lap, stroking the small head.

Brooke peeked, and when she saw the puppy, her head jerked up. "Dad! That's the one Lauren wanted!" Her dark eyes lit up. The puppy scrambled from Aunt Willa's lap, and headed toward Brooke. "Look, Dad, he likes me!" She hugged the puppy, burying her face in its softness. "I have to name him. I wish Lauren was here to help me." She put her face to the pup's head and brushed her mouth against him.

Aunt Willa and Jackson exchanged relieved glances.

Jackson cleared his throat. "There's only one problem, Pumpkin. *He's* not a him, *he's* a little girl, like you." His heart swelled when she raised her face to him.

"Oh, I'll call her Winnie!" At that moment Winnie turned in her lap and put both paws on Brooke's chest and licked her in the face. "She likes her new name!" Brooke squealed with laughter.

Aunt Willa glanced at Jackson, a pleased, relieved expression on her face as she stood. "I guess I'd better go add puppy chow to my grocery list."

"The shelter sent a small bag home with Winnie. The pet store next door donates a bag to new parents."

"Dad, can I keep Winnie in my room?" She hugged Winnie tighter, gazing at Jackson over the puppy's head.

"You *may* keep her in your room until we get moved. I'll get Winnie a crate."

He heard Aunt Willa smirk when she passed him on the way out. She called back over her shoulder. "It won't be long before time to dress for church—don't forget."

"I won't, Aunt Willa," Brooke promised.

Jackson's cell phone rang. Winnie's ears perked up and she barked, sending Brooke into a fit of giggles.

"Excuse me ladies, I'll take this scary thing to my room and leave you two to get acquainted." He and Brooke laughed as Winnie looked from one to the other, tilting her head from side to side.

"She's just like Winslow!" Brooke fell back on her bed with Winnie in a tight embrace.

Jackson's insides tightened at Clair's name on the screen. He started down the hall to his room. "Hello."

"I have bad news, Jackson. And there's no easy way to tell you. Lauren's gone back to Italy."

"What do you mean, gone back to Italy? I thought Lauren lived in New York. I don't understand. Why has she gone there?" He gripped the phone as he closed the door to his room.

"She's as much at home in Italy and France as she is in New York. Anyway, she's gone there now mainly because it's a long way from you and Brooke."

"I'm at a total loss here—Lauren loves Brooke. And I think she loves me, at least she told me she did. Why would she tell me she loved me and then cross the continent to get away from me? When did she leave?"

"That's what we need to talk about. She left early today. I'm not surprised that she left, just that it was so sudden. I wanted to let you know. I'm sorry, Jackson."

"Clair, do you have some time tomorrow? I'll drive to the city if you do. I need to understand what's going on. Will she be safe where she's going?"

"Oh yes, she's safe and well looked after. I'm free tomorrow. Come to the Belmont. We'll talk."

"Thank you. And Clair, if Lauren *has* changed her mind about me, I'll accept that. I wouldn't want her to stay if she didn't want to."

Clair sighed. "I won't try to give you false hope, but you may have to accept that fact in the end."

Suddenly, hollowness caved his stomach and weakened his legs. He sat on the edge of his bed. "I understand. I'll be there. Just tell me when."

"Come for breakfast. You'll have to leave early, but I figure you will be up early one way or the other."

"I'll come early, but breakfast isn't necessary."

"Breakfast will be ready at eight o'clock."

"Yes, Ma'am. I can hear my mother or Aunt Willa saying the same thing. Thanks, Clair. I'll be there."

"I'll be waiting. And Jackson—did you get the puppy?"

"Yes, I did. Brooke's happily mothering the little thing to death as we speak." He heard Clair's laughter and gave thanks they had *something* to laugh about.

"That's wonderful. I'm so glad. See you tomorrow."

He searched his mind, trying to make some sense of the last twenty-four hours. What had he said or done to cause Lauren to run from him? What had happened? He stood and hurried into the hall, pausing to listen for sounds from Brooke's room. Hearing her chattering to Winnie, he continued down the stairs to the kitchen.

"Aunt Willa, I'll be leaving very early in the morning for New York. Will you get Brooke to school and back?"

"Of course, I will," she said.

"Don't forget to send lunch money." He glanced to see her patronizing expression and hurried to earn points back. "I'm going to see Clair. She's known Lauren since she was eight. I need to talk with her and try to figure out what happened at the shelter yesterday."

"I think that's a wise plan. But since you'll be here tonight, I'm making you a healthy dinner, tilapia with grilled vegetables." Her no-nonsense glare quelled objections to her going to a lot of trouble.

"I'll look forward to it." He grinned at her relieved expression.

Willa puttered about. She had something on her mind. Jackson let her take her time bringing it up.

"Whatever happens, Jackson, you'll be all right. Lauren may have realized something about herself. Sometimes the weight of responsibility for a child can be scary." She glanced up at him. "And we tend to run from our fears just like we run from our grief." She sighed.

True. He could write a book about running from grief. "But *I alone* bear the responsibility for Brooke."

She sighed and might as well have added, *you men.* "I know that. But if she loves you in the best sense, she would not only *want* to share your responsibilities, she would *expect* to share them. She loves Brooke."

He walked around the island to where she stood folding clean tea towels. "What would I do without you?"

She laughed and pushed him away from the towel drawer where she stacked the clean towels inside. "Just take care of yourself for Brooke and me, promise?"

"That's what I'm trying to do, Aunt Willa."

He wanted to have a life again, and all because of Lauren, this lively and beautiful person. But how could he explain that to his aunt? How could he explain something that he didn't understand himself? Lauren had unknowingly helped him face his grief.

Would he be able to help her face her fears?

CHAPTER 38

he Villa

LAUREN TRAILED THROUGH THE VILLA. She loved this place and had from the first time Clair brought her here. But it seemed changed. Or was it her that had changed? She opened the wide shutters that closed off the view of the street and the front courtyard below.

As far as villas go, Clair's could be considered small, with just three bedrooms upstairs, each with a private bath.

A large open sitting room with comfortable furnishings connected the bedrooms without wasted space of hallways. French doors opened across the back of the airy sitting room onto the veranda. Ancient trees grew from ground level to shade the upper veranda.

The lower level consisted of a large foyer and great room with a formal dining room at one end. The ample kitchen angled off to the right side of the dining room. The master suite occupied the entire left side of the lower level, just off the great room.

Lauren turned from the window at a sound from downstairs. Mrs. Armato? She ran to the stairs and raced down. Flying into the large kitchen, she startled the short, pretty, dark haired woman. "Maria! When I heard you come in, I expected your mother." She hugged Maria and stepped back. "Sorry to scare you."

"No problem, Miss Lauren—what surprise! When you get here?" She studied Lauren's face. "Miss Clair, too? You should let me know! I would shopped for all your favorites, already."

"Maria—it's okay. Clair's not with me ... I'm alone." Lauren reached for a shopping bag and placed it with the others on the worktable.

Alone. Tears threatened.

Maria took her arm and turned her to the light. "You don't look so good, Miss Lauren. No? You ill?"

She shook Lauren gently.

"Goodness no. I'm just tired from a long trip. Where's your mother?" Lauren blinked her eyes dry and turned away from Maria. Reaching for the teapot she set it to warming.

"It's Papa. He not feeling so good, so, I help out to see him get better."

"Oh, Maria, I'm sorry to hear that, will he be all right?"

"Papa is old, some days good, some days bad." She sighed heavily and went back to putting the food away.

Lauren waved a hand at the supplies. "Does Clair have guests?"

"Yes. Young people; people of her father's. I think from New York." Maria busied about.

Lauren's stomach tightened. They must be clients of Charlie's. Please don't let it be someone she knows. "Who is it?"

"The name, David and Caroline Wheeler, yes?"

Maria wasn't familiar with their names and Lauren didn't recognize them either. She relaxed and poured two cups of tea.

"Maria, join me in a cup of tea, and then I'll help you prepare dinner."

"Tea is lovely, I have a cup, but dinner much later." she tapped her wristwatch. "Dinner, eight o'clock." She reached for the tea that Lauren pushed toward her.

Lauren glanced at Maria. "Any particular reason why so late? Americans usually eat earlier."

Maria shook her head. "Who could say, eh? Honeymoon, probably they see all Italy in one week."

Lauren shared a laugh with Maria, but a week in the villa with newlyweds didn't exactly fit the picture of the peace and quiet she'd looked forward to. When her cell rang, she glanced at it, hesitated and considered not answering it.

"Excuse me, Maria." Lauren took her phone and went to stand by the open kitchen door. "Hello, Clair."

"I see you made it. Is everything okay at the villa?"

"Oh, yes. It's so wonderful to be back. I hadn't realized how much I miss this country when I'm away from here." Lauren forced excitement into her voice.

"Oh, that's wonderful. Is Mrs. Armato there?"

"Maria is here now. Her father's doing poorly and her mother is with him, so she's filling in." Lauren gripped the phone.

"Oh, I'm sorry to hear that. Well, I just wanted to make sure you got there. I'm glad you're excited to be back in Italy. Don't work too hard and send me pictures of what you're painting. I'll talk with you later, bye dear."

Ending the call, Lauren stood quietly. There had been no mention of Brooke or Jackson. Did he manage to get Brooke the puppy? She longed to be in Valley Ridge with Brooke and Winslow. And Jackson.

"Maria, will you excuse me? I haven't unpacked yet and I'm very tired." She headed to the door. Maria didn't know that Lauren had arrived with nothing to unpack.

"Yes, yes Miss Lauren. Take your tea." Maria carried the cup of tea to her.

"Thank you, Maria," she mumbled and hurried upstairs.

* * *

MOMENTS LATER MARIA answered the kitchen phone. "Yes, yes?"

"Maria, this is Clair. Don't let Lauren know you're speaking with me. Can you talk?"

Maria lowered her voice. "I can talk, yes, Miss Clair. Miss Lauren went to her room."

"Good. Is she okay? I mean, does she seem her normal self?" Clair would have to confide in Maria. "I can't go into everything now, Maria, but my little friend is very unhappy and she may put on a front to fool you. But all is not well with her."

"I see, I see her front it not so good. She had tears on her phone."

"She did? Wonderful! I have things to do here, but keep me informed as to what she's doing. I know you and your mother will take good care of her."

"Yes, Miss Clair, we take good care of Miss Lauren. No to worry."

"Lauren said your dad wasn't well, will he be all right soon?" Clair had come to love this family over the years.

"Mama and me take good care of Papa too, but he is old, we shall see."

"If there's anything you need, Maria, all you have to do is call."

"Yes, Miss Clair, I know. Thank you, and no to worry."

Clair could see Maria nodding and dabbing her eyes.

"Bye for now, tell your mama and papa hello for me. I'll keep in touch." Clair finished the call to Maria and looked at the time. It was afternoon in Florence, but Jackson would be at her door any minute for breakfast. She was prepared to explain things to Jackson about Lauren's past as clearly as she knew how.

Minutes later the door chimes sounded. She took a deep breath and went to answer it.

"Good morning, Jackson, come in." She motioned him into the room. "For such a handsome man, you look awful."

He laughed and shrugged, running his hand through his hair. "I hope I don't look as bad as I feel."

Clair slid her arm through his and led him to the terrace where the table set ready. "Have a seat." She released his arm and touched a button on an intercom. "Mrs. Barton, this is Clair Weston, I'm ready for my breakfast order—and send plenty of coffee, please. Thank you." She glanced at Jackson. "I just spoke with Lauren earlier."

"She's okay?"

"She's fine. It's late afternoon there. I didn't mention that we were having breakfast. She needs to feel the sting of separation." She glanced up. "You needn't look at me like that. I'm not mean, I just know Lauren." She smiled at him and pushed a speaker button on the wall above the table when the door buzzer sounded. "The door is open, come in."

"Not for a minute did I think you were mean. I know better. It's just that *I'm* feeling that sting of separation you mentioned."

"I'm sorry. You may have to get used to the feeling until it goes away. I just want you to know that whatever happens, you're the first man she's shed tears over."

Jackson waited until the server had placed their food on the table and left before he spoke. "That's a good sign, I guess. I'll accept Lauren's decision, whatever. But I would like to know why she rejected me and maybe even understand it." He took the coffee she poured for him.

"Lauren lost her father when she was four. He died in an acci-dent in their apple orchard as Lauren sat playing close by. Her mother hated the weekend farm, but she worshiped Lauren's father. Immediately after he died, she sold the place and moved back to New York. She went to work in one of their friends' law office. She became a bitter woman and never stopped grieving. She never forgave Lauren's father for the accident that took his life."

"How awful for a little child. What kind of accident?" Jackson pushed the food around on his plate.

"A freak accident. He fell from a ladder while pruning a dead limb from an apple tree." Clair gazed thoughtfully into her coffee. "Lauren might as well have lost her mother too, for all practical purposes."

"I know that had to be hard on her, but lots of children lose a parent and still grow up to function normally. Brooke is very well adjusted, don't you think?"

"Oh yes, I agree, and Brooke is very well adjusted. But Brooke still had one caring, loving parent and your aunt to love her. Lauren's mother turned inward. She loved Lauren, but she became preoccupied with work. I met Lauren and her mother when Lauren was eight."

Jackson glanced at Clair. "Let me guess. The mother's own grief consumed her to the point that she forgot about Lauren and her grief? I almost did that to Brooke." He sipped the hot coffee. "Matt helped me see what I was doing."

"Well, be thankful for Matt." Clair smiled across the table at him.

"I was then, and I still am. Being thankful for Matt is as consistent as brushing my teeth." He gave the semblance of a grin, only to sober again moments later. "So you believe she's holding onto something from her father's death?"

"Not necessarily, but possibly. I just wanted you to know that Lauren had a rocky start."

Jackson gazed at Clair. "Too bad her mother had to work, Lauren might have done better if not for that."

"Her mother didn't have to work. Elizabeth Sara Collins chose to work. She held an esteemed position as an attorney, same as Lauren's father. She loved what she did. She also came from a very wealthy family, as did Lauren's father. Lauren's mother worked six days a week. My father was friends with one of the attorneys Elizabeth worked with." Clair leaned back and sipped her coffee. "I guess long hours at work was her way of coping."

"Clair, tell me what happened to Lauren. If not her father's death, then what?" He laid his napkin down and leaned back from the table.

Clair studied him for a moment. "The townhouse where Lauren and her mother lived was an exclusive complex. My father rented one of the smaller townhouses there for me when I turned eighteen. How Lauren's neighbor, a young single mother of two little girls, came to be living there I don't know. The mother worked from home, doing paperwork for a business downtown. She picked up her work every other day.

Lauren and the oldest of the girls became friends. Lauren might have been two years older than the girl—Debbie, Dede, something like that. I understood that the young mother had asked Lauren's mother if her daughter could call on Lauren if the girls needed anything in the time she had to be gone every other day." Clair continued as Jackson listened solemnly. "The day I met Lauren was the day I moved into my new place. She sat on the front steps of the townhouse and watched me park. I introduced myself and asked her if she would like to have a Coke with me. I realized later that I shouldn't have done that—being a stranger to her."

"She accepted your offer of a Coke?" Jackson sat quiet, his expression intent.

"Yes. We went merrily off to my place three or four doors down, I don't remember. But while she was in my apartment, the eldest of the two little sisters knocked and knocked on Lauren's door, needing help, we learned later." Clair brushed at her eyes and paused for a moment before going on. "It seems that the younger child had choked on a raisin and her sister ran to Lauren for help. By the time the young mother arrived back home, it was too late."

Jackson slowly shook his head. "And Lauren wasn't where she was supposed to be. She didn't know what had happened." He spoke softly. "A terrible accident to be sure, but Lauren was a child, she couldn't have been held responsible, or have done anything."

"Of course not. But the distraught mother blamed Lauren. She was the oldest of the girls and would have probably thought to call 911. But Lauren and I didn't know anything until we heard the commotion in the hall. The police were there. An ambulance came. When we went into the hall, the mother became hysterical." Clair paused. "She screamed at Lauren that she should have been there, that she was an irresponsible girl and that she should have been watching them, which wasn't true. Lauren didn't babysit the girls."

Clair sighed. Reliving the memory brought the pain back. "Someone called Lauren's mother from work. She arrived on the scene and reprimanded Lauren severely for being out of their townhouse. She shamed her for being irresponsible." Clair paused for a moment. "Mrs. Ashby tried to console the young mother, but the woman continued screaming accusations at Lauren, who cowered, terrified at my side. I finally got permission from her mother to take Lauren back to my place." Clair looked at Jackson. "She was physically ill the rest of that day. It was a full year before she began to get over it. I made friends with Lauren's mother, and I gave Lauren art lessons so that I could spend time with her."

"What happened to the woman and the other child?"

"They moved away."

Jackson shuddered and pushed his hand through his hair. "Poor little children. All three of them." He looked at Clair. "You were just a child yourself, Clair."

"I know. Lauren and I both grew up a little that day."

"I can see that Lauren would be traumatized, but I would think she would still want a safe, happy home. Why is she running from what Brooke and I represent?"

"People react differently. All I know is that Lauren avoids any close attachment that makes her responsible, for another person's well being. Her mother rode her daily about responsibility. I often thought that Lauren's mother punished Lauren for the accident that took her husband's life—I think she thought he was irresponsible because of the farm and she never let up on Lauren."

"Poor Lauren. But I would never expect her to be responsible for Brooke—"

"Jackson, love and responsibility go hand in hand."

"That's what Aunt Willa said. Did Lauren not have counseling?"

"No. Her mother didn't believe in it. I tried talking to her about it more than once. She informed me that all Lauren needed was to take her responsibilities seriously."

Clair rang for a busboy to clear their things. She rose from the table and walked to the rail of the terrace and stood quietly looking down. She turned to Jackson as he stepped to her side. "I told you I spoke to Lauren just before you got here." Clair touched his arm. "She's miserable, Jackson. My housekeeper told me so."

He began to pace and rub the back of his neck. "I had already planned to go to her. I have to make her see—" He grinned at Clair. "I'll take my advantage with me, Miss Brooke. Can you tell me where she's staying?"

Clair was already scribbling on a card. She looked up and smiled. "I figured you'd say that." She handed him the card. "But Jackson, just be prepared for the worst."

Jackson nodded, thanked Clair, gave her a hug and started toward her door. "Oh, and Clair, don't let her know we're coming." He hurried out the door.

Jackson stuck his head back in the door. "Could you tell me the name of the café where you painted Lauren?"

Clair ran to grab another card and scribbled more directions. She hurried back to Jackson with the card.

"It's just down the street from the villa. Good luck, and call me!"

CHAPTER 39

 esolved

LAUREN MADE it to her room before the flood of tears broke. She threw herself across the bed and cried her miserable heart out until sleep overcame her weariness.

Hours later the murmur of conversation drifting up from below the open window awakened her. Disoriented, Lauren lay still wondering who would be talking outside her window. Gradually she focused on the soft-turquoise shutters and remembered that she lay crumpled on her bed in the villa.

Suddenly an overwhelming longing for Winslow wrenched her heart. First thing tomorrow morning she would send for him.

Struggling up from the bed, she looked down from her window. The newlyweds were trying to put the top down on one of the tiny cars that tourist rent. The couple laughed softly, touching hands, they were happy and carefree. They had the rest of their lives together to make memories. Lauren watched them and thought about the carefree times she could remember. The beach house in Connecticut, the villa, and the summers in France and Spain with Clair's family were the only carefree times she could recall.

Oh, how she needed to talk with Clair. But she wouldn't call for fear of inquiring about Brooke and Jackson. How could she break the ties if she stayed on the phone asking about them? Tomorrow morning she would make arrangements for Winslow and she'd write her letters to Jackson and Brooke.

Her stomach grumbled; reminding her she hadn't eaten all day. She piled her hair into a loose twist on top of her head and straightening her shirt, headed downstairs. The kitchen was quiet. She hesitated; surprised that Maria sat at the long wooden table reading.

"Miss Lauren, you have nice nap? Your body need rest." She closed her book and going to the big iron stove, she retrieved a plate from the warming oven and put it on a place setting on the table. "Don't mind in kitchen?"

"I don't mind at all. I like it best in here." Lauren smiled at Maria and settled herself at the informal table. "Maria, this looks wonderful, but I hope you didn't stay late just because of me? I can wait on myself, you go home and relax awhile before bedtime."

"No, no, I serve the young people. Besides, what to do at home? My cat—that is all." She put the teapot on and got two cups ready.

"Oh, Maria, I know you miss your husband. I'm sorry." Lauren felt Maria's sadness. She wanted to cry for Maria, as well as for any and everything else.

"Always, I miss him. But I have many years good memories I think on still."

"Yes, I'm sure you do." Lauren stared at her plate unseeing. Maria had years of good memories to think on, while some of

Lauren's best memories were less than three months old. At twenty-six years old, her best memories were brand new.

"Miss Lauren, you okay?"

Lauren nodded, afraid to speak.

"I get you something else—"

"No, Maria, the food is delicious, it's just me. I don't know what's the matter … jet lag I suppose. I have a busy day tomorrow. I think I'll just take some cheese and bread and turn in."

"Yes, milk and cookies too, you get hungry later." Maria had the snack ready before Lauren was barely up from the table.

"Thank you, and don't make breakfast for me in the morning, I'll be going out early. Good night."

"Good night, Miss Lauren."

Lauren dragged her body upstairs. She hesitated at the bedroom door. Sounds from downstairs drifted up. Was Maria on the phone? Probably calling her mother to check on her dad.

* * *

THE GOOD NIGHTS sleep with open windows had improved her outlook. With new resolve to move forward and no looking back, she choked down the urge to cry.

Dressed casually and for comfort, she made sure she had the phone numbers to make Winslow's arrangements. She found paper, pen, and stamps. She had everything needed to write her letters. The writing supplies fit nicely into an old tote she'd found in her closet.

Coming into the kitchen she greeted Maria, "Good morning. I'll be gone for several hours."

"Morning, Miss Lauren, where … you go?"

Maria or her mother had never asked any of them about their daily activities. Caught off guard Lauren stammered, "No … no nowhere special."

Maria flushed. Her embarrassment compelled Lauren to explain further.

"I'm just going to the Café. The one at the end of the street ... the one where Clair and I always go, you know, the one with the striped umbrellas."

Maria's face grew even more red, her eyes widening as she nodded rapidly.

Making an awkward exit out the open door, Lauren glanced back to see Maria reaching for the wall phone. What *was* the matter with her? With a puzzled shrug, she bit into the apple she'd picked up as she passed the fruit bowl.

At the end of the street she slowed her pace, her gaze taking in the sidewalk café. They couldn't be the same, but the colorful umbrellas looked just as they had the first time she saw them. The trees were bigger and the awnings a little faded, but everything else stayed as always.

Settling her things on a table in *their* corner of the outdoor café, Lauren set about the purpose of writing letters. Her mind wandered to the painting that Clair had done of her sitting at this table—the one Jackson had bought. Lauren hugged her arms to the soft white blouse similar to the one she'd worn in the painting.

She reached up on an impulse and loosened her hair. Shaking her head and freeing her hair, the breeze lifted it away from her face. With her elbows on the table, fingers laced, she closed her eyes and propped her chin on her hands.

Lauren recalled Jackson's expression when he first saw the painting. She sighed; this would not help her forget him. She drifted deeper into thought.

"I love the painting, but I love the real thing more."

She heard his voice. The voice she loved. Lauren sighed, she must be going mad. How would she ever forget him? "I miss you, Jackson," she murmured.

"I've missed you too, Lauren."

Lauren's eyes flew open. Jackson stood in front of her with his hands in his pockets. Her face grew warm as a flush spread upward. She held her hands to her cheeks and tried not to gape.

"May I join you?" He ran a hand through his hair and waited for her invitation.

"Yes, of course—what—what *are* you doing here?" She wanted to laugh and cry at the same time.

"I just told you. I miss you. Valley Ridge is not the same with you in Italy. It's been raining ever since you left. The sun refuses to shine." He smiled into her eyes. "I'm not teasing." He pulled out one of the chairs and sat across from her.

"Oh, Jackson, you shouldn't have come." She lowered her face for a second then looked back up. "Did you get Brooke a puppy?"

"Not *a* puppy, *the* puppy. I didn't send you a photo because I knew I was coming to see you, and I'd rather Brooke tell you all about the puppy." He raised his hand and motioned. Brooke stepped from behind a large pot of shrubbery, hesitant at first.

Lauren stared past Jackson, not believing her eyes as she clasped her hands. "Brooke!" She jumped from her chair, stretching out her arms. Brooke flew into them. They hugged and laughed as Lauren lifted Brooke off her feet.

"Lauren, my puppy is a girl! And she's staying in my room until we move to the country."

Lauren sat down with Brooke clinging to her. She brushed Brooke's hair back from her face. "You have a girl puppy? What did you name her?"

Jackson pushed a chair nearer to Lauren for Brooke to sit on.

"Winnie. She likes it too." Brooke dragged the chair closer to Lauren's.

"That's perfect!" Lauren laughed, delighted with the name. "Did your dad help you pick it?" She glanced at Jackson.

Jackson shook his head. "Not one bit. She had Winnie picked out before Aunt Willa and I could utter a word."

"Lauren gave Brooke another hug. "How did you know where I'd be?" She looked from one to the other.

"Clair helped us. And poor Maria got caught playing middleman." Jackson said.

"Aha, so that's the reason for Maria's odd behavior."

"Yes, I owe Maria an apology." Jackson waved to a waiter. "I have to sample this famous coffee I've heard so much about." Jackson turned to Brooke. "I understand that Maria, our ally, is making cookies this afternoon and she needs help."

Brooke giggled and squirmed in her chair. "I'll help, I like to make cookies."

"Good, I thought you would. I need to talk with Lauren." He reached for Lauren's hand as her gaze met his.

* * *

BROOKE SETTLED HAPPILY into Maria's kitchen and the cookie making got underway. Jackson tucked Lauren's hand through his arm and told her to lead the way. They'd decided on a walking tour while they talked.

"I hope you won't be upset with Clair for talking to me. She thinks the world of you, you know."

"Yes, I know, and I could never get upset with Clair no matter what she did. Clair couldn't *do anything* to upset me." She laughed softly. "Don't worry about it."

"That makes me feel better. I had to know why you left us, and Clair knows you better than anyone else. She explained about your ... ah, reluctance."

"My commitment issues. Goodness, she did tell you everything, didn't she." Lauren glanced briefly at Jackson, her face warming.

"After Clair and I talked, I could see why you might feel the way you do. But Lauren, that's the good part about being with

someone you love, the sharing of things. The burden of responsibility is easier when shared."

"I've never shared my life with anyone except Clair." She
looked down as they strolled along the stone sidewalk.

"You've shared with Winslow." Jackson lifted her hand and
brushed his lips across it.

"Winslow's a dog, that doesn't count." She broke into light
laughter.

"Oh, sure it counts. Compassion is the same no matter who,
or what it's bestowed upon. And you're very responsible for his
care and wellbeing." He nodded his head and pursed his lips
when she questioned with a look.

"How did you get to be so kind and wise?" She leaned
against him.

"I think it happened when I met you. When you kindly let me
off the hook when I … uh, fibbed to Matt about where we met. I
think I knew I loved you in that moment."

"Oh, Jackson." She laughed again. "You intrigued me that day.
It seems like that was a lifetime ago."

They'd strolled for several hours when Lauren pointed to a
café up ahead. "There's a good place to eat when we're ready. The
food is great."

Jackson had her hand in his. He squeezed it. "How about an
early lunch? I haven't had much appetite lately, but suddenly I'm
starved."

"I'm starved too." They gazed at one another.

The food tasted delicious and the small café enveloped them
in its quiet and relaxing mood, they lingered several hours,
talking—without a hint of an argument.

Jackson stood and pulled Lauren to her feet. "Lets walk
some more."

After roaming the narrow streets most of the afternoon, they
ducked into another small café and ordered hot tea and a light

dessert. Jackson took both Lauren's hands in his and studied her face for several long seconds.

"Lauren, do you trust me?" He spoke quietly.

"I ... suppose. What do you mean?"

"Do you trust me as a person. As an honorable man who keeps his word."

"Yes, I do."

"Then come back to Valley Ridge. Marry me."

"Oh, Jackson, I can't. We barely know each other. And it's not you I don't trust. It's me." She sighed. "I've been the way I am all my life, and I'm not a teenager. What if I can't change? What if I won't change?"

"In the first place, I'm not asking you to change. I want us to share our life and future. We'll deal with whatever we have to, together."

"I can't promise to be the wife for you and mother to Brooke that you both deserve. I don't know if I could or not. Let's just enjoy the time you're here."

Jackson leaned back in his chair and rubbed his hand across his face. Weariness slumped his shoulders. "Brooke and I will probably leave first thing tomorrow. I don't want to see Florence in my state of mind. This is Florence, Italy, a city reported best viewed through the haze of love." He gave her a rueful smile. "I had to come try, Lauren. I love you." He stood and offered her his hand. They walked quietly hand in hand.

They arrived back at the villa in a quiet, somber mood. Just outside the door, Jackson hugged Lauren and she returned his embrace before they went inside.

"Mr. Jackson, the little one already sleeps. She play so hard." Maria chuckled.

"Thank you for entertaining her, Maria. I hope she didn't wear you out."

"No, no. Would you like food?" Maria looked from one to the other. "And plenty cookies." She chuckled.

"No, thank you, Maria, we've had dinner." Lauren answered for both of them after glancing at Jackson. "You go on home, and thank you again for keeping an eye on Brooke." Lauren gave her a parting hug.

Jackson glanced around the large kitchen. "It was nice of Clair to put Brooke and me up here in the villa. It's a great place." He sighed, pushing a hand through his hair. "I'll call tonight and make arrangements to leave first thing in the morning."

"Jackson, please, since you're already here, stay and see Florence. Brooke is excited to be here, let her see the city." Lauren stood close.

Jackson pulled her into his arms. "Brooke is excited to be here only because you are here."

She looked up at him. "Is that not reason enough?"

"The sooner Brooke and I get back to our lives, back to Valley Ridge, me to my work and her to the new puppy, the better." He breathed deeply, his shoulders broadening.

Lauren stepped away from him. "I love you both, you know that?"

"Yes, I believe you do. Just not enough to fight for us." They stared into each other's eyes for what seemed an eternity.

Blinded by hot tears, Lauren turned and fled up the stairs to the safety of her bedroom

CHAPTER 40

𝒶 lone Again

JACKSON TOSSED the magazine aside and glanced at his sleeping daughter. Brooke had been especially quiet in the taxi on the way to the airport. He worried about her attachment to Lauren, the main reason he hadn't lingered in Florence. To allow their friendship to deepen would just make it more difficult for Brooke. It would be bad enough already.

She'd been calm when they left early without seeing Lauren. He'd expected a hundred questions. Her quietness was puzzling.

Jackson put his head back and closed his eyes. The plane engines droned, numbing his mind, just not completely. The image of Lauren, her eyes brimming with tears before she fled up the stairs, played over and over in his head.

"Daddy, can I have some juice? I'm thirsty." Brooke rubbed her eyes and pushed onto the corner of his seat.

First class had comfortable reclining seats, he put his forward and slid his arm around Brooke and pulled her close. "Yes, you *may* have some juice. Are you hungry too? Would you like a sandwich?" He squeezed her tight and pulled her deeper into the wide chair at his side.

"No, sir. Just thirsty." She spoke softly as she wallowed against him pushing her face into his chest.

Jackson pressed the call button for a stewardess. He placed an order for drinks, a sandwich and fruit just in case. While they waited he reclined the chair and clung to Brooke, whether to comfort her, or himself he wasn't sure.

Once they landed in New York they took a shuttle to where the Dodge waited. Jackson threw their bags in the back and climbed in beside Brooke. "I have an idea, Pumpkin." He looked sideways at Brooke.

"What? What, Dad?" She began to smile.

"I've been thinking. We need a new vehicle and this old truck needs a rest. Since the long layover from Italy put us back in the afternoon what do you say we go car shopping?"

"Yes, Dad! Can we get one like Lauren's?" Her eyes brightened for the first time since they'd left Florence.

"You think we need one like Lauren's? Well, I kind of like the Range Rover myself. Lets go look at one."

"We could take Winnie and Winslow both in our new car, Dad." She smiled and clapped her hands.

Jackson let it pass that Winslow wouldn't be hanging out with Winnie. No point in going there yet.

Brooke's expression grew thoughtful as she looked at her dad. "What will you do with our truck if we buy a new car?"

He looked over and shrugged. "We'll keep it. I'll have it delivered to the house."

That answer seemed to satisfy.

"We'll have a surprise for Lauren when she comes home, won't we Dad?" Brooke giggled at the prospect.

"Brooke, honey, don't be disappointed if Lauren doesn't come back to Valley Ridge. She's happy living in Clair's villa. We want her to be happy, don't we?"

She ignored his question and turned to look out the window.

His nerves tightened. "Did I tell you we should be ready to move to the country house any time now?"

"We will? When? Tomorrow?" She turned and squinted at him.

Jackson laughed. "Tomorrow might be a bit soon. We have to line up the movers and Aunt Willa will need time to pack her personal things. Maybe by the end of the week."

"Okay. I can't wait to see Winnie. I missed her." She looked at Jackson with wide eyes, blinking hard.

"I'm sure she missed you too. As a matter of fact you better be careful when we get home." He gave her a serious look.

"Why?" Brooke returned his wide-eyed expression.

"Why? Winnie just may be so excited to see you, she might lick your nose right off your face."

Brooke burst into a fit of giggles and put her hand to her nose. "Dad-d-d, dogs can't lick your nose off!"

"I don't know … you've just never seen a dog that excited." He slowed the truck. "Here's the dealership. My, my, look at the colors. And we have to pick just one?"

They looked at each other. Brooke pulled a face and Jackson mocked her expression as he parked the truck.

* * *

As they approached Valley Ridge, Jackson reached for his phone. "Aunt Willa, we're almost home. We have a surprise. Stand at the kitchen window and watch for us."

"What do you mean, *you're almost home?*"

He held the phone away from his ear and winked at Brooke— he pulled the phone back and said, "I'll explain everything when I get there."

Aunt Willa did better than stand at the window. She had walked out and was standing by the driveway when the bright-red Range Rover slowed, turned in and Jackson parked on the drive.

"Oh, my goodness! What a pretty thing! I must say you look very snappy driving that, Jackson."

Brooke ran and wrapped her arms around her great aunt. "I missed you, Aunt Willa!"

"Mercy child, you haven't been gone long enough to miss me." Aunt Willa returned Brooke's hug, and looked to Jackson. "It was about time you got rid of that relic. I'm proud of you."

Jackson hugged her. "Oh, I didn't get rid of it, just retired it from active duty. And before you comment on the color, Brooke picked it."

Brooke beamed proudly. "Do you like it, Aunt Willa?"

"I think red is beautiful. I'd have been disappointed in any other." She led them into the house. "I haven't shopped for food, not expecting you two to be here."

"I don't imagine that either of us could eat anything. We had food on the plane. We're mostly just tired. Brooke needs to get her bath and go straight to bed."

Jackson looked around. "Speaking of Brooke, where did she fly off to?"

"You didn't see her scoop Winnie up and scuttle toward the stairs?" Willa smiled and shook her head. "You look awful, Jackson, and why *are* you home?"

"There was no point in staying. And the more Brooke is around Lauren, the more attached she becomes. I thought it best to get her back home, once I knew Lauren wasn't coming back.

"Dad—Lauren *is* coming back. She's coming home!" Brooke clutched Winnie in her arms.

They hadn't heard her pad softly into the room.

Aunt Willa threw a quick glance at Jackson.

"Brooke, come here, sweetie. Remember we talked about how Lauren is happy living in Clair's villa?"

"Yes, sir, I remember. But Lauren will come home. I know she will. She promised me art lessons."

It was his turn to cast a worried glance at his aunt.

Aunt Willa went to Brooke and knelt beside her.

"Dear, what makes you think Lauren will come back?" She put her arm around Brook's waist.

"Lauren's not happy in Clair's villa. She pretends, but she's not." Brooke buried her face in Winnie's warm fur.

Jackson stood and lifted Brooke and Winnie together. "Forget the bath, no school tomorrow. The time change has wiped us out. Brooke and I are closing the blinds and going to bed. We'll talk in the morning." He trooped up the stairs like an old, weary man.

With Brooke settled in her bed and Winnie tucked in beside her, Jackson went to his own room and closed the door. He'd have early coffee with Aunt Willa in the morning and fill her in. He had to call Clair and Matt though. Jackson stretched out on his bed and closed his eyes while he waited for the connection. "Hello, Clair. Yes, I'm back. You were right about Lauren, she's made up her mind to stay in Italy."

"Oh, Jackson, I'm sorry. I have to say, I'm not surprised. She'll regret her choice someday, not that it's any comfort now. Will you be all right?"

"I'll be fine. One thing I learned from Jenna's death, you don't die from heartbreak, it just feels like it."

Clair sighed. "You could consider counseling for yourself, Jackson."

"I'll be fine, it's Brooke I'm worried about. She's insisting that Lauren is coming home. I'd better go, Clair. I just wanted you to know. Thanks for everything."

"Bye, Jackson. I'll see you at gallery in a week or so. We'll talk again."

Jackson decided to wait and talk with Matt at the gallery. He couldn't go another minute without a hot shower. Pretending to be okay for Brooke's benefit had worn him to the bone. He just needed to wallow in self-pity and heartache until he totally disgusted himself.

After showering, he darkened his room and fell into bed, expecting to sleep around the clock. Instead, he tossed and turned until the clock on his night table read 3:20 in the morning. The thought of tossing and turning another three or four hours before time to get up was unendurable.

A walk around the lake was what he needed. Throwing on clothes, he slipped out of the house. The moon was full and bright. Concentrating on the pleasing new leather smell of the Range Rover, he suddenly remembered his rubber boots were still in the truck—at the dealership in New York. He'd have to settle for a stroll in the new gardens instead of around the lake.

Turning onto the drive, Jackson quickly tapped the brake. Partially hidden from the moonlight by the trees, a silver Range Rover was parked outside the closed gate. Eeriness sent blood pounding to his heart and his thoughts racing. This didn't make sense.

His new vehicle crept up the drive and eased to a stop behind the silver Range Rover. Jackson approached it, looking in the windows. Empty. Moving quietly on, he went to the gate and slipped through the narrow side panel. He scanned the dark grounds. Even though a full moon hung above he couldn't see anything. Blinking and straining, his vision slowly adjusted.

"Lauren?" He felt foolish calling her name into the darkness. He'd left her in Florence. Yet her SUV blocked his drive.

"Lauren?" A movement over by the new iron fence sent him toward it. He strained his eyes as he soundlessly moved in that direction. He raised his voice, "Lauren—is that you?"

"Yes, Jackson—it's me."

Jackson barely heard her whisper.

He hurried his step and walking up to her, pushed his hand

through his hair. "Haven't I seen you here before, Miss? This *is* private property. You're trespassing."

"Oh, Jackson." She fell into his arms, trembling and laughing. "I was terrified when I saw the lights. It didn't sound like your truck."

Jackson hugged her tight. "It wasn't my truck. I got goosebumps when I saw the silver Range Rover. I decided that thoughts of you had pushed me over the edge. I had to be dreaming, or going mad."

They clung to each other laughing and talking at the same time, giving kisses between words.

Jackson held her away. "What are you doing here? *How* did you get here? I haven't even been home long."

"From my window I watched you and Brooke leave in the taxi and my heart ached with physical pain. I got on the phone before you were hardly out of sight. I got a flight that I almost didn't have time to make." She paused. "I couldn't bear the thought of my life without you two a part of it."

"You shouldn't have worried. I had already planned on going back, without Brooke. I could hardly throw you over my shoulder and haul you to the airport with my young daughter watching. You and I were going to have it out—and I was supposed to win."

"You would have won." She smiled up at him.

"I know we haven't known each other long, I appreciate that concern. But I know we are right together. So, while I have you under the influence of moonlight, Lauren Ashby, will you marry me?"

"I want to tell you something first." She hesitated. "I'm an artist. I paint as Sara Collins. It has never been a secret, but I wanted to tell you."

"Thank you for telling me. I confess I've known for a while, and I've admired your work for years, so did Jenna. I was waiting for you to tell me."

She returned his hug.

"But now, I'm waiting for an answer."

Lauren tilted her head back and by the light of the moon, she looked into his eyes. "I will marry you, Jackson Montgomery, in one year if you still want me then. I promise."

"Fair enough." He tightened his arms around her.

Lauren sighed. With peace and happiness in her heart, she raised her lips to his.

She was home, at last.

CHAPTER 41

 he Gift

LAUREN LIKED Matt and Ally's idea of dinner at the club the night before the wedding. They insisted on Clair joining the four of them for the evening before the big day. Drew couldn't finish his work in Europe in time to make the wedding, but Clair had arrived two weeks ago to be with Lauren and serve as her matron of honor.

Lauren had served as Clair's maid of honor five months earlier.

Matt tapped his spoon on the side of his water glass.

"At the close of this last evening of their freedom, let's raise our glass to Jackson and Lauren. May you two continue to be our friends, but more importantly, may you continue to be friends with each other!" Laughter followed the toast.

Ally leaned close to him, smiling. "You and I have remained friends since we married."

"Of course we have, dear, but we're different. Everyday

drudgeries don't touch our magical life." He kissed her nose and feigned surprise when the others all laughed.

"Speaking of magical." Jackson looked at Lauren and raised his brows. "We probably should call it a day. I have a nine-year old bouncing off the walls at home." He stood, offering his hand to Lauren. "My aunt will have me up at dawn making sure everything is perfect for the wedding."

Lauren took his hand and rose from her chair. "But everything is perfect. The yard is beautiful, the weather promises pleasant temperatures and cool breezes. Tell Aunt Willa to relax."

Outside in the parking lot, Lauren and Clair bid Matt and Ally good night. Jackson lingered for a goodnight kiss and one last embrace before he climbed into the Dodge.

As they buckled up Clair looked across at Lauren. "Why does he insist on driving that old truck?" She laughed.

"Jackson loves that truck. It belonged to his dad."

"You know you're getting one of the best guys in the state of New York." Clair tilted her head and smiled.

"Of course I do." Lauren agreed, as she pulled out of the parking lot. Quiet for a moment, then she said, "Clair, thank you for being my friend. Jackson and I would not be celebrating the eve of our wedding if not for you."

"Of course you would be. Fate is the master planner." Clair put her head back on the headrest. "The part fate handed me was in being an opinionated, bossy, not-afraid-to-interfere friend."

Later as Lauren turned into the driveway and pulled into the garage, she said, "You may have something about the role fate handed you." She sighed, shutting off the engine. "But whatever, I'm indebted for life." They laughed and shared a hug across the console. The party mood carried over.

"Seeing you, Jackson and Brooke happy, cancels any debt."

Panic suddenly struck from out of nowhere. Lauren's hands grew clammy. Dr. Brickman's voice sounded in her head. *'Focus on what you want, not on what you fear.'* Caroline Brickman had taught her what she called visioneering, the concept of imagining a positive scene to replace a negative one of fear and doubt. Lauren called a familiar picture to her mind, one that she'd imagined so many times it felt as real as her hand in front of her face. *She, Jackson and Brooke stand fishing at the edge of the lake. Jackson and Brooke pause to watch her execute a perfect cast as Jackson had taught her to do. She laughs as they raise their hands in triumph.*

She breathed deep and relaxed—it always restored her balance. Tomorrow at three o'clock she would be fine.

* * *

LAUREN STOOD at the tall windows. "The weather couldn't be nicer if we'd placed an order for the perfect day."

Clair came to stand beside her. "True. Your wedding day is perfectly beautiful and so are you, dear."

"I'll be totally limp and wilted if you keep squeezing me every ten minutes." They laughed and hugged again.

Clair admired the back detail of Lauren's gown. Maria had insisted on the privilege of hand making it, the same as she had done for Clair. Gown design was Maria's main work in Italy. The gown fit beautifully in an understatement of elegant simplicity.

They waited in the large den that overlooked the back gardens. "I can't imagine why you didn't have the ceremony here in these beautiful gardens instead of at the other side of the house." Clair saw Lauren's secretive smile and stepped in front of her. "Why *did* you choose the other side?"

Lauren sighed. "It's just as beautiful on that side of the yard as this one ... but mainly it was sentimental. That's where I first saw Jackson. He practically accused me of trespassing and ordered me off his property."

Clair gaped. "What? I don't believe it! And you never told me. I could get my feelings hurt—"

Thelma opened the door with Brooke in tow. "Here's you helper, Lauren. Isn't she beautiful!" Thelma beamed.

"Beautiful is the right word." Lauren held her arms out and Brooke ran to her. "Oh, Brooke, you look so grown up with your hair like that." Brooke turned for inspection, proud of her new look.

"Aunt Willa took me to have my hair done and they did my fingernails too." She held her hands out.

"Miss Brooke, you make me feel positively dowdy."

"Dow-d-y? What's that?" She wrinkled her nose as the ladies all laughed.

"It means next to you, I'm an ugly-duckling." Lauren planted a kiss on Brooke's forehead.

Aunt Willa came into the room. "Everything is ready. The men are all in place." She checked Brooke once more. "You girls know you are to walk from the back garden through the archway to where Jackson waits." She nodded to Lauren. "Clair will go first then you and Brooke will follow."

Lauren smiled. "Yes, Aunt Willa. We'll be fine. We've practiced." She reached for Brooke's hand.

Aunt Willa handed Lauren her small bouquet of white roses, they hugged and she swiped tears from her eyes. The harpist began to play.

* * *

JACKSON TRAINED his eyes on the rose covered archway. The girls would come from the back gardens. Claude had patiently coaxed white roses to grow over the arch just for Lauren. Jackson antici-pated their entry. Clair, beautiful as ever, led the way. But his first glimpse of Lauren and Brooke as they stepped through the arch of roses would remain in his memory forever. Lauren looked down at Brooke's upturned face as they walked slowly. Happiness radiated from both faces. Pride and love swelled his heart. He glanced at Matt, surprised to see him struggling to keep his cool. He smiled at Ally and she returned his smile, giving him a discreet thumbs-up.

As if in slow motion, all sound hushed except the soft music of the wedding march. Jackson's glance swept to Lauren. She lifted her face and walking toward him, Brooke's hand in hers, they came together to stand at his side.

"Dearly beloved, we are gathered here ... "

* * *

THE NEXT THING JACKSON KNEW, Matt was pumping his hand in a teeth-jarring handshake.

"Congratulations, my friend!"

"Thanks Matt. That went by in a haze. I hope I got everything right." He pushed his hand through his hair and breathed out pent-up tension.

"You said all the right things. Trust me, you're married." Matt laughed. "Just keep smiling."

What seemed an eternity later, Jackson stole a moment alone with Lauren. "How long does this last?

"Until all the guests leave," she whispered.

Jackson glanced around the gardens at the crowd. "That could be a while."

"Oh, some people are already leaving. But why does it matter, are you expecting a home cooked supper?"

Several guests glanced over when Jackson put his head back and laughed loudly as Lauren smiled up at him.

"Oh, come on, Jackson, mingle."

Exactly three hours and twenty minutes later the last remaining guests congratulated them and made their way to where the valet had brought their cars up.

Matt, Ally, and Clair, along with Jackson and Lauren all sank into the white wooden chairs. The girls kicked off their shoes, enjoying the feel of the cool lush grass on their tired feet.

Thelma and Aunt Willa were in the house somewhere with Brooke.

Jackson and Lauren sat with their friends, exhausted but happy when suddenly Jackson turned to Lauren and said, "Say, what's for supper?" Tired and worn out, everything was funnier than it really was. They were all laughing like children when Aunt Willa and Thelma joined them.

Thelma kissed Lauren and Jackson and said goodbye. Aunt Willa was dropping Brooke off at her friend Mandy's house to spend the weekend. Then she and Thelma were heading to New York for a couple of days of shopping. Matt and Ally had dinner plans.

Drew was arriving around nine o'clock to spend the weekend in the country with Clair at Lauren's old house, which they were thinking of buying for weekends.

Finally, it was over, they were alone.

Jackson gave instructions to the cleanup crew before he and Lauren strolled to the front entrance of the house. He opened the door and lifted Lauren in his arms and carried her through to the great room. "Lauren Ashby Montgomery, welcome home," he whispered, his lips against her hair.

Lauren tightened her arms and hid her face against his neck for a long moment before she raised her face.

"Thank you, Jackson, for sharing your wonderful home with me. When I watched you leaving Florence last year, my heart whispered that wherever you are is home. I did fall in love with your house first, but now it would mean nothing to me without you in it."

"I'm relieved to hear that." He murmured.

She laughed softly. "You know I love you."

"Yes, I know. And I tease, but I'm glad you love the house and that it brought you to me in the first place." He carried her to the large windows and sat her down. Looking out to the edge of the woods, where they first met, he said, "That will always be my favorite place on the property. That's where I first saw you, where I found you in the moonlight, and where you became my wife." Jackson reached for her hand. "I haven't given you my wedding gift." He tucked her arm through his and they walked up the wide stairs side by side. When they reached the landing he turned her toward the studio and opened the door. Jackson led her across to one of the large windows.

"Stand here. See that statuary?" He pointed.

"The woman in the flowing gown?"

"Uh-huh, that one. Close your eyes."

"Closed." she murmured.

He gently turned her from the window. "Open your eyes." He handed her a package wrapped in white satin paper with a large white bow.

Lauren carefully undid the wrapping. Her eyes fell on the gift. The paper and ribbon slipped unnoticed to the floor. She stared at the small painting for a long time before she lifted her tear filled eyes. "The daffodils!"

"I want you to have it. It was Jenna's last painting."

"Oh, Jackson, it's beautiful!" She gazed at the small painting. "I've always wondered who had this." She hugged it to herself. "I tried to buy it before I met you."

"I know. The daffodils came from the foot of the statuary. They come back every spring. Jenna would be honored to have her painting in your safekeeping."

"Thank you. I will treasure it always."

Folding her into his arms he thanked God for giving him this gentle person to love.

"Jackson, when I got angry because you wouldn't sell me this house, Thelma told me something. She said that sometimes when God says no, it's because He has something much bigger and better in store for you."

He gazed upon her face, as she continued.

"I was just looking for a house. But He gave me a home, a husband and a child."

Jackson touched her face. "What about all the extra that He gave you? The noise, the clutter and a new dog?"

"Yes, I love it all." She laughed softly.

Lauren turned to the window and gazed once more upon the scene that had inspired Jenna as she added the final strokes to the small painting.

"Thank you, Jenna," she whispered. "I promise to love, cherish and care for all of your treasures. The rest of my days."

The End

Gentle reader...

Thank you for the gift of your time. I know you are a gentle reader if you enjoyed reading *Trespassing on His Heart*, the story of Jackson and Lauren. As you got to know them and their friends and family, you saw their gentleness and care for each other and the folks in their town.

As in real life, change happens, and so it does for this newly married couple. If you'd like to spend more time with Lauren and Jackson, you're invited to find out how they cope with married life, in *Tender Is The Heart*, **Book 2** in the **Valley Ridge Romance** series. available on Amazon.

I thank you...

First, I give thanks to my Lord always, for loving me. Without Him I could do nothing.

Thanks to my brothers and sisters and their spouses. You guys are like extra arms and legs— so necessary—I love you.

Words are little things to express my huge debt of gratitude to my daughter, Gayle, for her tremendous help and encouragement. From story plot to flow, first page to the last. And the times we'd say 'what if . . .' then spend ten minutes laughing and being silly before we'd brush tears of laughter from our eyes and get back to work. Thank you, dear.

Many, many thanks to my sister, and neighbor Ruth Allen. For reading every word and helping me work things out—and doing it in a kind, patient manner. Thanks for all the good suppers, too!

* * *

To my friends who supported me with encouraging words and the belief that *someday*, I would finish this book.
Thank you, Marsha McDonald, Katy Measures, Shirley Hicks, Sandy Duvall, Susan Ferguson, Dr. Leea Arnold, Nancy Connally, Mary Cretsinger, Bonnie King, Dana Scott and Danielle Davis.

* * *

And to the two beautiful ladies who grace the cover of Trespassing On His Heart. Thank you, Erin and Dovie Banta, for allowing me to photograph you for my book cover.

* * *

To very special friends,
Charlcie and Dorothy, thank you.

ABOUT THE AUTHOR

MaryJ lives in Oklahoma, in the Red River Valley. She writes fiction; stories of life and love. Written to please the gentlest of readers. Appropriate for ages nineteen to ninety.
When not writing, Mary paints landscapes and still life, or she's tramping her rural setting with camera in hand.

* * *

"Hearing from readers rates up there with shoe shopping and having coffee with friends."
Share your thoughts about this book. Amazon reviews are much appreciated.
www.maryjhicks.com
marehicks4@gmail.com